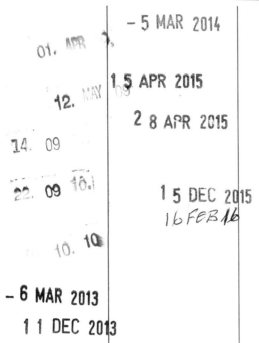

Pamela Fudge works as a part-time administrator at Bournemouth University. She has written poetry since she was a child and started writing fiction in 1983. Her first short story was accepted for publication in 1984 and since then her short stories have been published in most of the national women's magazines in the UK. She has also written *High Infidelity* and *Widow on the World*. Pamela lives in Dorset.

A BLESSING IN DISGUISE

When Alex Siddons becomes pregnant after twenty-five years of childless marriage, her life is turned upside down and her relationship with her husband, Phil, hangs in the balance. A child at their time of life is the last thing either of them wants or needs and yet, despite pressure from Phil, Alex cannot bring herself to terminate the pregnancy, even if it is the only thing that will save her marriage. Facing the prospect of life as a single mother, Alex finds unexpected support from within the Siddons family. Now she finally learns the true meaning of family and love.

Books by Pamela Fudge
Published by The House of Ulverscroft:

RELUCTANT FOR ROMANCE
ROMANTIC MELODY
WIDOW ON THE WORLD
HIGH INFIDELITY

PAMELA FUDGE

A BLESSING
IN DISGUISE

Complete and Unabridged

ULVERSCROFT
Leicester

First published in Great Britain in 2008 by
Robert Hale Limited
London

First Large Print Edition
published 2009
by arrangement with
Robert Hale Limited
London

British Library CIP Data

Fudge, Pamela, *1946 –*
    A blessing in disguise.—Large print ed.—
    Ulverscroft large print series: general fiction
    1. Middle-aged women—Fiction 2. Pregnancy—Fiction
    3. Single mothers—Fiction 4. Domestic fiction
    5. Large type books
    I. Title
    823.9'14 [F]

    ISBN 978–1–84782–588–9

Published by
F. A. Thorpe (Publishing)
Anstey, Leicestershire

Set by Words & Graphics Ltd.
Anstey, Leicestershire
Printed and bound in Great Britain by
T. J. International Ltd., Padstow, Cornwall

This book is printed on acid-free paper

This book is dedicated to my beautiful grandchildren, Abbie, Emma, Tyler and Bailey and to my step-grandchildren, Kimberly, Kiera, Chloe, Josh, Harley and Paige to whom I am also 'Nanny.'

Acknowledgements

My thanks go to all at Robert Hale Ltd, especially John Hale, Katy Williams, Gill Jackson and Shirley Day.

Many thanks also to the Midwifery Team at Bournemouth University, especially Elizabeth, Janine, Liz, Alison and Sue, who patiently dealt with all my queries regarding Alexandra's fictional pregnancy and the complications, and helped me to get my facts right. Also thanks to my stepdaughter, Debbie, who generously shared with me her own experiences of miscarriage and premature birth.

The support I have always had from my family and friends is — and always has been phenomenal. There is a blurred line between those who are fellow writers, like Pam W, Chris H, Nora, Lyndsay, Alan, Bruna, Cass and Janie, those I work with in the Admissions Office at Bournemouth University, like Pam M, Kate H, Kate T, Caroline, Sarah, Jill, Vince, Jane, Gail, Angela and Katrina, and those I relax with including Karen, Sally, Chris N, Jan, Robert M and Robert B. Everyone should have friends like mine because I am very blessed.

My love and thanks go to my sisters, Pat and Barb, my step-children, especially Allie, Rachel, Deb and Jay and my gorgeous grandchildren, also to my webmaster and step-son, Mark and his family.

Most of all, as ever, I would like to thank my children, Shane, Kelly, Scott and son-in-law, Mike. The love and support I receive from them is everything I could wish for and more. I could never thank them enough or love them more.

Finally, I could never forget Eddie and Frank who shared my life through two great marriages and left me with the best of memories.

1

'What do you mean you think you might be pregnant? *Pregnant*, Alexandra, at *your* age?' Phil looked stunned, but only for the briefest moment and then he burst out laughing. 'I've never heard anything so bloody ridiculous in my life.'

I felt like smacking him. I'd obviously been expecting a reaction but not, for some reason, an hysterical one. How could he just dismiss the possibility out of hand? Didn't he think I would have made pretty damn sure of my facts before even mentioning it to him? I wasn't some silly youngster just out of school, for heaven's sake, but a successful career woman with a clutch of qualifications under my belt and several years of lecturing behind me.

Trying to be charitable, I reminded myself I'd had several hours to get used to the idea, a long sleepless night to be exact, while for Phil this had obviously come as a complete bolt out of the blue. Even given the shock it must have been for him I couldn't help but feel it didn't excuse his utter insensitivity.

Calm on the outside, inside I was

absolutely seething and more than a little hurt, though I thought I hid it extremely well, merely placing scrambled eggs on wholemeal toast down in front of him with a little more force than was strictly necessary. Well, with enough force to crack the plate, if I was honest and I felt only disappointment when it didn't shatter on impact. *That* might have put an instant halt to his mockery.

I tightened my dressing gown belt, reached for my cooling cup of tea and wished I'd thought to get dressed before dropping my bombshell. I never was at my best first thing in the morning and, without make-up, was aware I probably looked every minute of my age. Phil, of course, was as perfectly groomed as ever, from the dark blond hair on his head — greying slightly now — to the highly polished shoes on his feet and didn't look as if he could possibly be nudging fifty.

'I'm *forty*-five, Phil, not a *hundred* and five,' I pointed out, then unleashing the seldom used sharp edge of my tongue, and itching to wipe the smug expression from his face, I continued, 'it's not unheard of for someone of my age to get pregnant and anyway I've already done a pregnancy test.'

'And?'

I finally had his attention. He appeared unconcerned but the scrambled eggs told another story, remaining untouched and beginning to congeal on the toast. It took a lot to put Phil off his food, so I wasn't fooled by his indifference for one minute.

I took a long sip of tea before I replied. 'And it was positive. The test was positive.'

For a moment he did look taken aback — but not for long — and then he retorted, 'Well, there you are, then, that doesn't prove anything. I don't know why you even bothered, Alex, those things are notoriously unreliable.'

With that he deliberately turned a page of the newspaper he'd propped against the teapot, and grasping the knife and fork made swift inroads into his Saturday morning choice of breakfast. It was as if the matter was too trivial for further discussion and was, therefore, dismissed. I was stunned. I had imagined a range of scenarios but complete indifference hadn't been one of them.

'You'd know all about that, would you? Anyway, that's not what it says in the instructions for use,' I came back, equally determined to have my say. Remaining on my feet in the belief it would give me an advantage I carefully placed my cup on the table. Withdrawing that very piece of paper from my dressing gown pocket, I threw it down next to the cup, and began quoting from memory, word for word, "Clearblue is more than ninety-nine per cent accurate from the day your period is due."

The leaflet was ignored, but the knife and fork were put down very deliberately and the newspaper was rustled and folded. It was clear Phil was getting annoyed, though I couldn't quite see why he was getting annoyed with *me*. I clearly hadn't got into this predicament on my own. When all was said and done, it took two to make a pregnancy happen and, if I *was* pregnant, he was damn well going to take his share of responsibility for it. When he finally managed to bring himself to look at me properly, I was able to match him glare for glare.

'And when *was* your period due?' he asked eventually.

'About two months ago.'

'About . . . ?' he echoed incredulously and I knew I finally had his full attention, 'but that means you're . . . '

'Ten to twelve weeks pregnant at a guess.'

'*If* you are.'

'If I am.'

'My God,' he said, suddenly ashen-faced and looking as if he had been punched in the solar plexus with great force. I guessed he was finally beginning to take the matter seriously.

'My sentiments exactly, but what are we

going to do about it?'

'First things first, Alex.' Phil sounded indignant and the remains of his breakfast were finally pushed to one side. 'I'm presuming there's a bloody good reason for you not mentioning anything about this until now, because there had better be.'

'Don't speak to me like that, Phil,' I said resentfully, drawing myself up to my full height, regretting the slippers that gave me no extra inches and reminding him, 'we haven't had a false alarm in years so I didn't think anything of it to start with. Then, when I realized I hadn't seen a period for a while, given my age, I just assumed I was starting the menopause.'

Relief flooded Phil's good-looking face and he even managed a smile. 'Of course, that will be it. You've started the change. My mother started hers around your age.'

'Thanks for the reminder,' I said wryly, finally taking a seat across the table from him and recalling what a song and dance she'd made about it being premature, which could easily have been put down to the fact she always subtracted at least ten years from her real age. I was reluctant to be the one to piddle on his celebration bonfire, but felt I had to point out, 'That doesn't explain the positive test result, does it?'

Phil dismissed it easily. 'A fluke,' he grinned, apparently happy again now he had it all clear in his mind and had decided we were back to the status quo. 'Nothing to worry about at all.'

I couldn't help feeling a bit disgruntled, despite my own sneaky relief at his certainty that there was no pregnancy but we *were* married, when all was said and done and had been for twenty-five childless years. I'd been sort of expecting a bit more in the way of interest — well, a lot more if I was honest — perhaps even a little bit of enthusiasm. The news, if it was true, had been a very long time coming.

'I did think you *might* have been pleased at the prospect of us having a child,' I said finally.

'*Pleased?*' he looked at me as if he couldn't believe what he was hearing. 'Twenty years ago — or even ten — nothing would have given me greater pleasure, but if I really thought for one minute . . . ' the sentence, ominously I thought, remained unfinished. It soon became apparent that Phil wasn't finished either.

'In fact,' he continued, 'a doctor's appointment might be a damned good idea. Not that I think there's even a remote possibility that you *are* pregnant,' he added hastily, 'but I

6

think, for both our sakes, we need to have any doubts in the matter removed.'

He rose to his feet and walked towards the door, paused and then walked back to pat me awkwardly on the shoulder and drop a distracted kiss on my cheek. 'I'll even go with you, if you like.'

With that parting shot he stepped into the hallway, hefted the golf bag full of expensive clubs on to his shoulder and said, 'I'll see you later,' without enthusiasm.

I went to watch him through the window over the sink, loading the sports equipment into the boot of his dark green Jaguar. There was no denying Phil was a very handsome man, he always had been, but I found it irritating in the extreme that his looks had only ever seemed to improve with the advancing years without any real effort being made on his part.

While the majority of women — including me — fought the ageing process tooth and nail, using every artifice available, some guys seemed to embrace maturity with ease and some — like Phil — even benefited from the odd wrinkle and smattering of grey hairs.

I couldn't help comparing his relaxed attitude to the passing years with my constant and strenuous battle to keep my youthful looks. I did feel I looked good for my age but

that wasn't achieved without a huge amount of energy being expended on my part. Much of my time, not to mention money, went into keeping up the appearance of youth and vitality. Gym membership alone ran into hundreds of pounds and then there were the regular trips to the hairdresser and beauty salon where styling and waxing didn't come cheaply or painlessly.

I was aware that not every woman in her forties chose to follow the route I had taken and, as highlights were expensive and calorie counting a complete pain, I almost envied them the more accepting approach to ageing. However, they weren't all married to Phil, who asked and expected high standards of all the people around him, especially those he employed within a very successful building firm and particularly from his wife.

As a consequence, I wouldn't have dreamed of leaving the house in the morning without a careful application of make-up, and the crucial time spent teasing my highlighted hair into a youthfully tousled style was of equal importance. So far I had fought against the idea of botox injections and collagen implants, but was aware the day couldn't be postponed forever if I didn't want to end up looking more like Phil's mother than his wife.

Life could be bloody unjust sometimes, I

reflected, when it came to the battle of the sexes, and having a baby at my time of life certainly wouldn't help me to keep either my looks or my figure.

Phil didn't raise his hand in farewell, as he would normally have done, but drove off without a backwards glance leaving me with my own hand half lifted. I stared after him, feeling extremely foolish and trying not to mind that he'd been so dismissive of the possibility of a pregnancy.

The sun shone on the quiet tree-lined road. The earlier frost leaving the thrusting green buds of early daffodils untouched in the half-moon of earth that was all that was left of the front garden once the sweeping in and out brick-paved driveway had been laid the year before, just after we had moved in.

Well, brooding about Phil wasn't going to get the baby a new bonnet, as my mother would have said — and wouldn't *she* have been surprised if the news turned out to be true. She'd given up on her only daughter producing a baby long before she'd died, but since she'd always appeared to take far greater delight in my failures than she ever had in my successes, I could only guess my inability to reproduce must have given her more pleasure than any grandchild ever could.

Even so, I didn't really want to think about having the baby that just *might* have made the difference in my mother's attitude towards me, and spun round determined to get on and not let Phil's cavalier manner get to me. I took one look at the mess of scrambled egg and neatly cut toast squares on his discarded plate and rushing to the downstairs cloakroom was violently sick.

To say I was shocked was an understatement, simply because I was *never* ill. Could it be the morning sickness I'd heard so much about, or just a reaction to the altercation with Phil? We so rarely disagreed about anything and I had been surprised by his reaction, I had to admit. I had expected a lot more in the way of support and understanding. Whether I was pregnant or not suddenly didn't seem to be as much of an issue as Phil's offhand manner about something that concerned him as much as me.

I went back into the kitchen deep in thought, where I polished off the remains of Phil's cold breakfast with gusto and then made fresh toast and ate it, piping hot and slathered with melting butter. I barely noticed what I was doing and when I did I put it down to the stress of the whole situation and refused to analyse the unheard-of binge further or to feel guilty about it.

Making my way upstairs, I stood in front of the mirrored wardrobes that Phil had insisted on and examined myself critically. I'd worked hard over the years to stay slim to the point of skinny and could not detect so much as the teensiest bulge, even when I turned sideways and thrust my stomach forward. I did however feel quite certain that my breasts were fuller and then wondered if it was another symptom that could be put down to the menopause.

Of course, what couldn't be put down to the menopause was the result of the pregnancy test I'd bought on the way home from work the day before and taken to set my mind at rest. The thought was laughable, though I'd never felt less like laughing. Even the woman in the chemist had assumed it was for my daughter and who could blame her?

No one could have been more shocked than I was when the word 'pregnant' popped up in that little window. It really was the last thing — the very last thing — I had been expecting. I must have aged a hundred years in a single moment and had gone to bed in a complete daze.

Was I pregnant? Was I? I splayed my hands over my flat belly and marvelled at the fact that if I was pregnant it had taken all of twenty-five years to arrive at this point. Yet I'd always been told, most emphatically, it became harder to get pregnant with the advancing years.

Still, there was no point in supposing and surmising, Phil was right about that — as he usually was about most things or so he would have me believe — and my weekly trip to the supermarket would surely have the desired effect of pushing the matter to the back of my mind.

Making myself presentable seemed to take even longer than usual, then throwing on a full-length coat against the early chill of the spring morning, I snatched my handbag up and hurried from the house without the usual meticulously prepared list.

I immediately spotted my elderly neighbour already out on the pavement, checking that the front gate had latched securely behind her, and almost stepped back inside rather than have to put myself out to be pleasant — then chided myself for being so mean-minded and pasted a smile on my face instead.

Vi reminded me a lot of my late mother in appearance, with her being of a similar age and build and always very upright and neat as a new pin. There the similarity ended, though, as I never saw Vi without a smile on her face and I couldn't have said the same of my mother.

My neighbour never left the house, winter or summer, without a hat suitable for the season jammed securely on to her head. On this occasion it was dark fur — almost certainly real — and it matched her gloves. I dreaded to think what the animal rights activists would make of Vi, but she always was a law unto herself. Her argument would probably be that as the animal was already long dead, there was no point in depriving herself of the warmth of its pelt.

'Hello, dear,' a warm smile lit her face the minute she spied me, 'you're out early.'

'Mmm,' I agreed non-committally. 'Going anywhere nice?'

The shopping bags rather gave the purpose of her outing away. A mixture of real leather and plastic imitations, a similar selection accompanied Vi on every expedition, whether to a charity shop, corner shop or super-market. She held plastic carrier bags in great disdain and had often assured me she wouldn't be seen dead carrying one.

Vi was a spinster from a moneyed background, but the inheritance tax had taken its toll and these days there was barely enough left for the upkeep of the enormous family home where Vi still lived in isolated splendour and genteel threadbare poverty.

Phil was always complaining that the house next door hadn't seen a lick of paint or a pointing trowel in years and was a complete eyesore as a result. My oft-repeated suggestion that, as a man with his own building firm he could do something about that at very little cost, always fell on deaf ears.

'Just going to get a few groceries,' she explained and went on to elaborate on her destination and the reason for her choice. 'I thought I'd pop to the big Sainsbury's as they've got 'buy one, get one free' on Whiskas this week and the mandarins are half price, too.'

Vi's life appeared to be devoted to retail therapy of one kind or another despite her lack of means. She adored snaffling a bargain, though I thought it strange that as an obviously educated woman she'd never managed to work out that the bus fare spent getting to out-of-town stores discounted any saving she might have made on her purchases.

Still, far be it from me to spoil her pleasure in claiming a good deal and for once I could do something about the travel costs. Anyway, I reasoned, doing my grocery shopping with Vi to watch out for would also leave me with even less time to think.

'I was just going there myself,' I lied merrily, as Waitrose was my personal preference for grocery shopping, 'can I give you a lift?'

'If you're sure, dear, that would be lovely.'

Moving at a speed that belied her years, Vi was up the drive and settled in the car before she'd finished speaking. I hid a smile, just suddenly extraordinarily glad of her company. You had to admire such an independent streak in someone who made no secret of the fact she was well into her eighties.

I was already halfway round the store, throwing items in the trolley with careless abandon due to the lack of a list, before I thought to pause in order for Vi to catch me up. I'd been shopping with Vi before and guessed she'd have made a beeline for the discounted goods shelves and would be having a great time hunting for taped up cornflake boxes and dented tins of Ambrosia rice or semolina.

It was obvious the damaged goods were only ever for Vi's personal consumption. I guessed she wouldn't take a chance on reduced pet food, refusing to cut corners when it came to Jaffa, her cherished and very spoiled ginger cat.

I'd reached the clothing department and since there was always a good quality range

15

on offer, I idled along the rails of skirts, tops and trousers, whilst I waited for my neighbour. Nothing caught my eye, so I headed past the shoes and handbags and rounded the corner into the next aisle, peering back over my shoulder as I went, fully expecting to see Vi puffing towards me at any moment.

When I turned back to see where I was going, I was brought up short. I hadn't realized they also sold children's clothes in Sainsbury's, and wondered why I'd never noticed before? There were the cutest little denim jeans and jackets hanging on the rails. A miniature version of the kind of thing most young men might have in their wardrobe, together with others embroidered with flowers for little girls. I lifted the hangers down and examined the tiny garments, completely enthralled.

Finally moving on, I found myself inexorably drawn to the tiny white vests, the Babygros covered in gambolling lambs and cotton-tailed rabbits, and wee socks that barely fit on my finger.

The array of disposable nappies, when I came to those, was mind-boggling. I found the choice totally confusing — boy, girl, premature baby to toddler — all available in so many brands. There had certainly been no

16

such thing when my mother had me or for some years afterwards. I could still clearly remember the rows of snow-white terry towelling nappies blowing on the neighbouring washing lines in the breeze when I was growing up.

I came to myself suddenly and was forced to ask what the hell I was playing at? I was shocked and more than a little horrified to find there were things in my trolley that had no right to be there. I bundled them back on the shelves any old how, careless of any rightful place and dreading to think what Vi would say if she saw me.

One thing was certain: the cat would have been well and truly out of the bag and all around the neighbourhood if she got wind of what was going on. Vi meant well but she couldn't keep a secret to save her life.

Somehow, I managed to go back and find her, coax her away from her bargains, through the checkout and out of the store — but the trauma didn't end there. I must have parked near the mother and baby section in the car park because we seemed to do nothing but dodge prams as we made agonising slow progress back to the car. I couldn't hurry more than I already was, with Vi lagging behind because she'd insisted on carrying the damaged and reduced potted plant she was inordinately pleased with.

At first I carefully avoided looking at the tiny occupants, but it didn't help. There were babies everywhere, in buggies, in those carry-seat things and still more being toted in harnesses by youngsters who looked as if they should still be carrying schoolbooks. There was one little child crying — screaming — and the young mother caught me looking.

She shrugged, 'Teething,' she offered, by way of an explanation. 'I'm going to my mum's when I've picked up some milk and bread, she'll know what to do.'

It was all I could do to dredge up what I hoped was an understanding smile before I hurried the last few steps to the car with Vi struggling to keep up. The feeling of relief as I closed the door on her and the pot plant and rushed round to the driver's side was overwhelming.

I refused an offer of tea with Vi and once she was delivered to her own front door I hurried inside my own and closed it firmly behind me, sagging against the wooden panels.

It was cool inside the house, and very quiet. There was a place for everything and everything was in its place. That was mine and Phil's life, calm and ordered and that — I reminded myself — was the way we liked it.

With the shopping packed away, I made tea, carried the tray through to the lounge, and sat down to enjoy it. The tea cooled in the cup as the inaction finally forced me to face some very unpalatable facts.

I suppose in my heart I had known — ever since I did the test and watched the 'pregnant' verdict appear — that I would eventually have to acknowledge the possibility that my life might very well have irretrievably changed. Ignoring the situation I'd been presented with was never going to be a real option, but I'd been in denial, I realized: either that or just shocked to the core.

It should have happened years ago, of course, when I could have been happy, excited at the prospect of a pregnancy, rushing out to buy tiny clothes and fluffy teddy bears the minute there was even a remote possibility that I might be carrying a child.

Well, it hadn't and I supposed if I really was pregnant — and I was still far from convinced — I would either have to learn to accept my condition — as would Phil — or, on the other hand, do something about it. What neither of us could do was keep pretending this wasn't happening. With two periods missed already time wasn't on my side and a decision had to be made, one way or another.

I was still sitting there when Phil came home, his mood obviously much improved by a good round of golf, the details of which he was keen to share stroke by stroke. Eventually, after fetching a cup and helping himself to tea, he got around to the subject of the morning's discussion.

'I've been thinking,' he said, and my back immediately went up to where it had been when he'd walked out and gone merrily off to the golf course.

I wanted to come back with a sharp, 'I should bloody well think you have', but held my tongue with difficulty, aware that constant sniping really wasn't going to help the situation.

'I might have been more supportive this morning,' he went on, and again I bit back a retort at this massive understatement, as he continued, 'You're obviously concerned — as I am — and though I'm sure there's no cause, you should make that appointment at the surgery and the sooner the better, eh? Whatever is going on, we can deal with it.'

I couldn't help asking, 'And if it turns out that I am pregnant, what then?'

There was a quick flash of what might have been irritation on Phil's face, but it was smoothed away so swiftly that I could have been mistaken.

'We'll cross that bridge — *if* we ever come to it,' he said and then changing the subject abruptly, added, 'we'd better be getting ready hadn't we?'

'Getting . . . ?'

'My dad's birthday meal.'

There was a distinct lack of enthusiasm in Phil's tone and it was all I could do not to groan out loud. A meal with the Siddons family en masse was going to be the far from perfect end to a far from perfect day.

'I'll go and run a bath,' I said without relish and forced my reluctant feet towards the stairs.

'I'll bring you up a glass of wine,' Phil offered and, after a slight hesitation added, 'and I wouldn't mention anything about you-know-what in front of the family. There's time enough when we know what's going on.'

I didn't dignify that with a reply. He should have known well enough, after all the years of being a rank outsider — a member of his family in name only — that they'd be the very last people I would dream of confiding in — about anything.

2

The restaurant was crowded and noisy, but above the chatter and laughter I could hear my mother-in-law's distinctive ringing tone imperiously demanding another 'more acceptable' table the moment we stepped inside the door.

A woman used to getting her own way — and also taking centre stage — she was apparently affronted to find the Siddons party seated towards the rear of the busy steak-house.

'Mon dieu,' Jacquetta Siddons threw out her arms in theatrical fashion, uncaring that every head in the place was turned her way, her proudly claimed French heritage coming to the fore, 'are we to be hidden away like a guilty secret? This is a celebration, n'est-ce pas? My husband he is eighty-five years old, he may not live to see another birthday.' At this point a lace-edged handkerchief was brought into play and touched to the corner of a dramatically made-up eye with extreme caution.

You had to admire her, I thought, though reluctantly, watching the scene as every

22

member of available staff ran round in circles trying their best to accommodate demands that were totally unreasonable.

The look on Phil's face was a mixture of exasperation and veneration, but he held back, steering me quickly round the corner to the bar area, thus placing us out of sight and allowing the whole thing to be sorted out to his mother's satisfaction before he made any attempt to join them.

'Did you get a chance to see who had made it for dad's meal?' he asked, ordering champagne to be delivered to whichever table the family ended up at once everything had been reorganized to Jacquetta's liking.

He had previously arranged a delivery of flowers for his mother and an elaborately decorated birthday cake for his father and these would be presented towards the end of the meal. The gestures would be expected, but largely unappreciated, as would Phil's offer to pay for the meal at the end of the evening.

I knew of old that if he were generous, Phil would be accused by his father of flaunting both his superior status and wealth but, on the other hand, if he did nothing and simply paid his share, he would be accused of being tight-fisted. Phil couldn't win in this situation; I knew that and so did he.

Where his father's approval was concerned, he would always be fighting a losing battle. Phil's relationship with his father bore striking similarities to that shared by my mother and me, it was one thing we had always had in common, so I knew how impossible it all was.

'I could only see Derek and Louise,' I said, risking a little peep round the corner, to where it was looking as if order was being restored now that Jacquetta's party had commandeered a large table at the very centre of the restaurant, putting another more accommodating family out, 'and it looks as if they've persuaded Martin and what is probably his latest girlfriend along.'

Louise was married to Phil's eldest brother Derek and Martin was their younger son. Martin was employed, along with *his* brother, in the family used car business, started by Derek — or Del as he was known — years before with a few dodgy motors and access to forged MOT certificates. To his credit, these days Del's business was far more respectable and made a good living for his family as far as I could gather.

As the mother of six boys herself, Jacquetta set great store by the size of the family each daughter-in-law produced. If she could be accused of having a favourite then Louise was probably it and could bask in the warmth of Jacquetta's approval for having done her duty. Being the mother of two sons and two daughters put her head and shoulders above the rest of us.

My childless status gave me zero rating within the family and was just another black mark to be added to all the others I was certain Jacquetta had against my name. I had long since given up trying to change my mother-in-law's lowly opinion of me, these days we were barely even civil to one another.

I peeped again. 'It looks as if it's safe to make an appearance now and the champagne's ready, so we can follow it to the table.'

I had been hoping the fuss of popping corks would mean we could slip unnoticed to our seats. I really should have known better.

'Phillippe!' Jacquetta — who had just that minute allowed herself to be seated — rose to her daintily shod feet with a shriek that had all heads turning in her direction yet again. 'My boy, my baby, let me look at you. You look tired, thin, are you eating enough of the right sort of foods?'

An accusing glare in my direction left me in no doubt that in her view I was totally incapable of looking after her precious son in an acceptable manner and this was despite the fact he had already survived twenty-five years of my ineptitude.

'Mum, I'm fine, mint in fact.' As always when Phil was with his family the local twang he had all but managed to extinguish from his accent became apparent. 'Happy birthday, Dad,' he had kissed his mother warmly, but shook his father's hand almost warily and passed him the very expensive and beautifully wrapped watch I knew he had spent literally ages choosing.

It was duly unwrapped, barely glanced at and tossed on to the table with an ungrateful, 'Yeah, I need to be watching the clock at my time of life.'

I gritted my teeth, and then again when I was summarily dismissed to sit between Martin's girlfriend and my sister-in-law, Louise, as far away from Jacquetta and her 'boys' as it was possible to be. There was a clearly defined pecking order in the Siddons family and I was most definitely at the lower end.

It was in my power to change that, I realized suddenly and it could be achieved just by opening my mouth. For a moment I was seriously tempted, just to view the uproar as the seating round the table was immediately rearranged and to see how it felt to be on the receiving end of Jacquetta's warmth

26

and approval for just once in my life. Something was stopping me, though, and it wasn't just Phil's warning about saying nothing.

It wasn't even just the doubt over the pregnancy that kept me quiet, but the indecision about what was going to happen next if, in fact, I *was* carrying a child.

In that one thing Phil was right, I acknowledged yet again. Twenty years ago — or even ten — the news would have been greeted by us both with total enthusiasm, but at this time in our married life did we really want the upheaval of the baby we'd accepted long ago just wasn't to be?

Never mind *older* parents, at our ages we'd be classed as positively *ancient*. There would be risks involved, risks to my health and that of the baby. If we were already having doubts about accepting a healthy child, those doubts would be multiplied many times over if there was even the slightest chance the baby might be handicapped.

I knew deep in my heart I didn't *really* want a child, not now, not at my time of life. I *was* too old, too set in my ways and I couldn't see Phil's attitude changing to the point he would welcome a newborn baby with open arms either. He had already made his feelings on the matter abundantly clear.

If I was being honest, I was seriously hoping against hope that he was right and the test result *was* a fluke so that in the end no decision would need to be made. It would make life easier all round. However, there was always the chance that it *had* been accurate in which case I was almost three months pregnant already and the time left available for choices was swiftly running out.

Abortion. I felt myself flinch at the very thought of it. It was a word I had been avoiding for all I was worth, but it really seemed as if it might well be the one I would be contemplating — and sooner rather than later.

'You're very quiet tonight, are you all right?'

I was so deep in my own very uncomfortable thoughts that I had to give myself a little shake before turning to find Louise's frowning gaze on my face. The question hung between us and for a split second I toyed with the idea of telling her the truth. I very quickly thought better of it, acknowledging that I hardly knew her, despite all the years spent as part of the same family.

From somewhere I dredged up a half-smile and indicating across the table to where the animated Jacquetta was holding forth, I said, 'It would be difficult to get a word in edgeways even if I wanted to.' Under my breath I muttered morosely, 'I doubt anyone would be interested in anything I have to say, anyway.'

My sister-in-law managed a rueful smile, 'Must be wonderful to have such doting sons. I wish mine were that attentive. Look at them hanging on to every word she says.'

It certainly looked that way, as between them Del and Phil encouraged their extrovert mother to become more and more outrageous. She sparkled away, lit up like a Christmas tree from the inside out, clearly adoring being the centre of attention.

The scarlet of Jacquetta's manicured nails flashed back and forth as every word she uttered was emphasized with fluttering hand movements. The nail enamel exactly matched an application of crimson lipstick that should have looked ridiculous on a woman of her advanced years but — along with a flawless mask of heavy make-up, and a youthful chestnut wig — instead gave her the appearance of a beautiful, if fragile, porcelain doll. As usual she was dressed from head to toe and very expensively in black.

I doubt if even Jacquetta's own children knew her real age since the exact figure had been veiled in secrecy for so long. How old she was could be of no concern to anyone but

29

her long-dead parents and herself, she insisted as, of course, she had every right to do. Early seventies was a figure bandied about within the family, though never in her hearing and since her eldest child was almost sixty even that was no more than an extremely dubious estimate.

I couldn't help smiling in spite of myself and in spite of what I felt was a completely understandable aversion to my mother-in-law. It was a relief to have my thoughts directed elsewhere, if I was being honest. 'She is amazing . . . '

'For her age,' Louise laughingly completed a remark that was all too common where Jacquetta was concerned both in the Siddons family, *and* outside of it. Noticing the way Louise's face lit up when she smiled, I thought, almost inconsequentially that she would be quite pretty if she only used a fraction of the cosmetics Jacquetta had at her disposal.

'How old is she anyway?'

The question came from Martin's girlfriend, who obviously didn't know any better than to ask it. She appeared to be all blonde hair, pert breasts hanging out of a skimpy top and very little real substance, though I was probably being too judgemental as usual and was just jealous of her youth. With good

30

reason, I acknowledged, since I was already well into middle age. Before too long I'd probably be taking a leaf out of Jacquetta's book and lying through my teeth about my age, too.

'I dare you to ask her,' Martin smirked, clearly aware of his grandmother's aversion to having any reference made to her age but seeming quite prepared to allow his girlfriend to take the risk of making an enemy for life.

The stupid girl already had her mouth open and was preparing to put her fashionably booted foot into it, when Louise protested, 'Martin, *don't* let Kayleigh get off on the wrong foot with Jacquetta or her life won't be worth living in this family. You do *want* her to be accepted by your grandparents, don't you?'

'Yeah course I do, mum. I wasn't thinking. Sorry babes.' He did look contrite and leaned over to kiss the girl on the cheek. She obviously had other ideas and turning her head swiftly met his lips with her own. In doing so, Kayleigh deliberately changed what should have been an affectionate but casual gesture into a full-blown and quite embarrassing exchange of tongues that went on and on. It stopped the conversation around the table dead.

Having taken the attention away from

31

Jacquetta, Kayleigh then graciously handed it back by saying, 'Whoops, excuse us, but I bet you remember how it is to be in love, Mrs Siddons.'

It appeared to have escaped Kayleigh that there were, in fact, three Mrs Siddons seated round the dinner table. It probably didn't escape Jacquetta — few things did — but she would simply have assumed that as the only Mrs Siddons who *really* counted the remark was directed to her.

The knowing gaze raked over the confident little blonde as if seriously toying with the idea of taking her down a peg or five. The heavily made-up eyes narrowed and I held my breath, then they crinkled as Jacquetta burst out laughing, 'Remember it, mon choux? I've never been out of love since the day I met my Randolph,' she blew her aged husband a kiss as if to emphasize her words. 'We could teach you youngsters a thing or two about love, believe me. Come back and see me when you've had six sons, as I have, and you'll tell me I was right.'

Everyone laughed, except Kayleigh, who merely looked confused — as well she might. It would have taken someone with a sharper view of life to see past Randy's crumbling eighty-odd exterior to the debonair cockney soldier of years gone by who had fallen in love with his mademoiselle at the tail end of the Second World War, and wooed her with motorcycle rides around the French countryside in a determined effort to win her heart and bring her home to England.

Having pursued her with a single-mindedness that had never been seen in him since, Randy had turned the young Jacquetta's head with promises of the life that would be hers in England, had married her and impregnated her with their first child all in a matter of weeks. From such an unbelievably romantic start it must have been downhill all the way for the young Madame Siddons.

It appeared the big strong soldier — faced with the task of providing for his rapidly growing family — quickly developed all the symptoms of the classic malingerer's 'glass back' followed by a growing fondness for another kind of glass, preferably kept filled with alcohol, which must have made the task of raising the brood something of a challenge for his young wife. To Jacquetta's immense credit she appeared to have simply got on with the matter in hand and, in all the years I'd known her, I had never heard her say one word to Randy's detriment.

Ever resourceful, and with a thriving black market still to be taken advantage of in those post-war days, it was a challenge that

Jacquetta had apparently risen to and without complaint as far as I was aware. The fact that her children had never known a day's hunger, even I accepted was entirely down to her efforts and for that alone she would always have my utmost admiration.

While Randy appeared to have spent his days tinkering with clapped out engines in the backyard and his nights in the pub — pastimes apparently unaffected by the painful back that prevented him from working to support his family — Jacquetta did what she had to do. Though I had my suspicions — and I had heard rumours to support them — that particularly in those early days, not everything she was involved in would have been strictly legal, I fully accepted her reasons justified her actions.

She'd sworn, years before, that her wheeling and dealing days were long behind her, but I had my reservations. Somehow I couldn't imagine Jacquetta growing old any other way but disgracefully and would never be convinced that the basic government pension would stretch to fill a wardrobe with the designer clothes and matching accessories she was so fond of.

The romantic tale of youthful love was being aired around the table — as it nearly always was on such occasions — this time for

Kayleigh's benefit, but you could see the girl was sceptical and who could blame her?

In Jacquetta you could still see very evident traces of the beauty she must have been in her day. In Randy however, all that remained of the debonair soldier was a passion for motorcycles that had never left him. The hair he'd grown longer over time, obviously to suit his fondly held biker image, was white now, but it still straggled past his shoulders. The reason for the goatee beard, however, remained a mystery to me. Hands that had once made a throttle roar now shook with the onset of Parkinson's and those previously firmly muscled thighs had shrivelled with age and inaction and could barely carry the frail old man these days, even with the aid of two walking sticks.

'He brought you on a motorbike — from France?' Kayleigh's tone held patent disbelief, as she looked from one to the other.

She had a point, they *were* an unlikely pair — and always had been — but a pair they were and it seemed they would remain so through all of life's ups and downs until death did them one day part. You had to admire such endurance in the present climate of marriages lasting barely long enough for the ink to dry on the certificate.

Unfortunately, a shared passion for the

family they had been blessed with did not extend — in Randy's case — to the youngest of their six sons. Perhaps the fact that Phil was undoubtedly Jacquetta's favourite had something to do with that, but it was often distressing to see — particularly for me as Phil's wife — Randy's very obvious and inexplicable dislike for a son he should have been proud of. No matter what Phil did, or how much he achieved, he'd never managed to win his father's approval — never mind his love. I felt it was quite possible that he never would.

I suddenly realized that Louise was speaking to me and, again, I had been miles away, this time watching the way Phil tried to engage his father in conversation only to have the old man continually rebuff him by turning back to his other son after barely acknowledging that Phil had spoken.

' . . . in the Echo,' Louise was saying. 'Del was so proud. 'Look what that brother of mine has got himself involved in now' he said, rushing indoors to show me the piece.'

'He's doing well,' I agreed, wishing his own father would even begin to appreciate just how well.

'Doing well,' Louise repeated, with a wry smile, 'there's hardly a building site in this county that doesn't have the board of Phil's construction company up on it.'

'Oh, is *he* Siddons Construction?' Kayleigh looked at me with real interest for the first time and added, 'God, you're his wife, aren't you? You must be *very* rich. Martin says you live in a stonking great house in Hightown Cliffs.'

When Martin joined in to describe the five bed and three reception roomed house where Phil and I lived, in greater detail than I would have dreamed he'd remember — never having been what you'd call a regular visitor — I didn't have the heart to tell them we'd probably been just as happy, happier even, in the little terrace property where we'd started our married life. They wouldn't understand, or even care, that this latest house in particular had somehow never really felt like home to me.

'That's the area where I plan to live when Dad's business really takes off,' Martin bragged enthusiastically, 'but I'd drive something a bit more flash than a Jaguar saloon.'

'You'd have to sell an awful lot of second-hand cars to make *that* sort of money,' Kayleigh pointed out, in a slightly disparaging tone, I thought.

'Actually,' Louise said defensively, 'the three of them make an extremely good living from the car trade. Del built that business up from scratch, eventually employing both of his sons, and our Michelle recently took over from me in the office, so it's a real family concern.'

'She was only saying . . . ' Martin was quick to excuse his thoughtless girlfriend.

'Well, I'd rather she didn't.' Louise's tone was sharp. 'Phil has no one to think of but himself, since Alex has always been independent with her own lucrative career. He could afford to take the kind of risks that he would have thought twice about if he'd had a family to support.'

'There's more to life than banging out kids,' Kayleigh muttered audibly, but luckily Louise didn't appear to hear her, not even when she continued for my benefit, 'I keep telling Martin he can forget about having four kids like his dad if he marries me, I think having a nice life is far more important.' This piece of wisdom was obviously confided to me as someone who, being childless, was perceived to have the same values.

She had jumped to the understandable conclusion that we'd had a choice in the matter and had obviously plumped for the material things in life instead of a family. I wasn't about to put her right. I was quite certain she'd make her own choices. She seemed like a girl who would know what she wanted.

It was a relief when Jacquetta finally settled down and the menus were passed around, until I realized I faced another dilemma. I could carry on burying my head in the sand and eat anything I wanted to, or I could acknowledge the fact I was possibly pregnant and make my choices more carefully while I made my mind up about what I wanted to do about it.

Even I was aware there were certain foods to be avoided during pregnancy, though I couldn't for the life of me remember why that was or why I was bothering to worry about it. I'd very probably already eaten lots of unsuitable fare in my ignorance of a condition that may or may not exist.

I couldn't explain then why I found myself avoiding any starters involving prawns, pâté, parma ham or mayonnaise, it just suddenly seemed like the right thing to do. The deep-fried mushrooms were delicious anyway and I couldn't remember seeing anything about shunning fungi in any of the literature I must have inadvertently come across when flicking through magazines and newspapers in the recent past.

For the main course I played safe with grilled chicken and salad, since I couldn't remember if red meat was good or bad, felt sure that anything with cheese was iffy and had never been a lover of fish dishes anyway.

There was champagne in my glass and I'd already had wine at home, but decided enough was enough and that as long as I took even a sip or two no one would notice that I wasn't really drinking. I was beginning to feel quite virtuous and hoped that Phil was noticing that at least one of us was behaving responsibly over the unexpected situation we'd found ourselves facing and acknowledging there may be a reason for caution.

It had to be Kayleigh who stirred things up just when everything was going reasonably well. That girl was born to cause trouble, as I'd already decided from watching the way she'd been annoying Louise with her thoughtless little comments. I'd never had much in common with my sister-in-law, but if this little madam was going to become part of her family then she had my sincere sympathy — and Martin would certainly have *his* hands full.

I'd been quite enjoying the food, managed to make polite responses when required and was looking forward to making a reasonably early escape when all hell seemed about to break loose.

'I only said . . . ' Kayleigh was protesting, managing to look smug at the fuss she had caused and surprised by it all at the same time.

'Well, don't,' Louise advised tartly, 'because you obviously don't know what the hell you're talking about.'

I was beginning to wish even more than usual that I could find myself elsewhere. Sitting slap bang in the middle of an argument was very far from my idea of fun and when it became apparent that it involved Phil and me and our lifestyle that really was all I needed. I'd thought Kayleigh was finished with that particular topic but it seemed I was wrong.

'Don't talk to her like that,' Martin snapped, 'she's entitled to her opinion — and I agree with her. No one even bothers to get married these days, let alone get tied down with a load of kids. It took dad years to build his business up with us lot hanging round his neck like a millstone. Uncle Phil had the right idea when he put his business first.'

'Mon dieu,' Jacquetta clutched a hand convulsively to her throat, 'how can you say such a thing? Family is everything.'

Throughout this exchange Randy had been silent and I don't even know what drew my gaze to him, but I was shocked at the expression on his face. Purple with suppressed fury, he suddenly brought his fist crashing down on the table with all the force his feeble strength would allow.

'I might have known this came down to *him*,' he roared in an apoplectic rage, 'him, and that bloody stuck-up wife of his, bleeding up-starts, the pair of them, looking down their long noses at the rest of us. Too bloody busy stockpiling money to think about having the family that would have made Philip's mother happy — and too bloody selfish. But there, it takes a man to father a child and I doubt very much whether Philip Siddons ever had it in him, even if that wife of his hadn't turned out to be sterile.'

In my heart I'd always known and accepted the very evident dislike he displayed towards Phil, but this was the first time I had seen it brought right out into the open quite so vehemently. The vicious nature of his attack left me totally speechless, though the same couldn't be said of my husband.

'Are you saying you're a man then, Randy? *Are* you?' Phil was on his feet his voice dangerously low and icily calm. 'It makes you a man does it, because you fathered six kids? No matter that you left it to your wife — a slip of a girl in a foreign country — to feed and clothe them from birth while you played with motorbikes or sat in the pub and claimed you were too ill to work. Well, you'll *never* be a man in my eyes and you're certainly not fit to be called a father.'

'Phil, Phil,' Del tried to be the voice of reason, 'Calm down, mate, think what you're saying.'

'Let him say away,' the old man put in with a sneer, 'for all his mouth *and* his money, it doesn't change the fact he's got no bloody lead in his pencil. It must eat him up inside that every one of his brothers has a family — even our Rich managed one kid — and he . . . '

I should have seen what was coming next, but I was as shocked as everyone else around the table when Phil suddenly blurted out, 'Well, that's where you're wrong, Randy, because Alexandra is pregnant *right now* and, let me tell *you* something, this is one grandchild you will *never* see as long as I have breath in my body.'

3

'Whatever possessed you, Phil?'

I was beside myself, walking up and down our tastefully and very expensively decorated lounge like someone demented — as indeed I was at that moment. The showy cream and pale wood of the furnishings and décor did little to soothe my mood.

'You *know* what got into me,' Phil was still bristling with anger and full of a righteous indignation the journey home had done little to dissipate, 'I wasn't going to let the hateful old bastard get away with *that*. You heard what he was saying.'

I paused in my pacing, 'Yes, I did,' I agreed, trying my best to be understanding, but feeling I had to add, 'it's nothing he hasn't said or hinted at a hundred — a thousand — times before.'

Phil stood in front of me and held out his hands palms up, 'But I had nothing to throw back at him before — and *this* time I did. It really was as simple as that and the words were out before I could stop them.'

'But we'd already agreed I'm probably not pregnant at all. You, in particular, had absolutely *no* interest in the fact that I might be, or if you did you certainly hid it very well.'

'So, I changed my mind on both counts.'

'What do you mean you've changed your mind? You've decided I *am* pregnant and you *do* want a child, just because it will get up your father's nose. That's pathetic, Phil.'

'He's no bloody father of mine.'

'He's the only bloody father you've got as it happens and that's why you have to put up with him and his vile insults — or that's what you've always told me.'

The sound of the doorbell interrupted a bitter exchange of words that was clearly going nowhere and we were shocked into silence for a moment, until Phil demanded, 'Now who the bloody hell can *that* be at this time of night?'

'One of us had better go and find out.' When Phil showed no sign of moving, I said resignedly, 'I guess that will be me, then.'

Marching into the hallway, I threw back the front door to find what appeared to be a deputation of Siddons family members on the doorstep. This included the party from the restaurant — minus Jacquetta and Randy — plus two more of Phil's brothers. To say I was surprised was an understatement, pleased I most definitely was not.

'Well,' my tone was less than enthusiastic,

the smile I managed was several degrees less than warm, 'to what do we owe this unexpected pleasure? Actually,' I went on, 'don't answer that, it has nothing to do with me. I suppose you'd better come in. Phil is through there.' I indicated his whereabouts with a jerk of my head in the general direction of the lounge. 'You can find your own way, I'll go and put the kettle on.'

I didn't offer anything stronger — which the men would undoubtedly have preferred — feeling we didn't need the effects of alcohol inflaming what was already promising to be a volatile situation, if similar scenarios from the past were anything to go on. There was always something to argue about in the Siddons family, especially if Randy had anything to do with it. The only difference — and the one thing that concerned me — was the whole thing appeared to be in danger of erupting right on my own doorstep this time.

The three men and Martin who, I supposed, was technically a man — though he didn't yet count as such in my eyes being so much younger — made their way into the lounge. I headed for the kitchen, followed by Louise and then by Kayleigh — the undoubted instigator of all this trouble. She appeared quite unperturbed by it all and was looking around with avid curiosity, obviously prepared to be impressed with the trappings of a lifestyle she made no secret of aspiring to.

'Would you like to go and have a look around?' I offered, a mite sarcastically and she leapt at the chance, almost childlike in her eagerness. We watched her wander off happily, touching this and that as she went, blonde head swivelling in all directions at once.

Louise shook her head behind the girl's back and leaning against a marble worktop, helped herself to a biscuit from the packet I'd just opened. I could see she was desperate to voice the question that was probably on each member of the Siddons family's lips at that point.

'You can go ahead and ask,' I invited, possibly because out of my in-laws — and there were many — she was the one I came closest to tolerating and also perhaps because by that time I badly needed someone to confide in myself.

Louise was a bit younger than Derek at fifty-four and had always appeared reasonably sweet natured, though we'd never had a lot to say to each other in the years we'd been part of the same family. Naturally fair, she still had very little grey in her hair and — as I noted every time I saw her — would have been quite attractive had she attempted to make the most of her looks with a touch of lipstick and mascara and a half-decent hairstyle. I had always thought shoulder-length hair on a woman in her fifties was a big mistake and it certainly did nothing for Louise.

I rarely saw this particular sister-in-law in a new outfit, though she did dress reasonably well for someone who appeared to have little interest in clothes. On this occasion the white blouse and black slacks were a safe enough bet but they made her look like a filing clerk.

She'd always seemed amazingly content with a lot in a life that included bringing up her family in the middle of the used-car lot where she still lived, surrounded by her children and grandchildren these days, who all had homes close at hand. If I was being totally honest, I had always kind of envied her, without really ever understanding why.

'Are you then? Pregnant I mean?'

'There that wasn't so hard, was it?' I managed a feeble smile, and continued, 'I really don't know for sure, Louise. You would know more about such things than I would. I have only the vaguest idea what I'm supposed to be looking for.'

She took another bite of her biscuit, a bourbon cream, before asking, 'Well, you must both have thought something was up for

Phil to say what he did. What indications have you had that you might be?'

I ticked them off and it only took two fingers, 'Missed a couple of periods, been sick once.'

'Not very conclusive, is it? Menopause, tummy upset?'

'*And*,' I went on, as if she hadn't spoken, 'one positive pregnancy test. It was Clearblue and I bought it from Boots,' I added, as if that made a difference. It might have for all I knew.

Louise straightened up and stopped chewing. 'They're . . . '

' . . . ninety-nine per cent accurate,' I finished for her. 'I know, I read it in the instructions.'

She chewed rapidly and then swallowed, coughing on the crumbs that refused to go down, 'I think you very probably are, then. How do you feel about it? Had you and Phil been trying for a baby?'

'I don't *know* how I feel about it, haven't the faintest idea' I stated flatly. 'We've been trying for a baby for almost the whole of our marriage, but gave up hoping a long time ago and accepted we would be childless.'

'Oh, Alex,' she said, her pretty blue eyes sympathetic, 'I'm so sorry, I never realized, but just assumed . . . '

'That we were too selfish to want a family 'spoiling things'. Don't worry we both guessed it was what everyone was thinking, both inside and outside of the family. We felt it was our business, not up for discussion or interference and so we never bothered to set the record straight.'

'Where's that tea, then?' Richard came into the kitchen, walked right up to me — as if we hadn't already met on the front doorstep — and kissed me on both cheeks, saying with a laugh, 'Well, Alex, you've set the cat among the pigeons now all right. How are you, darling?' He looked me up and down. 'No need to ask, really, you're just as gorgeous as ever. Our Phil is a lucky man.'

Richard, or Rich as everyone called him, was Phil's senior by almost two years. They were quite similar to look at, both handsome men though Phil was a sharper dresser, but there the similarity ended. Where Phil was bordering on being workaholic Rich was so laid back about everything he was almost horizontal. Even his wife taking off with his only child in tow to live abroad with another man, hadn't appeared to seriously phase him for very long.

If Rich was heartbroken he hid it very well, making sure he kept on good terms with his ex-wife in order that contact with his daughter could be more easily maintained and calmly picking up the pieces of his life and refusing to feel sorry for himself.

He made his living working on oilrigs — though in what capacity I had no idea, but assumed it was something managerial since it obviously funded a good lifestyle — and lived in what I'd heard was a very nice flat on the outskirts of Brankstone town when he was on dry land. Never short of money or female companionship, I'd always thought he had his life all arranged to ensure he got exactly what he wanted out of it and I admired him for that. Living to please only yourself sometimes seemed like a very good idea to me.

'Flattery will get you everywhere, you old flirt you. I'm as you see me, Rich,' I smiled up at him, admitting there was something likeable about him despite the Siddons label, 'fit and well — and not necessarily pregnant, so all the fuss could be for nothing.'

'That's as maybe, but it sounds to me as if Phil was provoked beyond endurance by the old man — as usual. Damned if I know what his problem is. He has more reason to be proud of Phil than any of us. He's made the Siddons name one to be reckoned with not only in Brankstone, but all along the south coast.'

Belatedly, I turned to put the kettle on,

saying over my shoulder, 'I gave up trying to work out what the problem was years ago. Could you get the cups out, Louise, they're in the cupboard just to your right there and you'll find a tray next to the wine rack.'

'Anything I can do?' Rich offered, adding as he saw me reaching for a foil wrapped package and filters, 'I wouldn't bother with the fuss of real coffee, love, they'll be just as happy with instant.'

'Del probably wouldn't even notice the difference,' Louise agreed, clattering crockery on to the tray, 'and we'd better get in there,' she tossed her head towards the lounge, 'before things get heated — as they tend to do in this family.'

In no time, with two extra pairs of hands at my disposal, we had trays loaded with cups, saucers, biscuits and pots of hot tea and coffee. I was not allowed to lift a tray.

'Just in case,' as Louise said.

'You know he doesn't mean it,' Del was saying as we entered the room.

'Yes, he *does*,' Phil argued, his mouth set in a mutinous line. It was a look I was all too familiar with and it didn't bode well for whatever discussion was taking place. 'He always means every bloody hateful word he says to me — and there have been more than a few over the years — and this time I meant what *I* said. He'll *never* get to see this baby. He's never been a father to me and he won't get the chance to be a grandfather to my child.'

'That's always assuming there *is* a child,' I put in, because I felt I had to say something to put the record completely straight.

This time it was Tony's turn to have his say. He was the next brother down from Del, who was the eldest at almost sixty years of age. The six of them had been born at two-year intervals, with Phil the youngest approaching fifty. Barry and Simon were the missing brothers aged fifty-six and fifty-four respectively, and the only ones not living locally.

'Don't tell me,' Tony was saying, 'that all this bust-up came about because Alexandra *might* finally be pregnant after all this time.'

'From what I can gather,' Rich put in, 'though I wasn't there when it all kicked off — it all blew up because Dad was goading our Phil, yet again because he has no kids.'

'Surely that Phil's business,' Kayleigh came wandering into the room and didn't hesitate to voice her opinion whether anyone wanted it or not. 'What's it got to do with anyone else?'

'Yes, thank you, *darling*, we can manage without your input. Who are you, anyway? You're not one of ours, are you?' Tony threw the girl a look of dislike, clearly not impressed by either her looks or wisdom.

'She's my girlfriend,' Martin's tone was belligerent, 'and she's entitled to her view.'

'As are we all,' I spoke in what I hoped was a soothing tone. 'Now, why don't we all sit down — we can bring in more chairs — and have a sensible and civilized conversation over the tea and biscuits.'

'Good idea,' said Rich, leaving the room momentarily and returning with a dining chair dangling from each hand.

Once everyone was seated the atmosphere lightened considerably. It was even agreed that Phil *did* have a point and the old man always appeared to have it in for him, for whatever reason.

'But he *is* an old man,' Del pointed out.

'Age doesn't excuse his behaviour, and it's hardly a recent thing,' Rich declared, surprising me, since he had always appeared to me to be particularly close to his dad. A shared love of motorbikes probably helped — though the two-wheeled monstrosity parked in *our* garage might have been a pushbike for all the difference it had ever made to Phil's relationship with Randy. 'Anyway, if he has a problem with Phil he should be man enough to admit it and sensible enough to sort it out. It's gone on for long enough in my opinion.'

'Thanks for that but it won't happen,' Phil said flatly, 'not in a million years and I'm passed caring.'

That this last remark was patently untrue was recognized by everyone in the room apart from Kayleigh, who obviously knew precious little about the Siddons family politics. Randy's spiteful and all too frequent attacks on Phil still had the power to hurt, probably because they were always unprovoked and mainly unfounded, but with a slight element of truth in most cases for authenticity, I guessed. Our perceived inability to start a family was a good case in point.

'I've had it up to here,' Phil brought the back of his hand up under his chin, 'with the old man questioning my ability to be a father. I wouldn't mind if he would once — just bloody *once* — question his own very evident inability to be a father to me. It's not just about biology.'

'Perhaps the fact that Alex is pregnant will make all the difference,' Tony appeared to have missed the point of the conversation entirely, but Phil soon put him right. No one took a blind bit of notice of my repeated but pretty feeble protests that the pregnancy wasn't even confirmed yet.

'It will be too little, too late, as far as I'm concerned,' Phil's tone was bitter, 'and I meant what I said before. This child will meet his grandfather over my dead body.'

'You can't do that to Dad,' Del was on his feet and intent on fighting his father's corner, 'he's old and sick. It wouldn't be fair.'

'I may be younger, but I'm sick, too. Sick of the way he's treated me all these years. Has he ever been fair to me? Answer me that and make sure you're honest.'

Del tried, you could almost see the inner struggle, but if he was looking for a convincing argument he had obviously failed miserably.

'You see,' Phil looked almost disappointed, 'you can't.' It was almost as if he wanted someone to convince him his father's treatment of him was all in his imagination. If they had, I'm sure it would have made him feel better. No one likes to think they are unlovable, especially to their own parent — as I of all people should know.

'More tea,' Louise offered into the silence that no one seemed able to fill.

'No, bugger the tea, I'm getting out the whiskey,' Phil said, heading towards the door. 'It's not often my brothers come to visit and I think that, and the fact I'm finally going to be a dad, calls for a celebratory drink.'

'I'll help you,' Kayleigh offered unexpectedly, and skipped smartly out of the door after him.

I guessed she was bored to tears with a discussion that would be of little interest to her and was glad of something to do. I thought of following just to make sure they found enough glasses but decided to let them get on with it. I was glad I had when the talk turned to something that had always puzzled me.

Randy's dislike of Phil was well known to all within the family. The old man hardly made a secret of it, spitting his bile in his youngest son's direction at any opportunity, both in private and public. Phil could do nothing right and as his wife, I often came in for similar treatment.

The one thing I had never understood was why Randy behaved that way towards Phil without any apparent motivation and certainly without provocation. As the talk continued in Phil's absence it soon became evident his father's victimisation went much farther back than even I'd realized and also that not one of the three brothers present had any more of an idea than I had about what exactly had initiated it.

'We've simply never talked about it,' Rich confessed and shrugging, he added, 'hardly acknowledged it either, if I'm honest. Mum always favoured Phil anyway — only natural really since he was her last baby — and she shielded him from the worst of dad's temper while he was growing up.'

'It really goes all the way back to when he was just a little *child*?' I was shocked and didn't even try to hide it. 'I hadn't realized.'

'Actually, it does, now I think about it,' Tony agreed, looking thoughtful. 'I think we all did our bit to protect him, like taking the blame for a lot of the things Dad accused him of doing — mostly without good reason.'

Del remained silent, but he was nodding thoughtfully and his unspoken agreement damned the old man even more in my eyes because, as a rule, he would normally defend his father against any accusation.

For the first time in all the years of being part of the Siddons family, a subject that had plagued and puzzled me had been dragged out into the open. By retaliating in earnest, possibly for the first time in his life, it seemed that Phil had finally brought his brothers to a point where they were willing to see things from his side.

'Even I sort of noticed,' Martin confessed, his tone reflective, 'but I thought there must have been some sort of fight — argument — from back before I could remember. I'd be really upset if my dad treated me the way Grandad treats Uncle Phil, but he's always bent over backwards to treat me and our

James exactly the same.'

'If I'm honest,' Del admitted, 'it's because of Dad and Phil that I'm extra careful with my kids, but I never realized it before. Isn't that funny?'

It was quite apparent that no one thought it the least bit funny. In fact, Louise looked close to tears as the truth began to come out.

'So . . . ' it was Tony's turn to speak, '*why* is he like it? What reason can he have to feel the need to vent his spleen on our Phil at any given opportunity?'

'Answers, please, on a postcard,' came Phil's voice from the doorway. He came in carrying yet another tray but full of glasses this time and Kayleigh followed close behind with a bottle in each hand.

'Is it because you're the youngest, and he didn't want another kid?' Martin ventured.

'Or because you were another boy and he desperately wanted a girl after five boys?' suggested Louise, going on to explain, 'Del was over the moon to have a boy after even two girls — though he'd have loved our Martin even if he had been another girl,' she added hastily and loyally.

There were various other suggestions, but they were in a pretty similar vein and then Kayleigh — well, it would have to be her, wouldn't it — came up with the one explanation that had possibly crept into everyone's mind during the course of the discussion.

'Perhaps you're not even old Randy's son,' she said blithely, 'has anyone ever thought of that?'

The silence in the room was deafening.

4

Kayleigh's careless words, placing a question mark squarely over Phil's parentage, were instantly dismissed as rubbish, but just the fact of her saying them made the possibility they *might* just be true a bit too real for comfort.

The suggestion that Randy might not be Phil's biological father was a bit like the news of my possible pregnancy, and once out in the open it had to be dealt with and discussed — as it was, endlessly and eventually drunkenly.

I thought our uninvited guests were never going to leave, but the good manners instilled into me so relentlessly by my mother throughout my childhood wouldn't allow me to give into my fatigue. In truth, I'd have loved nothing better than to simply go to bed and leave them to it.

'I still can't see the problem with simply asking your mother,' I told an extremely hung-over Phil when he finally surfaced the next morning, looking a bit green and exceptionally sorry for himself. 'She's the *only* one who would know for sure. She

61

surely can't do other than give you a straight answer to a straight question.'

He shook his tousled head emphatically then groaned from a movement that obviously pained him, pushing away the plate of bacon and eggs I had just that minute placed in front of him. Looking at the state of him I wondered why I'd bothered, since food was obviously the last thing on his mind.

'I can't do *that*.' He was looking at me as if I was completely mad, yet to me it was the one sane suggestion that no one had thought to make during long, alcohol-fuelled hours of deliberation. 'Ask my own mother if she's an adulteress? You know how much she thinks of the old man and always has. It's unthinkable, a ridiculous idea. She'd never have been able to bring herself to cheat on him, not in a million years.'

He scowled at me ferociously and I felt prompted to point out, 'Well, don't blame me, when it wasn't actually me who suggested she might have. It was Martin's girlfriend, if you remember.'

'Kayleigh doesn't know any better. The rest of you really ought to get a grip on reality.'

To be quite honest I was beginning to doubt my own previously unquestioned ability to decide what *was* real and what *wasn't* any more. I was beginning to feel that

I already had far too much on my plate to deal with and the Siddons family's unexpected and unwanted involvement in my life was just complicating matters even more.

The sudden show of care and concern actually grated a bit — well, more than a bit, if I was being brutally honest — after all the years of none of them appearing to give a tuppenny damn about whether Randy really did hate Phil's guts as much as he appeared to, or why on earth that might be.

'Fair enough, leave a subject that's bugged you for years if that's what you want, but we can't leave making a decision about the future of this pregnancy — that's always assuming there actually *is* a pregnancy — or our choices will be running out.'

I cut into the bacon in front of me, dipping the morsel into a deliciously runny egg yolk that I was pretty sure I shouldn't be eating, and then savouring the combined flavours greedily while I waited for his reply. I hadn't eaten a fried breakfast in years, but my usual thin slice of wholemeal toast just didn't appeal any more and a normally iron will-power where food was concerned seemed to have deserted me entirely over the past few days.

'Choices?' Phil looked mystified, but was apparently relieved to be off the subject he

63

never *could* deal with in anything approaching a rational manner. Why he couldn't just go to Randy and simply *ask* him what his problem was beat me and it always had. Though, if I were asked why I hadn't done the same with my mother I wouldn't have had an answer either. Who knows, the pair of them might just have come up with reasons that we could accept and even learn to live with.

'Yes, choices,' I repeated, excusing his vague response as being a direct result of the amount of drink he had consumed the night before.

No normal person would be able to think straight with that much alcohol swilling around the bloodstream. Reaching for Phil's cup, I refilled it with black coffee and placed it pointedly right in front of him.

He took a sip, considered what I'd said and then brightened. 'You mean what colour to paint the nursery? What make of pram? I suppose it's a bit early to be thinking about schools — but I definitely think we should go for private and give him or her a better start in life than we both had.'

I was so gobsmacked at this total about-turn that I almost had to pick my jaw up off the floor. '*Prams?*' I said, '*Nurseries? Schools* for God's sake? Have I missed something here? You were the one who said most emphatically that I wasn't pregnant. You laughed your head off at the very idea and you couldn't have made it any clearer that a child was the last thing — the *very* last thing — you needed to be contemplating at this point in your life.'

It seemed for a minute as if he was going to argue about it, but then Phil shrugged, 'So, I'm coming round to the idea. I did initially think a pregnancy was unlikely, but apparently those kit thingies are pretty accurate, and . . . '

' . . . *and* a baby would make your dad sit up and take notice of you for once in his miserable life. Keeping a grandchild from him would be the perfect way to punish him for all those years of neglect, wouldn't it?'

Phil didn't say a word, but the look on his face spoke volumes.

'Well,' I continued relentlessly, 'I'm sorry, Phil, but I'm not prepared to go through months of a pregnancy we didn't plan, to have a baby neither of us really wants, just so that you can score points over Randy-bloody-Siddons. I'm still not totally convinced that I *am* pregnant, mind you, but if I am, I'm telling you, here and now, I don't intend to go through with it.'

'An *abortion?*' There was sheer horror in

his tone, but I didn't even try to kid myself it was for the baby we may or may not have created, and I was proved right when he followed the remark up with another more telling one. 'You can't do that, everybody knows about it now.'

'And *that*,' I reminded him furiously, shoving the remains of my breakfast to one side, annoyed that he had managed to put me off my food, 'is all down to *you*. So, when I have the termination — if we find there's anything to terminate — you might want to do a follow-up story and share the news with all and sundry that I've had a miscarriage.'

Phil's mouth opened and closed, and when he couldn't find anything to say, I relented a little and said a bit more kindly, 'Phil, you said it yourself. I'm *not* pregnant. Two missed periods, one bout of sickness and a positive result from a test taken in a hurry upstairs in the bathroom, are hardly conclusive and are all easily explained away. You were probably right all along and it's the onset of the menopause. I'll get myself to the doctor's — tomorrow if I can get an appointment — and come away with a prescription for HRT, end of.'

He should have looked relieved, not disappointed. I couldn't understand his change of heart and I certainly didn't welcome it. He'd been right the first time — and I had come to accept that, as I did most things that Phil stated a firm opinion on — we couldn't become parents now, not at our age. The whole idea was ridiculous.

'You can tell the family I miscarried anyway, if you like, as soon as it's confirmed as a false alarm,' I suggested, 'that'll shut Randy up at least. It can hardly be seen as your fault that I couldn't carry a child to term. He thinks I'm useless anyway, and always has.'

'Only because you're married to me,' Phil pointed out, with bitter truth.

I shrugged. It didn't bother me, it never had. My mother and Randy had a lot in common. My own father had died while I was still in my teens, but up until his death I'd had all the love he had to give, which was probably just as well, because after his death my mother was even colder and more distant than she had been towards me before. Why she ever had a child I really had no idea because she clearly wasn't cut out to be a parent.

I had no doubt that if my mother had her way, I'd have gone straight from school into the first job I could get. Luckily for me, my father had left a watertight will — making it clear that he expected me to take up the university place he anticipated me being offered — with a sum of money held in trust to fund my years of study.

I had missed him so much and, starved of love at such a critical time in my life, it was no wonder I'd fallen for the first man to show me any real interest. The fact that Phil was a penniless labourer when we met did nothing to recommend him to my mother. She enjoyed pointing out, on every possible occasion that I had, 'married beneath me', but that she had 'expected no better', and I was, 'my father's daughter'.

The inference was that he must also have married beneath him, and that did not escape me, though my mother seemed to miss the irony of her dismissive words completely.

Thinking about my father, made me more than a little uncomfortable about the decision I was going to make should it become necessary. I wasn't sure he would have understood my reasons — I wasn't even sure I understood them myself — but the realization that my skills as a parent might mirror those of my mother definitely added weight to my argument against going ahead with a pregnancy if there was one.

That Phil's parenting skills wouldn't bear too close a scrutiny was another matter for consideration. Much as I loved him, I wasn't blind to his almost obsessional desire for a life that was run according to his needs and wishes. Easy going as I was, I went along with it to keep him happy, but I did wonder what effect he thought the disruption a baby would bring with it was going to have on that.

Considering options and implications in so much detail was making my head hurt. 'Can we leave thinking about all of this for another day?' I pleaded, collecting up his plate of now congealed eggs and bacon along with my own. 'Let's forget all about family problems, unplanned pregnancies and menopausal symptoms for a while. We have a free day for once, so why don't we just enjoy it?'

'How do you propose we do that?' Phil's tone was negative to say the least and I knew I was going to have my work cut out trying to fire up his enthusiasm. I poured him yet another black coffee and pushed the cup in front of him, determined to at least try.

In the end we went to the cinema — something we hadn't done in years — laughed our way through a Jim Carrey film, ate a bucket of popcorn and shared a Pepsi. We even held hands and kissed like teenagers. As we had back row seats it seemed like the right thing to do and for the first time in a long time we couldn't wait to get home to bed.

★ ★ ★

I had to wait three days for a doctor's appointment. It felt like three years and I chafed against a delay that made me increasingly certain that a child was on the way and even more certain that a child was the last — the very last — thing I wanted or needed in my life. The time for building a nest and rearing young was long gone as far as I was concerned — I was far too old and set in my ways. We both were.

To my annoyance Phil insisted on going with me and even helped me into the car of all things. Well, it wouldn't work and it wouldn't last, this solicitousness of his. He really needed to take a reality check instead of letting his family's warped values cloud his normally rational judgement.

The waiting room at the surgery was crowded and Phil visibly flinched each time anyone so much as sniffed near him. As a normally healthy male he had little cause to visit his GP apart from the yearly flu jab and a top-up for his tetanus when necessary. For anything else, like me, he'd always depended on the relevant remedy from the pharmacy.

Given Phil's limited, and always reluctant, dealings with the medical profession, his support on this occasion should have been touching. I did try to appreciate the effort he was undoubtedly making. However, it was becoming plainer by the minute he'd sooner be in any one of a thousand other places.

Feeling sorry for him, I touched his arm and told him, 'Don't feel you have to stay, Phil. Why don't you wait in the car, or go and buy a paper? I shouldn't be too long. I'm absolutely fine about going in to see the doctor by myself.'

'I wouldn't dream of it,' he assured me, adding, 'we're together in this — all the way.'

'Mrs Siddons.'

My heart leapt at the tinny sound of my name over the intercom. I stood up too quickly and my handbag fell to the floor. Phil bent to retrieve it, gathering up my purse, a couple of lipsticks and a pen that had fallen out without a hint of the impatience he might normally have shown. Then, taking my arm, he steered me firmly along the carpet-tiled corridor towards the doctor's office.

Dr Gerrard was waiting with the door open for us. 'Mrs Siddons — *and* Mr Siddons — it's not often we see either of you here. I wish all my patients were as healthy.'

The little joke raised polite smiles. Satisfied, the young man settled in the swivel chair behind his desk and indicated the two available seats on the opposite side.

'Please sit down. Now what can I do for you?' He focussed his attention on me, obviously because the appointment had been made in my name.

'She's pregnant,' Phil said proudly, getting straight to the point, only to have me cut in sharply, 'We only *think* I might be pregnant, Phil. That's why we're here, to have it confirmed that I am — or that I am not. Whichever is the case.'

It took real effort to keep a tetchy note out of my voice. Noting the GP's straight look in my direction, I could only hope to God the menopause really *was* imminent, in which case my worries would be over and we could go home and just get on with the life we had worked so hard to build together. Somehow, though, I didn't think it was going to be that simple.

'Right,' the doctor smiled at me and I immediately forgot the freckles and the mop of red hair and thought how very pleasant he was. He would surely understand that a woman of my age couldn't possibly be pregnant or that if I was I couldn't be expected to go through with it.

I couldn't remember noticing very much at all about him or his manner during my infrequent previous visits. Always in too much of a rush, I supposed and looking for a quick fix for whatever ailed me in the form of a prescription so that I could be on my way back to my busy life.

'Let's start at the beginning.' he continued encouragingly. 'What makes you think you might be pregnant?'

'Alex has missed two periods now.' Phil spoke before I had a chance, obviously determined to be in on the act.

'And the date of your last period was . . . ?' Dr Gerrard queried, looking at me and making notes with an old-fashioned fountain pen that scratched its way across the paper. I wondered how he ever read what he had written and why he didn't just use the computer like everyone else these days.

'It was the twenty-third of December.'

'Had you been trying to get pregnant?' He didn't even add, at your age, which immediately gained him many extra Brownie points in my eyes.

I managed a light laugh, 'We've been married for twenty-five years and never taken precautions,' I said ruefully.

The doctor looked from one of us to the other in silence, before curiosity finally got the better of him, 'You didn't ever think to seek medical advice regarding fertility?'

'In the end it didn't seem that important — to either of us. We accepted we would be childless and just got on with our lives. I expect a lot of couples do the same.' I seemed to be the one doing all the talking at this point.

The doubtful look on Dr Gerrard's face showed quite plainly he was far more used to childless couples anxiously seeking his help and advice, rather than just accepting what nature apparently wasn't willing to provide.

'Of course,' I went on, trying to push things along and at the same time endeavouring not to sound too eager or confident, 'I am forty-five years old, so the missed periods could be put down to the onset of the menopause, couldn't they?'

'That's certainly a possibility,' the doctor agreed politely, then he asked, 'Have you any other reason, besides the missed periods, for thinking you might be pregnant?'

'You've put on weight recently,' Phil pointed out helpfully, though he'd not mentioned noticing any such thing to me.

'I've been eating more,' I insisted quickly, but neither the doctor nor Phil responded, or even appeared to notice my comment come to that.

'Alex also did a home pregnancy test with a kit.'

'Just the one?'

I was sure I looked a little sheepish but I

carefully remained silent.

Phil spoke up, taking me by surprise, 'More than one. It was probably two or three.'

I stared at him, 'How did you . . . ?'

'I've been finding packets in the bin all this week. I was waiting for you to tell me,' he added accusingly.

'And . . . ?' Dr Gerrard didn't try to hide his smile.

'They were all positive,' I muttered reluctantly.

'*All* of them?' Phil looked gobsmacked as well he might, since I hadn't seen fit to share the use of the additional tests or indeed any of the results with him.

I felt as if I'd been caught with my fingers in the till but recovered enough to ask with an unconvincing laugh, 'Shop-bought kits can't be completely accurate surely?' which was pretty much in line with what Phil had said right at the beginning of all this.

'They are actually rarely wrong and would certainly not *all* be wrong. I think there is a very good indication that you are indeed pregnant. Congratulations, Mrs Siddons.'

Phil looked delighted, but unsurprised, as if he had just known the dreams and wishes he had so recently decided had been his all along were about to come true. The man was obviously far too used to getting his own way and I, on the other hand, was far too used to letting him have it. With no such intention on this occasion, I must have looked completely stunned. It just wasn't possible. There must be some mistake — there had to be.

'A couple of missed periods, home pregnancy testing kits, it's not exactly rocket science or even conclusive, is it? Well, *is* it? We don't want our hopes raised unnecessarily, do we?' I appealed to Phil continuing swiftly, 'only to find out it's all been a mistake and there is no baby.'

'I can understand your concern,' the doctor conceded, 'and I can examine you if you are both agreeable. It may be a little soon but at twelve weeks the enlarged uterus is often just palpable above the symphysis pubis.'

I hadn't the faintest idea what the hell the doctor was talking about, but if it meant putting an end to the ridiculous notion that I was pregnant, he could do whatever he liked as far as I was concerned.

Ushering me across the room and drawing the curtain around the examination couch, Dr Gerrard advised, 'Just remove your lower garments, Mrs Siddons,' and then to Phil, he said, 'it will just take a minute. It may be just as well to make an early diagnosis, given your wife's age. If she is indeed pregnant we can start dealing with practicalities that much sooner.'

'Oh, yes, indeed.' Phil immediately started

playing the concerned husband to the hilt, annoyingly relaxing into the part as if it were made for him.

I was undisturbed when the doctor joined me behind the curtain, as confident of the outcome as I could be. There was no baby — absolutely not.

Unfortunately, the doctor didn't agree, as he made quite clear when I was once again sitting beside Phil on the opposite side of the desk.

'But are you sure? Are you *quite* sure? There's no mistake.'

'I'm as sure as I can be. There is no mistake.'

That was the moment when for a beaming Phil everything went wonderfully right and for me it all went horribly wrong. A confirmed pregnancy was the one thing — the only thing — I hadn't been prepared for, as ridiculous as that might seem given all the indications to the contrary. I felt as if my body had suddenly been invaded by aliens and I didn't like it one little bit.

Listening to the GP and Phil discussing appointments for scans, tests, midwives and God alone knew what else, it seemed increasingly as if I was in the middle of a nightmare.

I could feel my heart thumping so hard

that it was a miracle I didn't suffer an immediate coronary. My blood pressure must be through the roof and I knew without checking that my face was burning a deeply unattractive shade of red. This could *not* be happening to me, there must be some dreadful mistake.

Sitting there in a state of complete shock, I might have been invisible for all the notice that was being taken of me and the trauma I was going through, as appointments were arranged and due dates — whatever they were — were discussed. I was actually glad of the temporary disregard, as it gave me time to make the huge effort necessary to gather my scattered thoughts into some semblance of order and decide on my next move.

I watched Phil impassively and it was like watching someone else's husband. This smiling man, full of enthusiasm for a pregnancy that shouldn't have happened, was a stranger to me. If asked, I would have staked my life on his agreeing with me that a termination was the only answer. He had said as much in the beginning, but somewhere along the way his feelings had changed. Unfortunately, mine — initially confused — had also undergone a change. It was clear to me that the idea of a child being born to middle-aged and totally unprepared parents

— though it might for the briefest while have seemed like a good idea — was ridiculous in the extreme.

I took a deep breath, realizing it was essential I remained calm. A rash word or action now could send my whole future spiralling out of control. What I needed, I realized, was time to think through the implications of a pregnancy — a family — at our time of life and to discuss with Phil calmly and rationally the consequences of keeping the child.

He was almost incoherent in his joy, but he obviously hadn't thought this through thoroughly. I had been doing little else, and my hands shook as I reached for my bag.

In my heart I may well have known that all the signs could not be wrong, but the sane and sensible part of me had refused to allow me to jump to the obvious conclusion, only for it to turn out to be the wrong one. Each day had been different as one day I'd believed wholeheartedly that I *was* pregnant, the next day I'd been convinced it was all a mistake, and now, finally, I had to face up to the fact of a confirmed pregnancy and Phil's changed attitude towards it.

A lot of what the doctor told me went totally over my head, though I tried really hard to concentrate. He seemed to under-stand completely, filling my hands with detailed notes, books and leaflets that I would be able to take in at my leisure.

Phil couldn't have been more solicitous. He took care to thank the doctor for the positive verdict, slipped a supportive arm around me as he led me from the surgery. I thought he might be in shock, too, but where I couldn't get a word out, he couldn't seem to shut up and babbled about cots and car seats, buggies and bloody baby baths until I could have screamed.

'You're very quiet,' he frowned at me across the car as I fixed the seat belt into place. 'You are pleased, aren't you? I know we weren't expecting that particular result, but . . . '

'I'm still in shock,' I managed, by way of explanation, 'I'll need a bit of time to get used to the idea.' I almost laughed at such an enormous understatement.

Phil was still watching me with a stupid understanding expression on his face. 'Oh, me, too,' he agreed eagerly. 'God there's so much to think about, so much to plan and deal with. Our whole lifestyle will have to change,' he smiled happily, 'but it will be a change for the better. We'll make the most fantastic parents.'

Why did I get the uncomfortable feeling Phil's enthusiasm for this unexpected pregnancy was really less about us — the baby's parents, and what *we* wanted — and was a whole lot more about Jacquetta and Randy the grandparents and what *they* wanted?

5

I didn't want to be the one to burst Phil's bubble, I really didn't, but he seemed to be under the misapprehension that, because he had changed *his* mind about the pregnancy so totally, I would simply follow suit. Actually nothing could have been further from the truth. The fact of the matter was — and after a lot of soul-searching I finally accepted it — I didn't want a baby, hadn't done for years, end of story.

It might be burying my head in the sand but, despite the doctor's verdict, the symptoms and the positive tests, I was still far from convinced that I really was pregnant. It just seemed too unlikely for words after all those years of nothing. If I *was* — and only time and the scan we'd been promised could confirm or disprove that — then I would tell him how I felt, but in his present buoyant mood I had a horrible feeling Phil would simply refuse to believe me.

In no time at all he seemed to have convinced himself that this was the best thing that could ever have happened to us, while I was just plain sorry it was far too late to take the 'morning after' pill.

I couldn't talk to Phil about my feelings and there was literally no one else. Phil and our marriage had filled my world since our wedding day, almost to the exclusion of anyone or anything else, I was beginning to realize. I enjoyed my working life as a lecturer in business studies, but keeping my husband happy within our relationship and supporting his business endeavours had always been far more important to me.

There was no doubt in my mind that such a blinkered attitude had made me lazy about making and keeping women friends. I got on well with my colleagues, but rarely socialized with any of them outside of working hours. That this was entirely my own doing and not due to any lack of invitations didn't escape me. I certainly didn't know any one person well enough to feel comfortable discussing anything of a personal nature, which left me in something of a quandary.

For the first time I regretted putting my job and marriage before my own needs and I had to rack my brain to think of someone — anyone — I could confide in, because if I didn't talk to someone soon I thought I would explode.

★ ★ ★

Del looked up from his perusal of a car's engine, almost banging his head on the raised bonnet. 'Hi there, Alex.'

He was obviously surprised to find me picking my way towards him — as well he might, I admitted to myself, feeling a bit embarrassed — I was hardly what you would call a regular visitor to their corner of the world. In fact I couldn't remember the last time Phil and I had called round to his eldest brother's for a chat and I knew for a certainty that I had never before visited Derek and Louise alone.

'Hi, Del.'

I looked at my brother-in-law in his greasy overalls, at the jumble of disembowelled cars and car parts, and wondered how Louise could bear living her life in the middle of what at best was a car lot and, at worst, little more than a scrapyard.

Then I remembered that in the early days of Phil starting his business, our small garden had been turned into a builder's yard, and wondered when exactly I had become such a crashing snob. It suddenly didn't take much effort to put a lot more warmth into my smile.

'You looking for our Louise?' Del lifted a querying eyebrow, and then laughing said, 'Well, you'd hardly be looking to buy a car from me today, would you?'

My smile widened even more as I teased, 'Depends what you have in stock. My first car was a mini. I bought it with money Dad left to me and did it up myself. I really loved that car and might be tempted by something similar.'

'Don't tell me, I can imagine,' Del was shaking his head, but he wore a huge grin, his teeth white against the oil streaks that covered his face, 'fluffy animals, dice and seat covers?'

'How did you guess?' I smirked, and wondered how come I was suddenly getting along so well with a man I'd scarcely exchanged two words with in the past, despite all the family gatherings over the years.

'Could be that Lou had one just like it.'

'I loved mine, too.' I turned to find that Louise had come to stand by the back door, and she advised Del to, 'Stop hogging my sister-in-law's company, Del, it's me she's come to see, I'll bet. Come on in, Alex.'

The kitchen of their detached home wasn't the showpiece of chrome and stainless steel that had been Phil's choice for our latest house, instead it had the feel of a farmhouse kitchen with the beamed ceiling and oak cupboards of a country home. There was a telephone hanging from the wall in one corner, and nearby a corkboard bristling with pinned up paperwork. Beside it was a calendar on which every date was covered in black scrawl, in addition notes were fixed to the fridge door with the aid of colourful magnets and young children's paintings and drawings were blu-tacked to the majority of the cupboard doors.

The ceramic tiles in my kitchen, on floor and wall, were pastel blue, the walls a wash of palest cream. The tiles above the work-tops here were a mish-mash of bright colours, and the walls, though also painted cream, were hung with a riot of family photos in unmatched frames. It was obvious that this cluttered room was the hub of a busy family home.

Louise saw me looking and smiled ruefully, 'I'm afraid it's not a patch on your fabulous kitchen,' she said. 'I was so envious the other night.'

'Oh, but this is lovely.' I didn't have to inject the note of enthusiasm into my voice because it was already there. 'This is really lovely.'

I don't think she believed me for a minute, but she ushered me to one of the solid wooden chairs at a big scrubbed table that looked as if it might have come from a real farmhouse. I could imagine them all sitting around it at mealtimes and tried to dismiss the pictures of Phil and I eating in our state-of-the-art kitchen or seated at either end of the long dining room table. Somehow the two images just didn't compare.

I had always loved our life — a life where we had no one to please but ourselves — so why, quite suddenly, did it seem to lack appeal?

The teapot and mugs that Louise brought to the table were the blue-hoop design of yesteryear, the tea was poured through a strainer, and the biscuits were home-baked.

'Oh, I didn't think,' Louise was apologetic, 'you might have preferred coffee.'

'Tea is always my first choice,' I insisted, though that wasn't always the case and sipped it with a great show of appreciation. Actually, it was rather good and tasted like the tea of my childhood. I was obviously buying the wrong brand of teabags, despite the fact they were wildly expensive, because my tea at home definitely lacked the flavour of this, served as it was in a thick pottery mug.

'Shouldn't you be at work?' Louise said, and immediately clapped a hand over her mouth. 'Oh, dear, I didn't mean that to come out the way it did. It sounded so rude, and I didn't mean that as a criticism. Perhaps you're on holiday?'

I shook my head, 'I'm not,' I admitted, 'and

I should be at work, but I pleaded a migraine and got someone else to do this morning's lecture. I can't seem to concentrate. In fact I feel like I'm going mad.'

'It'll be your hormones,' she said comfortably, 'they'll be all over the place right now. I was just the same when I was pregnant — with our Michelle especially.'

Louise patted my arm sympathetically and to my utter horror my eyes filled with tears, which then began to drip down my face. I never cried, not ever, but I just couldn't seem to stop myself.

'It'll be all right, you'll see,' she soothed, pushing a box of tissues in front of me, before pouring more tea into my cup and adding extra sugar.

'It won't.' I really burst out crying then and thought my heart would break as I heard myself say, 'I can't be pregnant, Louise, I just can't, and if I am I don't want the baby. There, I've said it now and you're shocked, I can see you are, but I don't, I really don't, though I know no one will believe me.'

'Darling,' this sister-in-law that I barely knew, despite the fact we'd been a part of the same family for so long, gathered me into her arms and rocked me back and forth as if I were one of her own weeping children, 'there, there,' she said, 'there, there. It will be all right. It will. You'll see.'

'How can it be?'

'Will you trust me?' Louise asked, 'when I tell you that things have a habit of turning out for the best, even when you can't always see at the time what that best might be.'

I stared at her, felt a smile start. 'You mean,' I said, 'that it will turn out to be a false alarm?'

She shook her head and I felt the slight hope that had started to build drain away, 'I can't promise you that. I just want you to take this whole situation and deal with what comes up one day at a time. Don't rush ahead and worry about tomorrow, next week, next month or next year. One day at a time has worked for me many times when the going looked as if it might be too tough to cope with.'

I just looked at Louise. I wanted to believe her and she was very convincing. I felt tired, emotional, and quite unable to cope with everything being thrown at me. Perhaps her way was a good one and she certainly did have more experience of change than I did. I felt myself relax slightly, the rigid set of my shoulders easing a little.

'That's better,' Louise said approvingly, rubbing a gentle hand on my upper arm. 'I was told once that we're never given more to deal with than we can cope with — I can see that you don't believe me — but I've always found it to be true. You're stronger than you think, Alex. Have faith in yourself.'

I don't know where Louise got her wisdom. I supposed bringing up four children on the limited income her husband's early precarious business ventures in the motor trade provided had taught her a few lessons. Things had turned out well for her in the end with her family grown, and the business doing well enough to provide a livelihood for several of them.

I'd always felt so sophisticated compared to my stay-at-home sister-in-law but I found myself hanging on to her every word and appreciating her common-sense attitude. After my visit with her I was calm enough to return to work and concentrate on the research needed for an article I was working on, and by the time I got home I was in an altogether more accepting, wait-and-see frame of mind.

Phil was home before me. I found him sitting at the kitchen table surrounded by the literature the doctor had provided us with, and some additional printed sheets of information that might well have come from the internet. I hadn't so much as glanced at even one of the leaflets in the house and wasn't aware that Phil had either, but a cup of cold coffee proved he had become totally absorbed.

'Omelette and salad all right for you?' I asked, as soon as I'd taken my coat off, refraining from comment on his choice of reading material.

He ignored my question and came back with one of his own. 'Did you know there's a big increase in the frequency of pregnancy complications in older mothers?' he demanded, pointing to the paperwork in front of him, just as if it was something I *would* know.

I shrugged, 'Is that what it says?'

'High blood pressure, pregnancy induced diabetes, bleeding, low-lying placenta.' He looked up, 'What's a placenta?'

'Um,' I searched somewhere in the recess of my mind, 'I think it's what the baby is attached to in the womb and where it gets its nutrients from — something like that.'

'The chance of pregnancy complications rises from 10.43 per cent for women aged 20–29, to 19.29 per cent for women aged between 35 and 39,' he quoted and in the little silence after his statement I knew we were both taking in the fact that I was several years older than the highest figure.

'That's why they have tests,' I pointed out.

'Oh, yes, the amniocentesis,' Phil said importantly, as if he were an expert which, of course, compared to me he obviously was. 'Prenatal diagnosis to tell you if your foetus has a problem such as Down's syndrome, spina bifida or cystic fibrosis and give you a chance to do something about it.'

'Like abort the baby?' I said brutally.

'I prefer to refer to it as a pregnancy termination,' he muttered.

'One and the same thing,' I didn't know why I was even arguing but there was something I didn't like about Phil's sudden apparent change in attitude. The inference appeared to be that I couldn't carry a healthy baby if my life depended on it.

'It's something we need to think about and discuss,' he advised, adding, kind of half-heartedly, I thought, 'though I'm sure it won't be necessary. Here,' he vacated the chair he was sitting in and indicated I should take it as he offered, 'I'll make the omelettes if you like, while you read through this literature. I've printed up some additional stuff from the internet — just so we can get a clear picture.'

'Thank you, that will certainly be helpful.'

My sarcasm was obviously lost on Phil as he busied himself collecting ingredients from the fridge and carried on speaking at the same time. I was impressed, because he wasn't exactly well known for his multi-tasking skills.

'The age of the mother has an effect on the birth itself, too, not just the pregnancy,' he cracked eggs into a bowl with all the expertise of Jamie Oliver and continued without looking at me even once, 'women thirty-five and over are more likely to have induced labour, diagnosis of foetal distress, epidural anaesthesia or forceps or ventouse delivery, and virtually all studies agree the rate of Caesareans rises with maternal age.'

It sounded as if he was word perfect, and I had to admit I was impressed. I didn't know half of what the information he was imparting meant — and I wasn't sure that he did either — but Phil had certainly been doing his homework. The question was: why?

By the time Phil placed an impressively fluffy omelette, succulent with mushrooms and melted cheese in front of me, my emotions were all over the place. I was pretty certain I wasn't going to be able to eat a thing, even if it was something I *should* be eating in my condition. I'd been all set to justify my reasons for not continuing with the pregnancy — if indeed there was a pregnancy — and now it seemed as if Phil was about to beat me to it in the biggest about-turn since Hitler conceded defeat at the end of the Second World War.

'And there's another thing to consider,

according to the information I printed up,' Phil took his place opposite me setting down his own plate of food. He even paused to tuck in with every appearance of enjoyment, and then chew thoughtfully for a long maddening moment before he continued, 'apparently inexplicably, more babies die, *in utero*, right at the end of pregnancy in the older group of mothers. So you could go right through the pregnancy, only to lose the baby right at the very end, and it would all have been for nothing.'

I thought I had heard enough, much more than enough, if I was honest, so I offered Phil a challenge. 'Okay,' I said, 'you've told me all the bad stuff you've discovered, now tell me something *good* about being an older mother. I take it there is something good to report?'

He shrugged, 'Apparently you'll be more confident and relaxed during pregnancy and not so bothered about what you look like.'

'Oh, well, *that's* all right then.' I pushed the omelette away untouched and asked outright. 'What are you trying to say, Phil? You *are* trying to say something in a very roundabout and long-winded way, aren't you?'

He had the grace to look a bit shamefaced, and tried to justify what he was about to reveal with a show of very unlikely concern, 'Anything could happen, and I'm actually starting to think that expecting you to go through a pregnancy at your age is a bad idea.' He sat back looking relieved and almost pleased with himself.

'Only yesterday you thought it was a great idea,' I pointed out evenly, 'so, what's changed since then?'

'Well, we didn't have all this information then. If you will read it through, as I have, the facts speak for themselves.'

'There's actually nothing there that the doctor didn't already warn us about.' I was surprised that I remembered anything the doctor had said but, suddenly, I did.

'I didn't take it all in at the time, but now I have I think you should have a termination,' Phil's words came out in a rush and, even as I was taking them in, I couldn't think for the life of me why I wasn't immediately feeling as relieved as hell.

This was exactly what I wanted, wasn't it? If I *was* pregnant — and there was at least some indication that I might be, despite the fact I'd been living in a state of denial since the shock of the positive pregnancy test — then I wanted rid.

Here was the solution to a problem I'd just wanted to go away from the outset. A termination could be arranged and carried out and we'd be back to square one. It would be as if none of it had ever happened.

Instead of the relief I'd expected, I felt instead an overwhelming sadness. It was almost unbelievable that this baby, miraculously and naturally conceived in an act of love after so many years of a childless marriage, could be so totally unwanted. The poor, poor little bastard had never stood a chance with us as its parents. I could have wept.

'Do you want me to phone the doctor?' Phil queried, as if the whole thing had been discussed at length and agreed by us both.

I found myself nodding numbly.

He reached out, patted my hand and said kindly, 'It's for the best. We both know that.'

He was right, of course. We couldn't possibly become parents at our age. You only had to look at the risks involved. The chances of a healthy baby — and mother — at the end of the pregnancy were, apparently, minimal. The facts spoke for themselves. Anyway, what would we do with a child at our ages? The whole idea was ridiculous.

Just as I had gone along with Phil's original enthusiasm for the pregnancy, without making my own feelings clear, I now went along with his determination to delete the whole episode from our lives. He *was* right it really was for the best, but I just wished it were happening to someone else and not to me — to us.

I'm not sure what made me ask, but something prompted me to say, 'What if — when it comes down to it — I can't go through with the termination? What then?'

That had Phil's attention. He stared at me and his expression was unreadable, 'What do you mean you won't go through with it?'

'That's not what I said. I said, what if . . . '

'I heard what you said, and to me it sounds like the same bloody thing. The end result is, you'll be saddling us with a kid neither of us wants.'

'We might change our minds when it's born,' I pointed out, reasonably I thought.

'*You* might,' Phil said emphatically, '*I* won't, and if you go through with this pregnancy . . . '

I was being bloody minded, but I didn't care. 'If I go through with this pregnancy — for which, incidentally, we are *both* responsible — what then?'

'You'll go through with it on your own.'

I was shocked to the core and I didn't mind admitting it.

'Do you mind telling me what's brought about this total change of heart?' I said quietly, 'because there's more to it than facts, figures and statistics from the internet, isn't

97

there? Lots of couples successfully have babies later in life whatever you've managed to dig up to the contrary.'

'Yes, and equally, lots realize how much a child will disrupt their lives and decide against it.' Phil stared at me, his eyes narrow and suspicious, 'Why are you doing this, Alex? Why start raising this now when it's already been decided. There's no point.'

'It was already decided by *you* before I even walked in the door,' I said, 'and there is a point when a child's life — our child's life — is at stake. This is going to be our one and our *only* chance of the family we once wanted so badly.'

'Yes, *once*,' Phil was getting angry, he was obviously far too used to getting his own way and for that I had no one to blame but myself, 'that's the whole point. That 'once' was a very long time ago. I'm too old — *we're* too old — to start bringing up kids now. I'm too set in my ways, I'd be a *terrible* dad . . . '

Where on earth had that come from? A frown pinched my brow and I stared at him suspiciously, 'What makes you say that?'

'Well, you know, me being born late in my parent's marriage made it difficult for my own dad to accept me.'

'He had no difficulty accepting your brother Richard and he's only two years older than you. It's not like there was a huge gap and *your* dad was only about thirty-five when you were born, for God's sake. That's hardly ancient. I don't know what his reasons were or are for his treatment of you, but that's not it, and if that's what he's saying he's not being honest with you.'

'You don't understand and neither did I, but today he finally explained it all to me, and he said . . .'

'I think I can guess what he said.'

'He was only trying to help.'

'Help?' I repeated, adding, 'Well, if you believe that, you'll believe anything. He doesn't want us to have a child, does he? This termination is *his* idea and you'll do anything — yes, *anything* — to get that cantankerous old man's approval.'

'That's not it at all,' Phil said furiously.

'That's exactly it,' I rounded on him, 'you wanted the child to get his approval and now you don't want it for the same reason. You're pathetic and not fit to be a father, so you're right about that at least.'

'What are you going to do, then, bring it up on your own? Because that's what it will come down to.'

'I haven't made up my mind what I'm going to do, but I will give the matter careful consideration, weigh up all the pros and cons, and *then* I'll let you know what I decide. And, let me tell you this, the thought of bringing up a child on my own doesn't worry me in the least.'

I marched out of the kitchen with my head held high and could feel Phil's gaze burning a hole in my back. Thankfully, the fact that I was shaking from head to foot couldn't have been apparent to him and nor could he have guessed that even the thought of bringing up a child *together* actually worried me quite a lot. The thought of bringing up a child *alone* scared me half to death.

6

I think Phil assumed I would give in and do what he wanted once I'd thought things over. I think I assumed I would, too, but as the days passed and I was nowhere near reaching a definite decision, I was beginning to get impatient with myself.

'Wait and see' was all very well in some circumstances — and it had often worked well for me in the past — but in the case of a pregnancy, unwanted or otherwise, it was something that just wasn't going to go away. I knew perfectly well that if I didn't act soon any choice we had in the matter would be taken out of my hands and Phil's, too.

It came as quite a shock when, very suddenly, it seemed as if my mind was going to be made up for me. Tutoring business matters was hardly a strenuous affair, but I was passionate about my subject and tried to inject real enthusiasm into my teaching. After one such session I had just reached my office when a slight feeling of discomfort had me hurrying to the loo believing a tummy upset was imminent.

At first I thought my period had simply

finally arrived, but there seemed to be an awful lot of blood. I cleaned myself up as best I could and, after making a makeshift pad from loo paper, shakily made my way back to my desk.

The colleague I shared an office with barely looked up from the papers she was marking, merely acknowledging my presence with a quick, 'Hi,' before returning to her task. I knew Julie wasn't being unfriendly, but was just eager to clear a pile of assignments before the weekend. A divorcee with grown-up children, she liked to make the most of her free time and who could blame her?

I sat for a moment or two, a bit stunned, before calmly telling Julie I was bleeding and asking if she would mind phoning for an ambulance. If she was shocked she hid it well and, showing great presence of mind, she wrapped my coat and hers tightly round me because I was icy cold by then and my teeth were chattering. While she was on the phone she must have also contacted Phil, though I was in such a daze I didn't recall her even asking for his phone number because he was waiting for me by the time I got to the hospital.

I think we both knew I'd suffered a miscarriage and, to his credit, he didn't say it was 'for the best', or anything else remotely trite, just told me everything would be all right and held my hand as we went for the scan that would confirm this diagnosis.

I started crying as the gel was squeezed on to my belly and really had no idea why. I had rebelled against the possibility of a pregnancy from the start, so I was hardly going to miss what I'd never believed I had in the first place. Part of me couldn't help but suspect that our very negative attitudes had played a big part in this final outcome and though my head told me this was impossible, in my heart I felt as guilty as sin.

I concentrated hard on ignoring what was going on and gripped Phil's hand hard. He gave mine a reassuring squeeze back as the midwife, nurse, or whatever she was, did whatever it was she was supposed to be doing, so that she could give us the news that would return our life together back to normal.

'There's your baby.'

That was a possibility I hadn't bargained for. My eyes flew open and I stared at the woman as if she had gone completely mad.

'Look,' she encouraged, turning the fuzzy screen a fraction more in my direction.

I looked, but even straining my eyes I couldn't see anything that looked remotely like a baby, though I could see a tiny rhythmic flicker like the ticking of a clock, slightly to one side.

'Is that . . . ?'

'The heartbeat?' Her smile widened, 'It certainly is.'

She went on to trace the skeleton, pointing out a leg, an arm, until the vision became clear, even to me, and there was no denying the child I was carrying. A child who would have been, she explained, one of a twin, but this one had somehow managed to cling to life as its sibling had slipped away.

I turned to look a Phil. His gaze was fixed on the screen, an unreadable expression on his face. I touched his hand, but he refused to look at me and just went on staring at the fuzzy image of our child. I couldn't begin to imagine what was going through his mind. How could I when I didn't even know what I was thinking myself?

I could have stayed in hospital, but I chose to leave with Phil. I was given to understand that the remaining pregnancy might not be 'viable' and that when you lose one baby there is a serious risk of losing the other. There was nothing to be done but wait and see and I'd just as well do that in the comfort of my own home — except there was suddenly nothing comfortable about my home. I felt as if Phil held me personally responsible for this latest development and his accusing gaze followed me wherever I went.

I don't know what he told his family but they were conspicuous by their absence, though flowers arrived from Louise and, surprisingly, also from Jacquetta. I successfully fought the urge to bin hers after a tussle with my conscience, she was Phil's mother, after all, and they *were* addressed to both of us.

With every passing day the remaining child's survival became more of a certainty and I must have appeared more accepting of the pregnancy, because in the end Phil seemed compelled to speak his mind.

'You agreed,' he said, in what he must have felt was a reasonable tone, '*we* agreed, that a termination was the best option.'

I overlooked the fact that I had actually agreed to nothing, acknowledging that my silence might have been construed as agreement and merely said, 'But surely you can see things have changed now.'

'I don't see how,' he said stubbornly.

'No, you don't, do you?' I felt a bit sad really. 'Before the miscarriage I might have gone ahead and had an abortion in the end. I might not. Had I realized I was pregnant sooner I probably would have, because I feel no more desire for a child at this time in my life than you do.'

'Well, then,' he murmured, as if that was all there was to it. 'Don't tell me you fell in love with a fuzzy image on a screen, Alex, that is so not you. You don't have a single maternal bone in that slender body.'

'No,' I denied, finding the strength from somewhere to voice my real feelings at last, 'I didn't fall in love with the image, but I was amazed and not a little impressed by the child's determination to survive. Had it miscarried along with its twin I could have accepted that, but now I feel it does at least deserve a chance at life. I've also finally realized that I have been given this one and only opportunity for the family that used to be my dream. I would be a fool to throw that away just on *your* say so. Especially as your decision has been heavily influenced by someone who definitely does *not* have your best interests at heart, let alone mine.'

'This has *nothing* to do with anyone else,' Phil insisted, not altogether truthfully I felt. 'I don't want a child, and neither do you, if you would only be honest with yourself. What about your job, everything you've worked for?'

'Christ,' I said sharply, 'just listen to yourself. This is a baby, not a terminal illness.

We don't have to give up a damn thing if we don't want to. Hiring a nanny would be the obvious answer to everything and then we'd have the best of both worlds. A baby need not disrupt our lives.'

I wasn't actually sure whether I was trying to convince Phil or myself by the time I'd finished talking, but he wasn't having any of it anyway.

He gave me a look. 'I know what you're trying to do, Alex, and it's not going to work. You won't like what I'm going to say, but I'll say it anyway. The words are *mine*, they are the way *I* feel, and I can't *not* say them just to make you feel better,' Phil paused, and then continued relentlessly, 'I don't want this child, I don't want any child. I don't care what the child wants — I don't even care what you want. I can't allow that to influence me. I'm being as honest as I know how to be.'

'But . . . '

'There *is* no but. You can have this baby, Alex, or you can have me. You cannot have us both. It's your choice, and I will leave you to make it on your own. I do love you, but not enough to be a parent to a child I don't want, and please don't try to tell me that even a bad father is better than no father because we both know that's a lie. I have absolutely no intention of allowing history to repeat itself in

107

the Siddons family.'

Phil turned on his heel, but not before I had seen the look in his eyes. Despite myself, and what I was going through, I did truly believe this was every bit as hard for him as it was for me. Even so, the sound of the front door slamming behind him sounded the death knell on our marriage. I knew for sure that if I wanted to go through with this pregnancy there was absolutely no doubt I would be doing it alone.

At forty-five years old you'd have thought I could handle anything that life threw at me, but I was very uncertain about how I was going to deal with this. I wasn't in any way, shape or form prepared for what I could only guess I would be letting myself in for.

An only child, I obviously had no experience of siblings or, therefore, their offspring, and had so little to do with Phil's family that I couldn't remember ever holding any of his numerous nephews and nieces. The few friends I ever had over the years were career women like me and most — like me — were childless.

Without Phil's dominant presence to influence my every move I had serious doubts about whether I'd be capable of taking care of myself, let alone a baby. In all these years I'd not had the responsibility for so much as a pet cat, so how would I cope with a helpless human being? I really had no idea at all.

Phil would change his mind, I assured myself. He wouldn't turn his back on his only child.

The words were hollow, but that hope was all I had to cling to. Time, I decided was what he needed. We both needed time to come to terms with what was happening to us.

Deep in thought, I almost leapt out of my skin when the doorbell shrilled. I hurried to my feet, convinced it would be Phil. He'd had a change of heart and come rushing back, having left, of course, without his key.

I was smiling broadly and ready to fling myself into his arms when I threw open the door — to find Louise and Rich on the step and by the looks on their faces there had been a death in the family.

'What is it? What's happened? It's not Phil is it?' I reached out, pulled Louise into the house, pleading, 'Tell me. He's had an accident, hasn't he? I knew I shouldn't have let him rush off like that.'

It was Rich who said, 'We haven't even seen Phil, not since . . . We've come to see you. To see how you are — you know — after . . . '

It wasn't often I'd seen Rich lost for words and then I remembered the flowers Louise had sent for the lost baby and realized they had come to offer sympathy.

'Let's put the kettle on, shall we?' I said, making my way through to the kitchen.

'You go and put your feet up,' Louise insisted, 'you should be resting after what you've been through.'

'I'm fine, really,' but she almost pushed me into a chair and got on with filling the kettle and reaching into the cupboard for crockery. At least after the recent nocturnal visit she'd remembered where everything was, I noticed.

'I expect our Phil has taken it hard,' Rich sat down opposite me, his usually cheerful face quite sombre.

'He's not happy,' I agreed, unwilling to have a go at him behind his back. Perhaps they all agreed with him anyway. I tried to change the subject. 'How come you're here with Louise? Not that there's any reason you shouldn't be, of course, but I just wondered where Del was.'

'Well,' Louise looked a bit uncomfortable, but went on, 'Phil phoned as we were about to leave. He obviously wanted to talk, so we left Del to meet up with him and Rich brought me over here.'

'She's rubbish at finding her way. Not safe to be let out really. I reckon she only ever drives to the corner shop and back, and I wanted to come anyway,' he smiled at me, 'to see how you are.'

'Oh, I'll survive,' I found myself smiling back a bit crookedly, adding, 'somehow.'

'You must be sad, though.' Louise brought the tray to the table and busied herself pouring tea into the mugs she must have found at the back of the cupboard. I didn't recall using them since we'd lived here. They'd never gone with the image of the posh new house, somehow. 'Oh, I know you had concerns, but you'd have managed, I know you would, and to have it happen for you at last and now this.'

'Actually,' I chewed thoughtfully on a Rich Tea biscuit, 'I don't think there's the remotest chance I'd have coped with twins — as it is . . . '

'*Twins?*' Louise and Rich expostulated together and Louise's eyes filled with tears as she pleaded, 'Oh please don't tell me you lost *twins*, Alex. That's so unfair.'

'I thought you knew,' I said, curiously, 'you sent the flowers.'

'Yes,' Louise agreed, 'we sent the flowers as a way of saying sorry because Phil told us you lost the baby.'

'He didn't say there were two?' I thought I already knew the answer.

Louise shook her head, but Rich just stared

at me as if he knew there was more to come.

'Or that I was still pregnant with one of them?' I said flatly, but again I already knew the answer.

Her jaw dropped so fast it nearly hit the table but she managed to shake her head again wordlessly.

That was when I knew for sure there was no hope for Phil and me. He had quite happily let his family think the miscarriage was the end of it, because he'd fully expected me to either suffer another voluntary miscarriage or to have the remaining pregnancy terminated medically in accordance with his clearly specified wishes.

He'd obviously been quite happy to accept all the sympathy, however, and allow it to be thought that we had no child from the pregnancy that had finally happened because I couldn't carry it to full term.

In that moment of realization, I thought I actually hated Phil. I did know the baby and I would be better off without him.

It was Rich who finally repeated, 'You're still pregnant?'

I nodded, 'With one baby, yes, I can't believe Phil didn't tell you.'

Louise looked troubled, 'I know it's probably none of our business, Alex, but do you want to tell us what's going on here?'

Rich stood up. 'I'll go if you like.'

I shook my head, 'There's no need. Phil will be telling Derek his version, you'd just as well hear mine and then you can make your own minds up. I've no one else to talk to anyway, that's what happens when you put your all into a marriage and career to the exclusion of everything else — you suddenly realize that's *all* you have.'

Rich laughed and the sound was harsh and grated on the ear. 'You don't have to tell me, though *I* wasn't even wise enough to save something for my marriage,' he said. 'In my own defence I did think my career was *our* future. My problem was I didn't put anything into the here and now of our relationship. I failed to see that my wife and child needed me to invest time in *them*, too. I was shocked when Jess left, but when I sat down and thought about it, I really wasn't surprised. I could see I'd got exactly what I deserved, but I truly thought you and Phil had got it right and really had it all.'

'We thought we did, too,' I agreed, 'then this happened, exactly what we once wanted, but far too late. It threw us into turmoil and neither of us knew what we wanted any more.'

'But Phil was thrilled . . . ' Louise began, looking puzzled.

'For a while,' I agreed, 'until Randy convinced him becoming a father at his time of life was a bad idea. He doesn't want a grandchild from Phil and me,' I could hear my voice rising but I couldn't seem to help it, 'and he's somehow managed to convince Phil that history will only repeat itself if he tries to be a father to our baby.'

Rich groaned, and leaned his head into his hands. 'Now why doesn't it surprise me that Dad had something to do with this? But surely Phil has a mind of his own, why on earth would he allow someone so obviously biased to cloud his judgement like that?'

'But I've been just as bad,' I finally admitted with great honesty, 'going from refusing absolutely to believe I was pregnant, to not wanting the baby but saying nothing because Phil was so happy and then going along with the idea of an abortion because that seemed to be a solution.'

'You want it now, though?' This came from Louise.

'I still don't really know *what* I want,' I admitted slowly, but very honestly, 'but I can hardly turn the clock back, can I? I don't think I'm equipped to cope with a baby at my age, or that I'm good mother material, to be honest, but this baby seems so determined to live. It seems that the very least I can do is to give the poor little so-and-so a chance.'

'And Phil?' Rich asked.

'Phil's made it clear it's him or the baby. He doesn't want it and he won't accept it. It looks as if I'm to make the leap from happily married and childless, to single-parent family almost over night.'

'He'll change his mind,' Rich said with a confidence he was obviously far from feeling.

'I hope you're right,' I said, 'because I don't think I can do this alone. Phil was right when he said I didn't have a maternal bone in my whole body.'

Louise shook her head and said, in a very firm tone, 'Whatever Phil decides, you won't have to do it alone, because we'll be here for you, won't we, Rich?'

'Of course,' he agreed stoutly, 'but I'm sure it won't come to that. Phil will come around, you'll see. It's been a lot for him to take in, so much has happened in a very short time. He'll make a great dad, and I'm sure that's what our Del is telling him right at this minute.'

Rich sounded convincing, but he obviously had his doubts because when they finally left he pressed something into my hand and murmured, 'In case you need to get away for a bit, Alex. Feel free to treat the place as your own.'

Surely he didn't really think it would come to that? I watched them leave and, if anything, I was more troubled than before. The fact that Phil had kept from his family the news of my continuing pregnancy was a real shock. That clearly was not the action of a man who had any interest in 'coming around' and accepting a situation that was obviously an anathema to him but, stubbornly, I clung to the hope that he *would* have a sudden change of heart because I didn't know what else to do.

In fact, with every passing day it became more apparent that the hope was a futile one. I couldn't believe the way our solid marriage had crumbled so swiftly around my ears. Even though Phil had made his feelings perfectly clear, I guess that in my heart I had not truly believed that he would suddenly change from a reasonably caring human being into the kind of man who would turn his back on his wife and unborn baby. It just goes to show how wrong you can be.

From a close and loving couple sharing a home, a life and a bed, we became strangers who couldn't even share a conversation without it turning into an argument. I didn't know where Phil was spending his time when he wasn't at work, only that he wasn't spending it with me. I grieved for all that I had lost through my own stubborn insistence in continuing with the pregnancy and questioned over and over again whether I was doing the right thing.

With everything that was going on, finding Jacquetta on my step when I came home from work at the end of a particularly trying day was the last thing — the *very* last thing I wanted or needed.

7

'What can I do for you?'

I knew I couldn't have sounded less helpful or welcoming and, quite frankly, I didn't give a damn. I had absolutely nothing to thank Jacquetta for. She might not *quite* have been the mother-in-law from hell, since she did at least stay out of my way on the whole, but her low opinion of me had never been a secret. She rarely even acknowledged my existence at family gatherings.

It was something I had lived with — without ever knowing the reason for it — through all the years of my marriage. Every effort I had made to be friendly in the early days of my relationship with Phil had been rebuffed until, very soon, I simply stopped trying.

'May I come in?'

It was on the tip of my tongue to refuse, but there was something about her demeanour that made me reconsider. Dressed from head to toe in very expensive black, make-up immaculate as ever, chestnut wig topped by a black satin cap-style hat, she looked much as she always did, but there was something in her eyes — a look I couldn't quite put my finger on — that made me open the door wider and usher her in.

Even as I turned to follow her I was regretting my action, but it was too late by then, I could hardly turn her around and throw her back out — much as it would have pleased me to do so.

Jacquetta paused, probably waiting for me to show her the way. I didn't recall her ever paying a visit to this house, though we had lived in it for over a year. I was aware she and Phil met up regularly for lunch, but where they conducted those meetings was of little interest to me. That it would be well away from Randy's hostile presence went without saying.

I found myself leading her into the lounge. Somehow I just couldn't see us sitting cosily in the kitchen sharing a pot of tea.

She looked around with undisguised curiosity. 'It is very — elegant,' she said, 'the sort of house I once could have seen myself living in — if things had turned out differently.'

Her home these days was a warden-controlled flat rented from the local authority and adapted to cope with Randy's failing health and limited mobility. Before that it had been a council semi but very smart and kept in good repair and redecorated regularly by her sons. I wasn't sure exactly what she meant, except that she had, perhaps, expected better. I found I wasn't curious enough to ask. I just wished she would get to the point of her visit and then leave.

'Will you take a seat?' I felt obliged to offer, cursed as always by the good manners my parents had instilled in me as a child.

She sank elegantly on to an armchair, crossed her black-silk encased legs daintily and, for the first time, looked directly into my face.

'We've never got along,' she said in a crashing understatement, 'but there is no real reason for that.'

No real reason, apart from the fact she'd detested me from the word go and had made no secret of the fact she had never thought me good enough for her favourite son, but perhaps she didn't see those as reasons.

'I've always admired you greatly,' she continued.

Now that *was* news to me and I could feel myself gawping at Jacquetta like some kind of imbecile. As a lecturer I was rarely lost for words, but she had me there and I couldn't think of one thing to say in reply to such a blatantly untrue statement.

'You did not realize this?'

I shook my head helplessly.

'You are clever, talented, independent. I do

not expect to have a daughter-in-law so smart and I am envious of you always — and not a little in awe. I do know my son would not be where he is today in business without you behind him — and that makes it hard for me to understand the way he behaves to you now.' She paused, and then seemed to find her voice again. 'You lose his child, no fault, no blame, but it is clear to see he punishes you for that. Why?'

I wasn't sure how much she knew — or how little — about recent events, and didn't know how to reply. All the other stuff I wasn't about to fall for and couldn't fathom her reasons for telling me now. There was never anyone less admiring of my place in society than Jacquetta. She had no use for a childless daughter-in-law and whatever else might be accomplished was immaterial in the light of that great failing.

'Have you tried asking him?' I said finally.

'He will not talk to me about this. He speaks with Randolph — after all the years of hate between them — and he also tells me nothing. In the end I have to come to you, as one mother to another, to tell you how I grieve for your loss, and how ashamed I am that my son — your husband of so many years — has let you down so badly when you need him most.'

121

I'd never seen Jacquetta cry, not once, not ever, and I was horrified as one tear quickly followed another, generally wreaking havoc on the heavy mask of make-up. My instinct was to take her in my arms but there was too much bitter history between us and I didn't have to fight the urge very hard or for very long.

'You must go back and ask your husband why he is so determined to convince Phil that besides being a lousy son he will also make a lousy father. He's succeeded, of course, because however much he denies it, Phil will still do anything — and I do mean *anything* — to get his father's approval, even if that means getting rid of his child.'

'Mon dieu,' Jacquetta put her hand to her throat, 'but Randolph loves his grandchildren, he would not do such a thing.'

I didn't argue, just looked at her and watched the doll-like face crumple even more. I didn't have to justify my remarks, aware that she knew the truth as well as I did. Randolph — for his own unexplained reasons — did not want a grandchild with Phil as the father.

Watching her struggle was difficult, but I had to allow her to work things out for herself, to tell me what exactly she knew without any prompting from me.

'What has happened, Alexandra? Have they forced you into an abortion between them?' The heavily made-up eyes were full of tragic tears, spilling over and causing more sooty tracks through the layers of foundation and blusher.

In spite of myself, I did begin to feel sorry for her. To discover the two men she loved most in the world had feet of clay must have been hideous but, as I had to remind myself, she had stood by for years and allowed the damaged relationship between Phil and his father to develop when her early intervention might have made all the difference.

I relented a little and told her, 'The baby was miscarried naturally,' she visibly relaxed, so I added with deliberate cruelty, 'but not before Phil had already made his desire to get rid of it quite clear. To be fair,' I added, trying very hard to be, 'I was fairly easy to manipulate and had all but agreed because I wasn't at all sure I wanted a child so late in life either.'

'Understandable,' Jacquetta said with a nod. 'You have the nice life, the nice home you have both worked so hard for and rearing children is not easy at any age.'

I confess I was shocked that she appeared so understanding and felt obliged to point out, 'You managed it.'

'I had no choice,' she said simply, 'but to get on with it. I burned my bridges in my home country by running off with Randolph. My family disowned me. I was alone in a foreign land, married to a virtual stranger when the babies began to arrive. I was young, healthy, what choice did I have but to manage the best way I could.'

'It must have been difficult for you.'

'Not the life I was promised, or the one I would have chosen, but the clock can never go back.' Jacquetta's tone was rueful.

'No,' I agreed, thinking of my own situation. I hadn't intended it, but found myself offering, 'Shall I make tea?'

'That would be very nice,' Jacquetta accepted graciously, and I wondered why we couldn't have been this civilized years ago. 'I will come and help you, you are not long home from hospital and should be resting and recovering from your ordeal.'

It was becoming increasingly obvious she didn't yet know about the surviving baby. I guessed Rich was back on his oil rig and Louise must have kept the knowledge to herself thus far, perhaps still expecting Phil to 'come round to the idea' and 'do the right thing' whatever that was.

'What I don't understand,' she said suddenly, fiddling with the cups and saucers, 'is why Phillipe is behaving so badly towards you when he has got what you say he wants. Is he not happy that the baby is no more?'

Tired of playing games, I said bluntly, '*That* baby is no more — its sibling had other ideas and decided to stay in the womb. I'm still pregnant, Jacquetta and Phil is angry with me because of that.'

We both jumped as a cup smashed to smithereens on the ceramic-tiled floor. Standing side-by-side we stared at the shards of crockery scattered around our feet.

'No,' she said harshly, reaching out a hand as if to ward me off, 'the child survives and Phillipe still wishes to be rid of it. I cannot believe this of him.'

I shrugged suddenly past caring and bitterly regretting the offer of tea. I should have known this new softer Jacquetta was just a figment of my own imagination. 'Believe what you like,' I said harshly.

'But this is history repeating,' she said, and she sounded so sad. 'It is just exactly how Randolph behaved and why there is this bad feeling that goes all through the years. I cannot bear that it happens all over again.'

'I think,' I said, intrigued by her comments and willing her to tell me more, 'that we had better sit down and talk about this properly.' I carried the tray, reset with fresh cups, across to the table, urging Jacquetta to be seated while I took a brush to the broken china.

'Now,' I went on, joining her and reaching for the teapot, 'I think I deserve to know the family history, don't you?' and she nodded sombrely.

Jacquetta seemed relieved to share what must have been a huge burden for her to have carried for so long, the words poured out in a torrent of grief and I finally understood just how closely history *was* repeating itself.

Despite her youth, Jacquetta had loved Randolph, though she was the first one to admit he was not the man she had thought she was marrying. He had great charm, she said, and I had to believe her, despite having seen absolutely no evidence to back up her claim. Of the two of them, she soon realized she was actually the stronger and she took charge of the running of their lives, but always in such a way that Randolph's male ego never felt threatened.

'He couldn't cope with the responsibility, you see,' she said simply, 'but still must always feel he heads the household. In his heart he accepts what we both know. He had let me down, and badly, but we played a game so that his pride should not become damaged. In his own way he has always loved me. I have never doubted it. The children were his way of tying me to him. I knew that. But after five he thought enough was enough — and I agreed. However, accidents happen and another baby was expected. Randolph was not happy, though why one more child should make any difference I could not see and I desperately wanted the child. Then I miscarry, just like you, and we think that is the end of the matter, but there was another baby to come and that was my Phillipe.'

'He was one of a twin, too?' I stared at Jacquetta.

She nodded, and said again, 'History, it repeats. Randolph *never* wanted that baby, but the child was very special to me, and he became the one huge bone of contention between us. I should have walked away with my children — I could have survived without Randolph, but,' she added, 'Randolph could not have survived without me.'

'In any case, making everything right for one son would have meant leaving five others without a father. Randolph punishing Phillipe over the years just for being born has been his way of punishing me. He was — and is — jealous of the bond between us. I thought — hoped — that time would change things and when that didn't happen I simply prayed that my love would be enough.'

'Could you never talk to Randolph, make

him see how unfairly he was behaving towards a defenceless child? Surely you could make him see, he's always loved you so much.'

'I tried but it made no difference. Phillipe loves *you*, but will he accept this child?'

I shook my head.

'However,' she was suddenly brisk, 'it is early days and I think he may yet see sense. Give him time, my dear. Please, will you give him some time to come to his senses? I am convinced he will eventually do the right thing. Phillipe is *not* Randolph.'

'I know that,' I agreed, 'and I wouldn't want you to think that I entirely blame Phil for his reluctance to welcome a baby into his life at this late stage. I cannot say, hand on heart that I'm happy to find myself pregnant at my age either, but the thought of the alternative doesn't make me happy either. Presently, I am just going along with the situation, but I have no feelings for the child and if going ahead with the birth signals the end of my marriage, I fear I never will have.'

'You've been through so much at a very emotional time — and with no support, I'm afraid — I would think that makes your reaction very normal. It is early days and would be strange, I feel, if you were overwhelmed with love for the little one who is the cause of all this upheaval.'

I stared at Jacquetta — a woman I'd had good reason to detest for more years than I cared to remember. For all of her bravado, her certainty that things would even yet turn out right, I could see the doubt I felt in my heart mirrored in her dark eyes. She looked old, afraid and more vulnerable than I had ever seen her. She also looked a mess, with her chestnut wig awry and the sooty streaks of her tears marring the porcelain mask of make-up she habitually wore.

I dredged up a smile from somewhere, but resisted the urge to touch even her hand. 'Why?' I said softly. 'Why have we never talked like this before, Jacquetta?'

'I never thought you would heed me. You are so clever, a career woman, independent and wise. I could not compete.'

'It wasn't a competition for Phil's love, you know,' I told her. 'You are his beloved mother and will always have a very special place in his heart. I know you love Phil, but I love him, too, and that should have brought us closer together,' I paused, 'Did you think I would look down on you? Did you?'

Jacquetta dropped her gaze, so I knew I had finally hit on the truth.

'You couldn't have been more wrong,' I said quietly. 'I've never liked you, mainly because it was your behaviour towards me above anything else that made me an outcast in your family, but I've always admired and respected you for the way you did whatever had to be done to ensure your children didn't go hungry. If I can be only *half* the mother you are I will be more than happy to continue with this pregnancy.'

I thought she was going to cry again, but Jacquetta swallowed hard and kept her composure. 'Thank you, you pay me a great compliment. It is more than I deserve from you. I see now I have been very wrong in my judgement of you. I have not been a friend to you in the past but, given time, I hope you will allow me to be a friend to you in the future.'

Her parting words were, 'My son behaves like the fool, but give him time and he *will* come to his senses. I am quite sure of this.'

I just wished I had her faith, but then she could not have known that Phil had already moved into one of the spare bedrooms and was giving every impression of staying there indefinitely.

When I tried to talk to him, and try I did, his answer was always the same. I couldn't keep the baby and the marriage. He had made his choice in the matter and I should do the same. He wouldn't stand in the way if

130

a baby was my priority, but I should just let him know once I had finally decided and then we would talk about the future.

It was obvious we couldn't go on like that and the day of my twenty-week scan brought matters to a head. I thought right up to the last moment that Phil would appear — to offer support if nothing else. It was his baby after all and he should have been grown up enough to take responsibility for that.

I wasn't angry, just very sad that it should have come to this, and very aware that I was still far from thrilled to find myself thrust into a situation I wasn't in any way prepared to deal with.

It was obvious one of us had to make the first move and I supposed it was going to have to be me. That being the case, I made a point of waiting up for Phil to arrive home.

He strolled in at two-thirty in the morning, threw his keys carelessly on to the hall table and almost jumped out of his skin when he saw me standing by the kitchen door.

'Bloody hell, you gave me a fright. I thought you'd be in bed.'

It was the most he'd said to me in weeks, but he didn't actually look at me while he was speaking.

'I thought we should talk.'

'It's a bit late for that,' he said, a touch

belligerently. 'You've chosen to carry the kid over and above my wishes, there's nothing more to say.'

'If your mother hadn't done the same, you wouldn't be here.'

'You leave my mother out of it.'

I swallowed my anger, knowing a row would get us nowhere.

'Phil,' I said, hating the pleading note that crept into my tone, 'If I could bring myself to do what you want I would. I love you — you know that — and would do anything for you . . . '

'Except this one thing.'

It wasn't a question and I agreed reluctantly, 'Except this one thing.'

Phil shrugged, 'Then it's as I've said, there's nothing more to say. It's over.'

I was shocked and didn't try to hide it. 'Just like that,' I said.

'Just like that.'

'Are we talking about a divorce here?'

It was Phil's turn to look surprised, but he recovered swiftly, appearing almost relieved, I thought. 'If you like,' he said.

I couldn't believe it had come to this in so short a time. It was like talking to an unfeeling stranger, but I still couldn't believe he meant it.

I crossed the hall, took his arm and shaking

it, I looked up into his dear familiar face and asked earnestly, 'Are you sure, Phil, are you quite sure this is what you want?'

Without a second's hesitation, he replied, 'Yes, this is what I want, but the blame has to be yours. You've given me no choice in the matter, and I hope you'll remember that when you're bringing up a kid that nobody wanted — alone.'

With that he spun on his heel and went upstairs. I stood in the hallway watching his ascent and smelling again the whiskey on his breath, the perfume on his clothes and the smell of sex on his skin.

8

The next morning, early, I packed enough clothes and toiletries for my immediate needs and left while Phil was still sleeping off the excesses of the night before.

I wondered if this was the scenario Rich had imagined when he'd slipped the key to the front door of his flat into the palm of my hand. I even wondered if he had already known I was fighting a losing battle to save my marriage, because there was obviously a lot more to this situation than I had ever realized.

Had Phil started the affair before or after he knew about the expected baby? Had he already made up his mind our marriage was over and the pregnancy had merely given him the excuse he was looking for? If that was the case his behaviour was even more despicable than I could have imagined. Using the conception of an innocent baby — his own child — to suit his purposes was about as low as you could get in my opinion.

He could have the house. I'd already decided that. I had *never* liked it anyway — it had been Phil's choice. I was only just beginning to realize that almost everything about our marriage was, in fact, Phil's choice.

I was more than capable of earning my own living and finding a new home for the baby and me. I was aware I couldn't stay at Rich's indefinitely, but for now I was more than grateful for his generous and thoughtful gesture. At least I didn't have to worry about where I would be laying my head for the next few nights.

It was at times like these you realized who your friends were and a time like this forced me to acknowledge yet again how sadly lacking my life was in that department.

I became aware of Vi watching me from her front room window as I loaded a couple of holdalls into the boot of my car. I waved cheerily, hoping she would think I was merely doing a stint of guest lecturing at another university, as I did from time to time.

She lifted a hand in reply, but I thought she looked forlorn and I promised myself I would take the time soon to let her know what was going on. She would be pleased about the baby at least, even if she couldn't grasp the foibles of the modern marriage. How could I expect her to understand when I had trouble with it myself?

The silver BMW that had also been more Phil's choice of a car for me to drive than my own, purred into life and I drove away from my home, marriage and the life I had known for twenty-five years, without looking back.

'It's just you and me now, chum,' I told the baby, and then realized it was the first time I had recognized it as a person and addressed it as one. It felt strange, but not in a bad way, so I carried on. 'We'll be okay. Pick up things as we go along once you're born and manage somehow. I suspect that's what most people do anyway when they start a family. It's not exactly something you can train for, is it? I never heard of a Ph.D. in motherhood.'

It felt strange to think of the two of us as family but that's what we would be. I'd gone from one kind of family of two to another, but this one came with a whole lot more responsibility attached. I just hoped I was up to it.

The first step to a new and very different sort of life was always going to be daunting, but at least I had this temporary home to go to, thanks only to my brother-in-law's generosity and forethought. It was a damned good job I'd thought to pick up the address book next to the phone before I left, though, because otherwise I wouldn't have had a clue where to go.

Apart from sending cards bi-yearly on birthdays and Christmas, I'd had no reason to know where Rich lived. I doubted if Phil had visited this brother at home any more than he had the rest of his siblings, and I certainly never had. We met them only at family gatherings and these were usually held in impersonal hotels or restaurants. Certainly no one would have expected Rich to host such an event in his home, him being a single guy with a job that took him away for weeks on end.

Realizing with a jolt that I must be in the general locality of Rich's home, I pulled into the roadside to consult the book again, prepared to pull the A to Z from the glove compartment if more detailed instructions became necessary.

A sharp rap on the passenger window almost had me jumping out of my skin. A grinning face peered in at me. It belonged to a tall guy who appeared to be bent almost double, dark hair trimmed to within an inch of its life, sporting the sort of moustache that made him look at best like a Spanish bandit or at worst an extra for the 80s group The Village People. He was gesturing impatiently for me to lower the window. It whirred smoothly a fraction of the way down at a touch of the button, but I was careful to keep the doors locked and the car in gear, wondering who he was and what he wanted.

'Can I help you?' I sounded haughty even to my own ears.

'Nope,' he beamed at me, 'but *I* can probably help *you*. Looking for somewhere specific are you? Lived round here on and off for most of my life so I can probably point you in the right direction quicker than a book.'

'Mallory Court?'

'End of the road — see the curve there? — big brick building just on the right. You can't miss it.'

'Great, thanks.' I had my finger on the button to close the window, but I wasn't quite quick enough.

'Visiting or moving in, are you?'

'Moving in,' I managed through gritted teeth, cursing the good manners that wouldn't allow me to shut the window in his face and drive off.

'Looks as if we're going to be neighbours then,' he went on chattily, 'so which flat are you moving into? Number two is empty.'

'I'm not buying,' I found myself telling him a shade reluctantly, 'Just staying for a while in number five, a relative's flat.'

'Oh, Richard Siddons,' he nodded, 'I've got a lot of time for Rich. Cousin, is he? Never too busy to help out when he's got a minute to spare. He's been a tower of strength to me.

Not many about like that, I can tell you.'

I didn't put him right about the cousin bit. It was close enough I felt. I was intrigued about the tower of strength bit and wondered what it entailed. The guy seemed perfectly genuine in his gratitude and learning that Rich found time in his busy life to accommodate a neighbour's needs was a bit of a revelation. I couldn't recall Phil ever so much as passing the time of day with Vi.

'Hop in,' I offered, releasing the locks — having decided that the man was quite obviously who he said he was. He was around my age, looked entirely respectable and had the kindest eyes of anyone I could think of. He obviously knew Rich reasonably well and I saw no reason to mistrust him.

He folded his long length into the passenger seat, loosened the colourful Doctor Who type scarf wound round his neck, and within a couple of minutes we were in front of the building, which was indeed red brick. An imposing Victorian building that had obviously been converted with care into several flats without spoiling the exterior. I had to admit to some surprise, since I had always pictured Rich living in a bachelor pad in a modern purpose-built apartment block.

'That's Rich's parking place,' the guy indicated to an empty space to the right of

139

the steps to the front door. 'Number five is top floor, but there's a lift. I'll show you. I'm Winston, by the way,' he put out a hand, and the grip was firm when I took it. 'Flat number one, the only one with a door to the garden, and you're welcome to use it any time, long as you don't mind my mum's old dog keeping you company out there.'

'That's very kind of you,' I said, and meant it, realizing I was finally — and very belatedly — learning to recognize friendship when it was offered and to be less picky about from whence it came. Having friends was surely going to make a difference to my new life and I found myself hoping Winston would be the first of many. He seemed like a nice guy.

There was indeed a lift, so small you would get two people in at a squeeze, but a lift nevertheless, and one that whooshed me and my bags very efficiently to the top floor of the house in seconds. Number five was the only flat on that floor, so I had no near neighbour to pop in to borrow a cup of sugar. In my new frame of mind I wasn't sure whether to be pleased or sorry about that.

The key slipped easily into the lock and the door swung open to reveal a minute hallway with oatmeal carpeting and walls of a similar hue but a shade lighter. There was a black leather jacket of Rich's hanging in solitary splendour from one of a row of brass hooks. Slipping off my own full-length camel-coloured woollen coat I hung it alongside.

Looking around with interest I went from room to room. The oatmeal carpet was evident throughout the flat, as were the light colour-washed walls. It was very much a male abode with brown leather and oak wood furnishings favoured, but there were paler cushions and lamps to soften the masculine effect.

It was a home, not a showpiece, but uncluttered, with obviously a place for everything and everything in its place, as my mother would have said. The only pictures in evidence were of Rich's daughter, Amber, and they traced a path through her life, from babyhood to the pretty teenager she had obviously become. Very much a younger version of her dark-haired, brown-eyed mother, there was little of the Siddons genes in evidence.

The second bedroom came as a complete surprise. It had obviously been furnished and decorated with this girl very much in mind, from the feminine frills and flounces, to the big cream teddy bear sitting on cream lace bedcovers and the assortment of porcelain dolls arranged on the beech chest of drawers.

Had Amber ever visited to make use of the

room or did it stand in readiness, just in case? Digging deep in my memory I felt sure from the little I had learned about his life that it was always Rich who made the journey to the States and not the other way around, but I could have been wrong.

Not liking to trespass into a room so obviously set aside for someone of such great importance in his life, I had no choice but to take up residence in Rich's own bedroom. It was evident the bedding was freshly laundered, and that space had been made in the wardrobes and drawers for me to place my things. I could have wept at this show of kindness to a sister-in-law he really barely knew — despite all the years we'd been related — and couldn't help wondering who had offered support to Rich when *his* marriage had broken down. I did know it hadn't been Phil or me and felt suddenly ashamed.

Giving myself a brisk shake, I set to and emptied the holdalls, which didn't take too long and then made my way into the compact kitchen. I put the kettle on made coffee black and strong, and, finally, gave way to the tears I had been holding back since the unmistakable evidence of Phil's infidelity had assailed my nostrils the night before.

It was lunchtime before my mobile phone

burbled into life. I didn't need to check for the name of the caller. It was quite obvious that Phil must have finally managed to rouse himself and discovered my earlier departure from the marital home. I couldn't bring myself to listen to his excuses or — worse — his lies and left it to ring. There seemed little to be said at this point.

I went into the kitchen again and checked the contents of the cupboards, fridge and freezer and found everything I could possibly need packed tidily away. There was even long-life milk in cartons to eradicate the need for a dash to the shops before I could enjoy a cup of tea.

Nothing but the partially drunk cup of coffee had passed my lips since a solitary meal the previous evening, eaten before I'd realized what — I couldn't really say 'who' since I didn't have that piece of information yet — was keeping Phil so busy elsewhere. I still had no appetite, but realized I should eat, for the baby if not for myself. I was beginning to feel quite light-headed and not a little bit nauseous.

I poked through the contents of the freezer in a desultory fashion finding nothing that appealed, despite the choice available, and then leapt about two feet in the air when the housephone suddenly shrilled into the silence.

I went to the kitchen door and stared at the instrument jangling on its rest, wondering how on earth Phil had worked out where I was, and why the thing didn't click into answerphone mode and just take a message.

Then I got angry and asked myself what I thought I was playing at, behaving like the guilty party when *I* hadn't done anything wrong, and finally snatched up the instrument.

The voice at the end of the line wasn't Phil's, and the breath whooshed out of me with relief. I obviously wasn't ready to speak to him yet.

'Winston,' my laughter was tinged with hysteria, 'you did give me a fright. I wasn't expecting any phonecalls with Rich away.'

'Just thought you might like to share supper,' the voice was gruff but kindly, as he went on, 'only I've made way too much pasta and, as you've just moved in, you might not feel like cooking.'

My first instinct was to refuse, but I managed to override it by reminding myself of my new 'friends' policy. Winston obviously had no ulterior motive, given the fact that his mother would be sharing the meal with us.

Before I could have second thoughts, I heard myself saying, 'That is kind of you, I'll be right down, I'm absolutely starving.'

I was quite sure neither my mother nor even the more liberal Vi had ever been adventurous enough to try a pasta dish. No doubt it would be seen as a bit new-fangled and foreign for their meat and two veg palate, so I looked forward to meeting Winston's mother.

She still hadn't joined us when I was about to tackle my second helping of a tuna pasta bake that was so delicious I felt sure I could manage another heaped plate without any problem at all. I sat back in the chair with a contented sigh still eyeing the remaining slices of what was obviously homemade garlic bread like a greedy child.

'You eat it up,' Winston encouraged. 'You look like you need feeding up, if you don't mind me saying so.'

'Oh, no, really, I couldn't manage another thing and, anyway, there'll be nothing left for your mother.'

'My . . . ' Winston looked at me sharply.

'Your mother,' I repeated, 'I thought she lived here with you, you mentioned the dog was hers.' I nodded at the elderly Border Collie who dozed on the mat in front of the real flames of an old-fashioned coal fire.

'Oh, I see,' he said quietly. 'Well, of course, she did do — up until her death at the end of last year.'

145

My hand flew to my throat, 'I'm so sorry, I had no idea.'

He smiled, but he still looked pretty upset and I felt dreadful. 'Of course you didn't. How were you to know? I'm getting used to being on my own now, but it is taking time. It was always mum and me. She brought me up on her own, so it only seemed right that I should come home to take care of her when she needed me.'

I envied them what must have been an extremely close relationship, and was suddenly reminded of how clear my mother had made it that she preferred the impersonal care of strangers to anything I could have offered at the end of her life. It both saddened and heartened me to realize that people like Phil and I were probably the exception rather than the rule when it came to dysfunctional parents.

'Mum would be happy to see you eat up her share of the pasta,' Winston encouraged. The heaped serving spoon hovered over my plate again, but I shook my head regretfully. 'A couple of spoonfuls of tiramisu, then,' he offered, clearly not willing to give up easily.

'Not another thing, but I'll help you wash up.'

'You'll do no such thing. I have all evening to deal with the dishes.'

I found I was in no hurry to rush off and that I was actually enjoying Winston's company as much as I had enjoyed his food. Settled in one of his deep armchairs, I smoothed the head of Lisa, the elderly dog, and listened as he reminisced.

There were photos of his youth and childhood all around. The son of a single parent, when single parents were still frowned upon, it couldn't have been easy for either of them, but Winston had obviously been devoted to the mother he'd lost to cancer just a few months before and obviously still missed greatly.

'You remind me a lot of her,' Winston said, his eyes unashamedly moist, but lips smiling. 'You can tell me to mind my own business, but will you keep your baby? I'm only guessing that there's a problem of some sort, because you are wearing a wedding ring, but have come here alone.'

I stared at him open-mouthed, 'How did you . . . ?'

'Know you were having a baby?' he finished for me. 'I've been a press photographer for years and learned to spot a pregnant celebrity a mile away. You have the same bloom about you, and that look in your eyes that says you're enjoying a secret you can't share.'

If Winston was shocked when I burst into tears, he hid it well, just passed me a box of tissues, made another pot of tea, and finally he listened as I poured my heart out.

At the end of it all he said quietly, 'My mother always said what can't be cured must be endured, but it sometimes comes as something of a shock when things unexpectedly turn out for the best in the end. Even hanging up my camera to nurse my mother has given me time to rethink my future and decide that's a life I no longer wish to be part of. Perhaps this — Phillip, is it? — really isn't cut out to be a dad, not everyone is, but you *were* made to be a mother or I'll eat my hat.'

'Not the Stetson hanging in the hall?' I managed a watery smile as I added, 'It'll give you terrible indigestion.'

'Now, you know where I am,' Winston reminded me as I left to make my way back upstairs. 'You won't find me plaguing the life out of you, but I might just ring up now and again — to check you're okay and not needing anything.'

'Thanks, Winston, I'd appreciate that.'

At the top of the building I stepped out of the lift and into Rich's flat to be met by the burbling of the mobile phone I had left sitting on the coffee table. Six missed calls, all from Phil and I had deleted them all by the time it started to ring again. This time I pressed to connect, with a good meal inside of me, and Winston's common sense to bolster my confidence I felt I could deal with my wayward husband and anything he might have to say.

'Where are you?' were his first words.

'That's actually none of your business,' I said flatly.

'Don't be ridiculous I'm your husband. I have a right to know what you're playing at taking off like that.'

'Just as I have a right to know when you're playing around.'

The sharp intake of breath couldn't be mistaken, but Phil recovered quickly. 'What do you mean by that? I don't know what you're talking about. Has someone said something?'

I could hear the panic in his voice and, knowing the way his mind worked, thought he was probably visualizing half of everything he owned coming my way. He was certainly aware I had more than earned my share over the years.

'They didn't need to. I haven't used Anaïs Anaïs for years and there were other less subtle signs and smells, so please don't treat me like a fool.'

'It shouldn't have happened, Alex. I know

that, but I couldn't cope, you know, with everything that's been going on. She was a sympathetic ear, not much more than that. It wouldn't have happened if you . . . '

'So,' I interrupted the flow of words and then paused momentarily, 'let me get this straight. It's *my* fault that I became pregnant, *my* fault I only lost the one baby instead of both, and *my* fault you can't face your responsibilities, opted out and had an affair to make yourself feel better. Oh, bugger off, Phil, you make me sick.'

I slept fitfully, once I had turned the mobile off. For all my bravado, the assurances that I could manage on my own, I had been terrified ever since the moment Phil had made it clear he was withdrawing his support if I didn't do what he wanted and abort the surviving foetus. Him rushing into the arms of another woman almost immediately, when it became clear I wasn't going to comply, was something I *hadn't* bargained for.

I guess I had thought if I sat it out he would eventually relent and had put myself through weeks of living with a cold and calculating stranger as a result. At least I supposed this way I wasn't left with any false hopes of a touching reconciliation.

I needed to plan for my future. It was a future as far removed from the comfortable past I had enjoyed as it could possibly be. I had grown complacent, I could see that now, but who wouldn't after twenty-five years with the same person? I had seen our comfortable life as a working couple going on into an equally comfortable retirement with no money worries and no real surprises. Phil had been my whole world and now, suddenly, I was shocked to find I didn't actually know him — I probably never had — and certainly didn't like him.

The picture of the ideal life so carefully pieced together over the years, hadn't allowed for changes of any magnitude — I could see that now, too — but surely we could have rearranged it with a bit of effort on both our parts, and made room for the life we had created. However, rather than change the picture, Phil had decided the answer was to erase the change and pretend it had never happened. To my shame, I had very nearly gone along with it.

In the morning it was a relief to realize the arrival of the Easter bank holiday weekend spared me the necessity of making the effort to go into work, but I fully acknowledged I was going to have to make decisions about my future with the university, too. Strangely, the thought of leaving didn't fill me with the dismay it would surely have done just a few short weeks ago. Suddenly my job — like Phil — wasn't the be-all and end-all in my life. I actually had other priorities.

For the first time in years there was no sense of urgency to be up and doing, and there was no one to please but myself. I took a breakfast of cereal, juice and freshly ground coffee into the lounge and enjoyed what early morning TV had to offer along with the meal as I contemplated my future with amazing calm.

From somewhere I seemed to recall that the baby's due date was early October. That being the case, I could finish up the teaching year and take the summer off to find somewhere permanent to live and prepare for the birth. The thought was daunting, but no longer as frightening as it had been.

I would be all right. We would be all right. I placed my two hands around a still non-existent bump protectively. My decision was finally made. My only real regret was that I hadn't made it sooner and given Phil no other option but to accept the pregnancy right from the start. I couldn't help thinking it just might have made all the difference in the world but fully accepted regrets really were a waste of time.

We should at least be talking to each other in a civilized manner, I realized ruefully.

Hurling insults and accusations were going to get us precisely nowhere. This child had survived, in spite of us, and deserved a mother and a father. Whether we decided to make the split permanent or not was neither here nor there; this baby's welfare really should be our main concern.

With this in mind, I eventually picked up the phone and dialled my home number, quite certain in my mind that Phil couldn't do other than agree with me. I had been mulling it over for most of the day and done a pretty good job of convincing myself but, even so, my heartbeat accelerated when I heard his voice and it wasn't with pleasure.

He sounded friendly enough when he realized who was calling, even pleased to hear from me, and he listened to what I had to say without interrupting. There was, however, a noticeable chill in his tone when he finally spoke.

'So,' he said, 'let me get this straight. You expect me to play the proud father to a child I had no interest in from the start?'

'That's not strictly true, is it, Phil?' I reminded him in a reasonable tone, reminding myself I was doing this for the baby. 'At the beginning you were . . .'

'A child, moreover,' he continued pompously as if I hadn't spoken, and I could have sworn I heard a woman's voice in the background prompting him, 'that — as my father has so rightly said — I cannot even be certain is mine.'

I felt as if I had been punched in the stomach and had all the breath knocked out of me. It was as much as I could do to say a word but somehow I managed to say several.

'For that remark alone, I will never, ever forgive *him*,' I said, 'or *you*.'

Putting the phone down, I accepted that — baby or no baby — my marriage really was well and truly over.

9

News obviously travelled faster in the Siddons family than I'd realized so I was surprised to find Louise together with Rose, another of the sister-in-laws I barely knew, on my step — well, the doorstep of Rich's flat to be precise — the following morning.

A shopping trip wasn't high on my list of priorities for that day with my marriage lying in tatters around me, but for some reason they seemed keen to drag me out for some Saturday morning retail therapy to, 'Cheer me up'.

I guess a sleepless night had left me looking less than my best and the concerned comments my appearance evoked brought everything tumbling out along with quite a few tears. I couldn't believe I was, yet again, confiding in my husband's family but, whoever came up with the phrase, 'Better out than in', certainly knew what they were talking about.

'I can't believe it of Phil,' Louise looked shocked, as did Rose, so it was obvious they hadn't heard the full story. 'I knew you wouldn't have walked out for no reason,' she added, which was even more telling.

'Randolph Siddons has a lot to answer for,' Tony's wife added, shaking the tousled blonde head of springy curls that looked surprisingly chic on a woman who had to be in her fifties, 'because I can see all of his influence in this. He's always been a vindictive old sod and I've no doubt it will give him real pleasure to bugger up Phil's life and make it look as if he was doing him a favour.'

'He's never liked me,' I said.

'Nor me,' said Rose.

'Me neither,' Louise concluded, 'and I'm quite sure Jacquetta only tolerates me because of the children.'

'Head and shoulders over the rest of us you are, Lou,' Rose pointed out without animosity, 'a couple more kids and you could have had the *full* royal seal of approval, as it is you're certainly the nearest thing this family has to a Princess Royal.'

'The obsession with grandchildren makes it all the more difficult to understand Randy's determination to reject this one,' I said, placing my hands protectively over my belly, 'and to make sure Phil does the same, unless . . . '

'Unless?' Louise repeated, staring at me.

'Unless Randy simply wants to get rid of

me and he's willing to forgo the grandchild to achieve that, I told you he's never liked me. He must know this is my last chance to have a child with Phil — and he *does* know it's Phil's baby I'm carrying, no matter what he says — but Phil could go on to have children with anyone.'

'It's more likely that he's trying to cut Phil down to size,' Rose said shrewdly. 'He must know — as we all do — that Phil wouldn't be where he is today without you behind him.'

I murmured a protest at this point, which was dismissed by both Rose and Louise. I was amazed they gave me so much credit for Phil's success. I'd never thought I counted for much in the Siddons family, but after the visit from Jacquetta and now this, it seemed I might have been wrong — except where Randy was concerned anyway.

'She's right, Alex,' Louise sounded genuinely upset. 'That man has never done anything for his youngest son's good. He hates it that Phil's done so well and probably you for helping him do it.'

'Shows him up for the useless bastard he's always been and Jacquetta's pride in Phil's achievements always rubs salt into the open wound,' Rose was nodding in agreement.

'He couldn't be that bad — could he?' I looked from one sister-in-law to the other, and then we all nodded in unison and said as one voice. 'He could.'

'The thing is,' Louise said, 'what are we going to do about it? He can't get away with this.'

'Randy isn't entirely to blame,' I pointed out, 'Phil does — after all — have a mind of his own.'

'But he's tried for years to get the old man's approval, hasn't he?' Rose said quietly. 'As old as he is he must be very confused with Randy suddenly turning into his best friend and advisor. He obviously doesn't know what to believe any more.'

'Mmmm, must be difficult for him,' I nodded ruefully, adding with more than a touch of sarcasm, 'on the one hand there's the wife who gave him twenty-five years of love and loyalty and is carrying his first child, and on the other there's a vindictive old man who never gave him so much as the time of day. I can see it wouldn't be easy.'

'This is getting us nowhere,' Louise said suddenly, 'and we're supposed to be here to keep you company and take your mind off things. We haven't done a very good job so far. I'm sure Phil will come to his senses sooner or later.'

'I wouldn't hold your breath and it won't do him any good,' I said firmly, 'too much has been said and done to turn the clock back. In any case, he has someone else in his life now, so it really is off with the old and on with the new. He doesn't let the grass grow under his feet, does our Phil. Now,' my tone was brisk, without so much as a tremor I was pleased to note, 'are we going shopping today or tomorrow?'

The questions came thick and fast as we squeezed ourselves into the tiny lift for the journey to the ground floor.

'Are you quite sure? Who is it?' came from Rose.

'Yes, I'm sure, and I've no idea.'

'Someone we know?' from Louise.

'No idea.'

'How could he do it?' came from Rose again.

'No idea.'

'Are you *quite* sure?'

'I'm positive. Now, can we talk about something else?' I pleaded, and though I'm sure they were bursting to ask me a lot more, they both made a huge effort and neither Phil nor Randy was mentioned again.

It was a real novelty to be shopping in female company. Phil was a reluctant shopper at the best of times and, on the rare occasions I did manage to persuade him to join me, he was unreasonable, too, expecting split-second decisions to be made over this dress or that suit with precious little input from him. The annoying thing was, he had always been swift to venture an unfavourable opinion when you were dressed for an evening out, and it didn't help at all for me to point out, 'but you said you liked it in the shop'.

Louise and Rose were great, holding this and that up against me, enthusing over colours and shapes. I found that I was having a good time in spite of myself, and in spite of the fact my life and marriage were in pieces.

When we ended up in Mothercare it seemed to be by common consent. It was like being let loose in Aladdin's cave with my sisters-in-law's enthusiasm even beginning to rub off on to me. In no time a basket was filling up with all manner of tiny garments until I felt obliged to protest.

'It's too much, it's too soon,' I was laughing, but there was also the realization that still a part of me wasn't expecting to see this pregnancy through to the end. Too much had happened, one child had already miscarried, there was every chance the same was going to happen to this one. I couldn't take the chance, couldn't allow myself to plan or to care — not yet.

'But, Alex,' Louise looked at me strangely, 'you must be at least four months by now. You've had the amniocentesis test, haven't you? The serum screening for Downs?'

I found myself staring back, and for a moment it was as if she were speaking in a foreign language. I shook my head to clear it and then found myself telling a half-truth. 'I think I must have missed the appointment, you know, with all that's been going on.' When, in reality, I had simply decided not to bother.

'No harm done,' Rose rubbed my arm and smiled, 'appointments can be remade.'

She was holding a tiny pair of knitted bootees and I could suddenly picture a baby's tiny feet in them — my baby's feet. My heart melted a tiny bit at the thought and for the first time I allowed myself to hope that the family so long denied to me was going to become reality — in spite of Phil and his bloody father.

Rose went to put the bootees back on the shelf and I took them gently from her hand and put them in the basket. 'Let's keep those, shall we?' I said, and then stared at Louise when she asked, 'Now, are you going to breast-feed?'

She'd been ushering us across the store as she spoke and now dangled a nursing bra for my perusal. It looked far too big, and I said so, and wondered why they both burst out laughing.

'Easy to see you haven't had a kid,' Rose smirked, but not unkindly, 'I could have given the likes of Jordan a run for her money after giving birth, both times. Bazookas doesn't begin to describe the proportions mine took on.'

'Jeez,' I said ruefully, 'I didn't realize how much I had to look forward to.'

'Come on, you've been on your feet long enough.'

Louise took charge and I found myself whisked to the pay desk where I wasn't allowed to pay for a thing, then with a sister-in-law on each arm, I was almost frog-marched to the nearest Costa coffee house.

It was when I was on my way back from the ladies that I heard Randy's name mentioned again, and Louise apologized as soon as she realized I was back in the vicinity.

'Unfortunately,' she said with a frown, 'it's not just your family he interferes in.'

'Oh?'

'No,' Rose put in, 'Lou was just telling me he's been encouraging young Martin to buy one of those high-powered motorbikes that are all the rage now.'

'Mmm,' I nodded, 'and the only reason Phil keeps that bloody great monstrosity of his in the garage is in the hope it will get him on Randy's good side. He hasn't ridden it in years, but keeps it roadworthy and polished — just in case. Just in case of what I have no idea.'

'I wouldn't mind if getting a bike was Martin's own idea,' Louise took over the explanation, adding, 'well, I would, because they're so dangerous, but that's beside the point. Martin has no interest in motorbikes and I don't need that silly old biker putting thoughts into his head that aren't there.'

'Exactly.' Rose agreed, and I found myself nodding, before I asked, 'He's not thinking about getting one, is he?'

'No, he's not,' Louise said, 'but no thanks to Randy or bloody Kayleigh, either, because she was all for it, of course. I think she has this picture of herself in tight fitting leathers and shaking all that blonde hair loose as she removes her helmet. Now it's caused no end of friction between her and Martin.'

'You wouldn't be sorry to see that romance over and done with, would you, Lou?' Rose asked, looking sympathetic.

'You're right, I wouldn't be at all sorry, but it won't happen. Our Martin is besotted with her, though I wouldn't say it's reciprocated. The girl has ideas above her station, I can tell you. She's out for all she can get, far more than my boy will ever be able to give her, but what can I say? It's his life, though it won't be much of one with her bleeding him dry.'

I thought Louise had summed her up pretty well, but didn't think it would help to say so. Instead I said, 'Don't worry, Lou, things have a habit of turning out for the best.'

'You can say that,' she said in amazement, 'even now?'

'It's what you once told me, and you were right. Phil might not be much of a support right now — but you both are,' I pointed out, 'and Rich has given me a roof over my head. I've a lot to be thankful for under the circumstances. I'm sure the future will take care of itself. For now the only thing concerning me is how I can get into the house to collect a few more of my things without bumping into Phil.'

'Ah,' Rose brightened, 'I might be able to help you there, because Tony definitely said that Phil and Randy had something planned for bank holiday Monday. He said it was just like the secret squirrel club, with all the whispering. I don't think even Jacquetta knows what they're up to. Do you want me to run you round there?'

'Bless you, no, that's okay. I can manage easily.'

'It shouldn't be you out of a home, you

know, Alex,' Louise said seriously, 'you've done nothing wrong.'

'Except getting pregnant without prior agreement,' I smiled wryly. 'Don't worry, I never liked the house anyway.'

'But, I thought . . . We thought . . . ' Rose was staring at me.

I laughed, suddenly realizing what they all must have thought. 'You thought it was my choice to rattle around in a mansion, a show home. Looking back now, I don't even think that's what Phil really wanted, either. We were probably at our happiest in our first little end-of-terrace. I think all the trappings of success were only ever a ploy to gain Randy's attention and his approval, so it was all for nothing, because it didn't work. Nothing's worked — until now. Perhaps I can find it in me to be happy for Phil — one day.'

'You have a bigger heart than me, then,' Rose said stoutly. 'I just think he's an idiot. I can't help feeling he's going to wake up one day and realize he's lost a whole lot more than he's gained.'

Back at the flat, my sisters-in-law took their leave, 'Now are you sure you don't want to come over to us tomorrow?' Louise offered, 'you'd be more than welcome and we'd love to have you.'

'Or come to us. It might be a bit quieter

than Lou and Del's with our kids living out of the area. No offence Lou, but your house can be a bit — well, *busy* is an understatement — with your lot in and out.'

'None taken,' Louise assured her, 'and you're quite right but it's up to Alex to decide what she wants to do.'

'I think I'll just spend a quiet day, if you both don't mind. I need to do a bit of thinking and, anyway, Winston's invited me to lunch.' Two pairs of eyebrows shot up, and I went on quickly, 'Don't look at me like that, another man in my life is the last thing I need, and a pregnant married woman is the last thing Winston needs in his. He's Rich's ground floor neighbour and a bit lonely since his mother died and missing having someone to cook for. I've never had a man cook for me before and I find I quite like it. I think we're having haunch of venison followed by blueberry pie.'

'Sounds lovely, Alex, you enjoy it,' Louise encouraged, with Rose adding, 'but don't ever be on your own if you would prefer company, we'd love to see you, any time, wouldn't we, Lou.'

'Definitely.'

I found myself enfolded first in Louise's arms and then Rose's, and wondered why it had taken so long for them to become the family they always should have been. Perhaps, as I had already suspected, I had simply been too self-sufficient, too wrapped up in my comfortable life with Phil and my career to make the effort needed to make and sustain other relationships.

What had happened in my life recently had been a real wake-up call and it had made me aware of just how foolish it had been to isolate myself from the outside world. I seemed to recall a saying about no man — or woman, come to that — being an island and I was finding out, the hard way, just how true that was.

That evening, with the television playing in the background, I began to make a list. It was a sad moment to sit with pen poised over that pad because, had things been different, I'd have been making a detailed inventory of baby requirements, maybe planning a colour scheme for the nursery with Phil, but it was definitely a case of first things first.

Before I could plan for a new beginning alone with my child and a very different kind of life, I must deal with the mechanics of ending my marriage. Just a few short weeks ago both of those things would have been unthinkable.

Divorce. How stark the word appeared, scrawled in black ink across white paper, but

I realized it was inevitable. Pointless to sit around waiting for Phil to have a change of heart about both the child I was carrying *and* his new love. It was hardly going to happen, was it?

I was going to need a solicitor. For myself I wanted nothing, but I had a child to consider and grand gestures wouldn't keep a roof over our heads and food in our bellies. While I had no intention of taking Phil to the cleaners, neither was I prepared to let him get off scot-free. A fair deal was no less than the family he'd discarded in such haste deserved.

The next thing on the agenda had to be a house. It had been more than generous of Rich to offer me his home, but it had left him with nowhere to stay when next he was on shore leave or whatever it was they called it. I'd lost track of time with everything that was going on but according to the scan I was already around halfway through the pregnancy, which gave me a relatively short time to find somewhere permanent to live and get settled in.

The more I thought about what lay ahead the more terrified I became, those were only the first two things on what was obviously going to be a very long list and I hadn't even thought about the birth and bringing up a child yet.

I really didn't want it — this life I had so recently been given. Until these last few weeks my biggest trauma had been fitting a hair appointment into a busy schedule, the only thing Phil and I ever really disagreed about were holiday destinations. How on earth had we come to this? Could there really be no going back for us?

The phone ringing was a welcome diversion and I snatched it up quickly, fully expecting to find Winston on the other end, since he was the only person to have phoned me on the house line since I'd moved in.

'Alex, it's me. I'm coming home.'

The room spun and tilted as I listened to Phil's voice and, in that moment, I knew I could — and would — forgive him everything that had gone before. All those years of marriage couldn't just be dismissed and discarded. If Phil really wanted to give our relationship another chance then I was more than prepared to meet him halfway and I sincerely thanked God for giving me that chance.

Everything was going to be all right after all, and I found myself smiling for what felt like the first time in a very long time.

10

For one long blissful moment my world was right again. There was no problem that couldn't be overcome. I'd always known our love was strong and now it would show us the way to go forward — together.

'I'm coming home,' Phil said again, 'but I don't want you to worry.'

It took a moment or two for me to realize he wasn't making any sense. Why was *he* coming home when it was *me* who had left? Why would I worry and what about? Something wasn't right about this call, but for the life of me I couldn't think what.

'Alex, are you still there?'

And then it came to me, and the hopes that had soared sky high immediately plummeted back to earth to shatter into a million fragments. It wasn't Phil at all, but his brother Rich who sounded so remarkably like him on the phone that for a short while even I couldn't tell the difference. The haze of happiness that had surrounded me for far too short a time dispersed in an instant, leaving me flat, tired and so disappointed that I wanted to weep over my own foolish and futile dreams of a reconciliation that was obviously never going to happen.

'Yes, Rich,' I said, my tone remarkably calm, 'I'm still here.'

'I wanted to tell you myself that I was coming and not for you to hear it from someone else and start worrying. I have somewhere to stay. I'll be with Winston downstairs, so you'll see me coming in and out of the building, but I shan't disturb you.'

He sounded almost anxious and I was quick to reassure him. 'This is your flat, Rich, and you must come in and out whenever you want. I will obviously be looking for somewhere permanent to live before the baby is born, so I won't inconvenience you for too much longer.'

'Somewhere *permanent*?' he sounded shocked. 'Bloody hell, Alex, to be honest I've been expecting Phil to have come to his senses before this and was surprised you weren't already back home. What *is* his problem? Is he mad?' Then he laughed, a harsh sound that grated uncomfortably on the ear, 'But who am I to judge him with my marital history? Perhaps I can talk to him, though, help him to learn from my mistakes.'

'You're welcome to try, Rich,' I told him without enthusiasm, 'but I think you'll be wasting your time. Did you know he was having an affair?'

The silence on the end of the phone was all the confirmation I needed. The rumours must have already started, and then Rich said, 'I was hoping it wasn't true.'

'Do you know who with?' I didn't really want to know, but I couldn't seem to stop myself asking, but then hurried to add, 'No, don't answer that. I just hope it's no one I know, and preferably not someone young and gorgeous.'

Rich snorted, but I didn't know quite what to make of that.

'About the flat, Alex,' he said, changing the subject, 'I just wanted you to know it's yours for as long as you want to use it. Stay and have the baby there if you'd like. You could use Amber's room as a nursery, it's been standing empty for long enough and it's probably high time I accepted she will never want to use it.'

'Oh, but . . . ' I began.

'Don't try to humour me, Alex,' Rich didn't sound angry, just sad as he continued, 'as a father and a husband I screwed up big time, and I accept that. I just wish I could prevent my brother doing the same and having to live with all the same regrets as I have for years to come. Anyway,' his tone became brisk, 'the offer of a home for you and my nephew or niece is there and when I

172

say 'for as long as you want it' that's exactly what I mean.'

'Thanks, Rich.' I couldn't think of anything else to say.

★ ★ ★

Winston was almost excited about the imminent arrival of his expected lodger when I joined him for lunch. It was obvious he'd been extremely lonely since his mother's death — and though he must have made many friends in his line of work he gave the impression he wanted to leave that life, and anyone connected to it, behind. It seemed to include a personal relationship that his difficult choices had caused to end, though little was said about it.

I gathered, from the little he gave away, that Winston had taken Princess Diana's death — and the press involvement — badly, but it had taken his mother's illness and subsequent death all those years later to give him the strength of mind to turn his back on the only life he had known up until then.

However, everyone needs a friend as I had so recently discovered and it was obvious Winston was looking forward to enjoying Rich's company and was determined to make him comfortable during his visit.

'I've decided it's time I cleared out the wardrobes,' he said, and threw open the door to what had been his mother's bedroom to show me he'd already made a start.

'You have been busy,' I praised, looking at the clothes piled high in the middle of the bed and, realizing immediately to whom they had belonged, added, 'and very brave.'

'I had no reason to do it before, but Rich will need somewhere to hang his things, and there's no real point in keeping it all, is there? Mum isn't coming back, but she had some nice things and they might do someone else a bit of good.'

'Very good quality,' I agreed, lifting a scarf, feeling its silky texture and smelling the faint perfume that still clung to the folds.

'Would you like to keep it?' Winston asked, his dark eyes brimming. 'That was one of her favourites and the colours will suit you. I know she would be happy for you to have it. Mum would have liked you a lot.'

I didn't really want it. Wearing a dead woman's things, even my own mother's — or perhaps especially my own mother's — wasn't something I would relish, but didn't know how to say no without disappointing him and maybe distressing him further.

'Thank you, Winston, would it upset you if I wore it now?'

I don't think I could have said anything that would have pleased him more, and once the scarf had settled around my neck I soon forgot to mind where it had come from.

'Do you need a hand with this? I know it can be painful, it wasn't so long ago I was packing up my own mother's things.'

A sad and lonely business it had been, too, particularly with all the conflicting emotions. Phil had been 'too busy' at work to help, even on a weekend, and there was no one else I felt I could ask. There are times in your life when friends really are indispensable and I wondered why I hadn't realized that before.

'I would like to help, Winston.'

He seemed to think for a moment and then he relented, 'Let's have lunch first, then. It's all but ready.'

In the end, Winston dished the food up while I made a start. He'd decided to pack his mother's things into suitcases, 'as if she was going on holiday.'

'I won't be needing the luggage,' he assured me, 'I've seen enough of the world to last me a lifetime.'

'Your mum did like her clothes,' I said, sitting before a steaming plate, piled high with succulent slices of venison, at least four vegetables and golden roast potatoes. 'Did she enjoy her food, too?'

'She had the appetite of a bird even before she got sick,' Winston said ruefully, 'but she was a grand cook until her illness became too much and I had to take over. I didn't have a clue, living in hotels as I did, but I learned my way around the oven and hob pretty quickly when I had to, and now it's become something of a hobby for me.'

'Well, you're the best cook — male or female — I've ever met,' I said with complete honesty, 'I've never tasted anything as delicious as these roast potatoes and I thought I was a dab hand with Sunday lunch. Rich will think he's died and gone to heaven while he's living here.'

Belatedly, I wished I hadn't brought death into the conversation, given the circumstances, but Winston didn't seem unduly perturbed, and almost beamed at me across the table.

'With the two of you around I shall feel as if I've gained a new family,' he assured me, 'especially with the baby coming. What about you? I know you lost your mum, but do you have family apart from Rich and your estranged husband, Alex?'

I shook my head. 'My dad died years ago, when I was in my teens, and you already know my husband and I are having a few problems at the moment.' I was aware of the

176

understatement and I'm sure he was too. 'Rich is only my brother-in-law, so it was very kind of him to put himself out the way he has, and risk upsetting his own brother into the bargain. I think he thought — hoped — any separation would be more temporary than it has turned out to be.'

'Perhaps Rich can talk some sense into his brother,' Winston said as he placed a steaming blueberry pie on the table alongside a jug of thick cream, 'get across the regrets he has about the break up of his own marriage and the part he played in it.'

'Perhaps.' I didn't add just how unlikely it would be that Phil would listen and I didn't allow any thoughts of my marital strife to detract from my enjoyment of the crumbly pastry and sweetness of the fruit beneath. Curiosity made me ask, though, after a couple of mouthfuls, 'How can you be so sure I'm not the one who needs the talking to?'

Winston didn't even reply, but his look said an awful lot. I had to remind myself that he was obviously very biased and didn't know Phil or anything about our life before the split.

'Wow,' I pushed away a dish that had been practically licked clean — I'd been sorely tempted to do just that but good manners forced me to resist, 'that was delicious. Now, rather than fall asleep in the chair, shall we make a start on the drawers once the washing up is done?'

'I won't have you washing up,' Winston's tone was emphatic, 'as you're a guest, and I can't keep you working, either. It wouldn't be right. The drawers can wait for another day.'

'If you leave it, you will find it hard to work up the enthusiasm to start again,' I told him with the authority borne of experience. 'Take it from one who knows — and I didn't share the close relationship with my mother that you obviously enjoyed with yours — it really is better to keep going once you've started. I'm at your disposal today for as long as you want me.'

'Must have been my lucky day when you moved in,' Winston said with feeling, and as we sat smiling at each other I added, 'Actually, I think it was mine. If I've learned nothing else lately, it's the importance of having friends, especially in times of trouble.'

Leaving him to clear the table, I went back to the bedroom where his mother had spent the last weeks and months of her life lovingly cared for by the son who had obviously adored her.

I couldn't help wondering why there weren't more relationships like that. Obviously they all had to end sometime, no one lived forever after all, but the joy of a happy family was something to aspire to and yet so many relationships fell by the wayside.

I had always thought Phil and I had a good marriage but, if I was being honest, I could never have imagined Phil nursing me through an illness, much less doing such a thing for his mother, despite the fact he doted on her.

Deep in thought, I had worked my way through the two top drawers of neatly folded underwear, scented with pretty homemade lavender bags. I removed the bags, and reminded myself to leave the drawers open when I was done, deciding it was unlikely Rich would appreciate the delicate flowery fragrance clinging to his pants and socks.

Smiling, I turned my attention to the third drawer, which needed a good tug to bring it open. This one was filled with nightdresses in a myriad of rainbow hues. I would imagine their purchase would have been Winston's way of ensuring that, even when his mother was unable to get up and about, she could still take pleasure in her appearance.

I packed these away quickly, mindful that the sight of them might bring back painful memories for him, and then found at the bottom of the drawer what I took to be another nightdress neatly folded and wrapped in tissue. Obviously special, it had been packed away with great care. I thought it might well have been the last thing she had worn before her death, as it was evidently something of great sentimental value.

Setting it carefully on the bed, I lifted the tissue back to reveal a very old christening robe. Made of pure cotton, so different from the polyester and cotton of the modern day, it had clearly been laundered and pressed before being carefully packed away.

The gown might well have been hand-stitched, I wasn't enough of a needlewoman to tell, but it was beautifully made with frills and ruffles to the front and little tie closures to the back. It was evidently very old and had been greatly treasured.

'Ah,' Winston's voice from the doorway made me jump, 'you've found the christening gown.'

I looked at the garment spread out on the bedcover. 'It's beautiful,' I said, touching the sweet ruffles reverently.

'I was baptized in that,' Winston came to stand beside me, 'so was Mum and her brother — and their mother before that and the babies in the family who died as infants, as many did in those days. I don't know how old it is, but it must be a hundred years or more.' He seemed to pause, to think and than he offered, right out of the blue, 'I would like you to have the gown for your baby. If you would like it that is.'

I looked at the dress longingly, but I knew I couldn't take it. It belonged to Winston's family, not to mine, and that's what I told him.

'Mum's brother died years ago and he had no children. I never married or gave my mother grandchildren — how could I with the life I led, never knowing where I would be from one day to the next? I'm sure that upset mum, but she hid it well and said we were each entitled to make our own choices. I don't think she ever gave up hope that it would be used again, though.'

'And it will be,' I promised, and folding the gown with infinite care I tried, but failed to picture my baby wearing it. I couldn't help wondering if there was ever going to come a time when I would feel something more than surprise that I was finally pregnant so long after I had given up on it happening and a mild curiosity about the baby I was carrying.

With the wardrobes and drawers empty and open to let the air get into them, and photos and personal belongings removed, it seemed that all trace of Winston's mother had been erased. When I voiced my concern that perhaps we had been too efficient, he assured me that it was possible to let things go and to move forward without losing any of the memories that held a person dear.

'To be honest,' he said, as if it had only just occurred to him, 'leaving the room as it was made life *more* difficult, not less. I could never walk in there without picturing mum as she was at the very end of her life, now I will find it easier to focus on all the happier times. I might even give the walls a coat of emulsion eventually and get some new bedcovers.'

'Do you want to put the cases in the boot of your car, then, Winston? Then you can decide on the charity you'd like to benefit and drop the stuff off on Tuesday morning.'

Without a word, Winston squared his shoulders, lifted a suitcase in each hand and made his way to the front door. I think we both knew it was best to carry the job through while he was in a positive frame of mind.

'I think I'll go for 'Help the Aged',' he said, 'that way we can help all the old folks and not just the sick ones?'

'Good idea,' I nodded, going in front of him to open doors and the car boot.

With one more trip the job was done and we went back inside to enjoy a cup of tea in companionable silence, each of us lost in our own thoughts.

Tomorrow, I was beginning to realize, I

faced a similar task, but this time I would be removing all trace of my own existence from what had been my home. Tomorrow was about accepting that my marriage really was over and that it was time for me to move on, too.

11

Easter Monday dawned bright, but a few dark clouds scudding across the sky gave a hint of rain. The weather seemed to tell of what was to come because, though I woke in a very positive frame of mind, I was quite certain there would be tears before the end of the day. It wouldn't be realistic for me to expect that it could be otherwise.

I wondered how Phil was spending the day, and how come he was spending it with a father who had previously resented even a minute of his company. Then reminding myself it was absolutely none of my business any more, I collected a roll of black bin-bags from the kitchen cupboard and mentally added that to the growing list of items I must replace before I relinquished the flat back to Rich.

Mindful of the baby's well-being, I ate a good breakfast of honey and porridge with a chopped banana on the top, I even added a trickle of cream and could just picture the look of pure horror on Phil's face if he'd been witness to this feast.

Keen on watching his own weight, he'd

been even more enthusiastic about watching mine over the years, making it clear middle-aged spread was not something he would tolerate in either of us. Enjoying my food with a clear conscience was something of a novelty for me, as were the womanly curves I was developing. I wasn't sure that I was unbiased enough to venture an opinion, but I did think my new shape suited me.

I drove past the house in Hightown Cliffs a couple of times to make sure the coast was clear, but there was no sign of Phil's green Jaguar and so I turned into the curved driveway and parked up. It was only as I approached the front door that it struck me the locks might well have been changed in my absence. When the key slid smoothly into the lock and turned easily I breathed an audible sigh of relief.

The house, beautiful as it was, certainly didn't feel like home. If I was honest it never really had felt like home to me. I'd always liked cosy and simple, while Phil's taste had tended to run towards showy grandeur, especially in the latter years of our marriage, when money was more plentiful. I hadn't realized until our separation, just how much of a compromise our relationship had become — with me doing most of the compromising it now seemed in hindsight.

I'd always been content for Phil to have his way in most things and if that made me a doormat, so be it, but it really came down to the simple fact that if he was happy so was I. I hoped that he was happy now, because I was suddenly sure that one day very soon I *would* be happy again, as unlikely as that might seem given my present circumstances. I certainly didn't intend to live a life filled with regrets.

There were signs that two people had been occupying the house. Two cups in the sink, two glasses left on the coffee table, with lipstick traces on one of each. Upstairs the bed had been left unmade and I wondered that Phil would put up with such sloppy housekeeping, and immediately reminded myself again that it had absolutely nothing to do with me.

Most of my things had been banished to the biggest spare room, some of it bagged up and the rest of it thrown across the bed or draped over a chair. I refused to be offended, especially as it certainly made life easier for me and set to folding and packing until the front doorbell brought my head up with a start.

I couldn't help laughing at myself as I went downstairs. It was hardly going to be Phil ringing at his own front door, was it? I was still smiling as I opened the door and found Vi beaming back at me.

'You're home,' she said, but she looked uncertain — as well she might since she would certainly have been aware that another female had taken up residence in my absence.

'Not exactly,' I said, 'but don't let's talk about it on the step. I've just about finished what I came here for, so perhaps I can come round to you for a quick cuppa. Is that all right? I don't really want to be in here any longer than I have to, so if you go and put the kettle on, I'll join you in a few moments.'

The car was soon piled high with numerous half-filled bags due to common-sense dictating that I restrict the weight of the contents in each, but at least I had saved time tramping up and down the stairs by just tumbling the bags from top to bottom.

A lot of the clothes could join Winston's mother's at the charity shop — I'd already decided that. Most of them would be totally unsuitable for a new and very different life that awaited me, so it was definitely going to be a case of 'off with the old and on with the new'.

Closing the front door was almost a relief as if I'd metaphorically closed the door on the past and every step I took from now on would be a step forward. The future belonged to me — and to my child — Phil had no part to play in it.

I left the car sitting in the drive. Well, it hardly seemed worth moving it, for if Phil returned he could recognize it just as easily if it was parked outside of Vi's. I actually hadn't been very long at all so far and after a quick cup of tea with Vi I'd be on my way.

Vi was upset by recent developments, as I would have expected her to be. How on earth could she hope to understand what had happened when I didn't fully understand it myself.

One day I had been — or so I'd thought — happily married and with a very nice life, the next the whole façade had crumbled with a speed that took my breath away. The solid foundation I had firmly believed our marriage to be built upon had turned out to be no more than shifting sand. With hindsight the miracle appeared to be that it had lasted as long as it had.

Given her age and narrow upbringing, it was hardly surprising that Vi was scandalized at the current goings-on next door. I'm sure she would have liked to discuss Phil's bizarre behaviour, but I refused to get involved, telling her, very clearly, that what Phil did and who he did it with was no longer any concern of mine.

'Tomorrow I will be seeing a solicitor,' I told her, and though I hadn't given such an action any thought until that moment, it suddenly seemed entirely logical and part of the whole process. 'For myself, I want nothing, but there is the child to consider.'

I'd forgotten that Vi didn't know about the baby, but she became so excited, even under the circumstances, that a little of her pleasure rubbed off on me and I enjoyed telling her about the christening gown I had been given.

I also admitted, 'I still find it very difficult to accept the pregnancy, Vi, perhaps because so much has happened. I do worry that I won't love the baby when it's born or even that I will blame it for everything. I'm still so confused.'

'It would be a small wonder if you weren't,' Vi said comfortably. 'I think for the moment you have enough to deal with, day by day, and worrying ahead isn't going to help, is it dear?'

I shook my head.

'I think some mothers fall in love with their baby while it's still in the womb, some the day it's born, and still others take a little while after the birth, but there are very few cases when it doesn't happen at all and, even then, help and advice is readily available.

That's my understanding anyway though, of course I'm no expert.'

'You talk a good deal of sense, though, and I feel better for listening to you,' I told her honestly. 'I don't think I'll worry too much from now on, just deal with every day as it comes — I have to say that method seems to be working surprisingly well so far.'

'You have a good head on your shoulders,' Vi insisted, getting up to put the kettle on again, 'and you won't go far wrong if you follow your instincts.'

Looking at my watch I couldn't believe how the time had flown by. 'No more tea for me, Vi,' I said, 'I must be going. I was meant to have been long gone by now and wouldn't relish bumping into Phil, or his lady friend, not yet.'

'Now, you will keep in touch.'

'I promise,' I said, 'now I have your number in my phone, and you must come over to me, perhaps meet Winston and maybe Rich, too. I can pick you up. I must go.' I found myself giving her a hug, which wasn't a bit like me, but I felt better for doing it.

Itching to be gone now, I was just about to hop into the car and drive off, when I realized I'd left my jacket in the house hanging on the back of a kitchen chair. Part of me wanted to leave it there and just go, but that was just plain ridiculous and, anyway, it was one of my favourite coats.

I had just slid the key into the lock when a voice behind me said, 'Mrs Siddons?'

I turned to find a gentleman wearing a long mac standing behind me. He must have followed me up the drive, but I hadn't even realized he was there. If I hadn't seen that Vi was still watching from her doorstep I might have been nervous.

'Yes,' I said abruptly, only just stopping myself from adding, 'who wants to know?'

Apparently satisfied I was who I said I was, the man flashed identification and said he was from Brankstone police. My immediate reaction was to suspect Phil of reporting me for trespass or even breaking and entering.

If it wasn't that, I had no idea what the police could want with me and, curious, I said, 'You'd better come inside.'

I waved to Vi to show her everything was all right and led the way into the lounge still wondering what Phil might have taken it into his head to report me for. Even after his actions of the past few weeks I still found myself surprised by how bloody petty he was being. He must know there was no need for this.

We sat down facing each other in two of the armchairs and he said, in a serious tone,

'Is your husband Philip Siddons?'

'Yes.'

'Does he ride a Triumph Bonneville motorcycle?'

I almost laughed out loud, but the man looked so solemn it would have seemed rude. I did smile slightly as I told him, 'Whatever this is about you've come to the wrong place. Phil owns a motorbike for his own reasons, but he has no interest in riding it.'

'Are you quite sure?'

The man, middle-aged and balding, but with a kind face, I noticed belatedly, was looking at me very seriously, and who was I, after all, to say if Phil had returned to his youth and a long forgotten love of two wheels?

'There's only one way to find out,' I said, 'I won't be more than a moment.'

I thought I already knew what I would find. Phil's Jaguar was parked in the double garage, as was his four-by-four. Of the huge black motorbike there was no sign.

'It's gone.'

The guy must have wondered why I didn't know what my husband was up to, but I just couldn't bring myself to tell him we were living apart, so added nothing further and simply sat down again, waiting for him to tell me what this was all about.

When he placed Phil's wallet, keys and watch on the coffee table between us, it finally dawned on me that something was very wrong, and a feeling of dread swept through my body.

'What's happened?' I said, almost forcing the words from between clenched teeth.

'There's been an accident involving two men on a motorbike, one middle-aged and one elderly man. Can you identify these items as belonging to your husband?'

'Yes. Where is he? Is he hurt? Can I go and see him?'

Everything was forgotten in that moment. Phil was hurt and he needed me.

'Unfortunately, the crash was fatal, both the driver and pillion passenger died at the scene.'

Well, I think that was what was said, but though his lips were moving the man was making no sense at all. Phil couldn't be dead — he just couldn't, because that would mean it really was all over. I wanted to stand up, to run away, but my limbs had turned to water.

He was still talking, telling me he realized I was in shock — how would he know that? — but that he still had to ask me some questions. He spoke and I must have replied because he kept making notes. Then he asked me if there was someone I could contact, but

I had no next of kin because Phil was my husband and Phil was dead, and now we would never have the chance to put right the wrongs between us.

'Perhaps your neighbour?' he was suggesting, and then the lounge door flew open and suddenly Rich was there, on his knees beside me, holding me so tightly that I could hardly breathe.

'And you are?' the man asked.

'I'm Philip Siddons' brother, Richard,' Rich sounded angry, and he swore at the man, telling him he should have waited, should have known someone would come immediately to be with me when I was told.

Vi came in, came straight across to me, 'Oh, my dear, my dear,' she kept repeating, taking my hands as Rich stood to usher the man out, having a furious whispered conversation with him on the way.

I stood up suddenly, telling Vi, 'Phil's dead, Vi. He was on that bloody motorbike and it crashed. Why would he be on the motorbike, he never took it out of the garage.'

Then I noticed that Rich was back, standing in the doorway, and the look on his face suddenly told me everything I needed to know.

'It was Randy, wasn't it? The elderly man on the bike with Phil was Randolph bloody

Siddons? Nothing, and no one else would have tempted him anywhere near that machine, except that bloody man. I'll bloody well swing for him, I will, I'll kill him,' and then I remembered, 'but I can't even have the satisfaction of that because he's done for them both, hasn't he? Well, he's really done it this time, hasn't he? I don't know what Jacquetta is going to say.'

Rich was by my side in a stride, holding me close, shushing and rocking me, with Vi standing close behind patting my back and telling me everything would be all right. I knew she meant well but I wanted to tell her to stop, that everything couldn't possibly be all right now and it never would be again.

Louise came, and then Rose came, and they cried the tears I couldn't seem to manage. I was glad that someone could cry for Phil's untimely passing, because I couldn't. Not while I was expecting him to walk through the door at any minute and ask what everyone was doing there.

We drank tea, talked in hushed tones about what had happened, and all the time it felt as if I were in the middle of a dream and could wake up at any moment.

Perhaps, I found myself thinking longingly, all of the past dreadful weeks had been a dream and I would wake up next to Phil in the king-sized bed upstairs to another very normal day. A normal day in a normal life in which unwanted pregnancies, infidelity and separation played no part.

It was Easter Monday and Phil might have gone off for a day of golf, leaving me to potter round the house and garden, listening to the pop music that I loved and he detested as I worked. Later we would probably go for a meal — Indian was his preference and Italian was mine — or to a show or maybe the cinema. I was easily pleased, just happy to have him home and in the relaxed mood that came from a good round of golf. Feet up in front of the TV would have suited me, but Phil usually had to be up and doing.

If this were not a dream he would be up and doing no more. Impossible to imagine all that energy and enthusiasm stilled forever, I could only imagine there had been some dreadful mistake or that I was indeed going to wake up very soon.

Time dragged along, copious amounts of tea were made and drunk by the people who filed in and out of the house. Cups were placed in front of me at regular intervals where they remained untouched until they cooled and were removed — only to be replaced with fresh cups moments later.

People — well meaning, I'm sure — took

my hands, some hugged me, some kissed my cheek, they all said how shocked they were that such a thing could have happened, what a great guy Phil had been. They had one thing in common — they were all strangers to me.

Suddenly there was a stir, muffled sounds as another visitor arrived, and I really felt as if I'd reached the point when I couldn't take it any more. I had arrived at the house that morning in the hope of removing my belongings from Phil's life and his home. Instead he had turned the tables on me and removed himself from my life totally, efficiently and forever. I didn't know how I was ever going to be able to accept that — for Phil and me — there really was no way back.

My eyes burned from the tears that wouldn't fall, my lips were frozen and unable to form the words I wanted to say. I wanted to run but I knew my limbs wouldn't obey me, yet if I stayed I didn't think I could bear one more platitude or one more well-meaning but senseless, 'Sorry'.

I stood up, and at the same time the door of the lounge was thrust open and Jacquetta stood there flanked by Derek and Anthony, who had obviously been trying to prevent her reaching me.

'Sorry,' Del said — that word again, 'we tried to stop her coming over but she insisted.'

Wig askew, make-up smeared, Jacquetta threw her arms out and pleaded, 'It's not true, Alex. Tell me it's not true.'

Faced with her grief, I felt my own composure crumble as I confronted the fact that Phil really *wasn't* coming home ever again and wondered how on earth an unplanned pregnancy had brought us to this.

★   ★   ★

It was a strange time, totally unreal, as we went through the motions and dealt with the aftermath of an accident that had claimed two lives. That it should never have happened was uppermost in all of our minds. Phil and Randy had no business being anywhere near a motorbike, let alone racing it — as it appeared they were — along winding country roads on the outskirts of town.

Phil's helmet must have done its job because he didn't have a mark on his face, when I plucked up the courage to go and see him later that same day. I knew I would have to do it or I would never accept that he was not going to come home again. He looked just the same as he always had, but with a peaceful expression in death that had not been his in life.

A post-mortem would reveal the extent of

the injuries that had caused his death, but while he was still my Phil, before any of the necessary procedures were carried out, was when I said all the things I would like to have had the chance to say while he was alive.

How I was sure we would have found a way to work things out, but that even if we hadn't got back together I was still certain he would have found a way to accept the child we had created and gone on to be a great dad.

I told him that I loved him, that I always would, and that I would try to understand and accept that his final actions had come from an overwhelming need to be accepted by his father.

I could not bring myself to pay a similar visit to Randy. There was nothing I could find to say to him, and everyone said it would be too much for me in my fragile state. I flatly refused to contemplate a double funeral and hoped that Jacquetta understood that on this occasion I had to take my own needs into consideration as well as hers.

After the post-mortems, there were death certificates, funeral arrangements, flowers and cards and my choice would have been to miss it all by hiding away in Rich's flat where few people could find me. Instead, I went back to the house that Phil had been so proud of and worked to erase every trace of his infidelity until I could almost convince myself it had never happened.

At least I could comfort myself that the reputation of a solid marriage would remain unblemished as only a handful of people had any idea it had ever been in trouble.

On the day of the funeral I would have liked to have followed the coffin with Jacquetta by my side, but the Siddons family were — apparently — sticklers for etiquette and so I found myself supported by Del as the eldest son, followed by Louise who was taking care of his mother, Phil's coffin was carried aloft by the remaining four brothers.

'My Way' seemed like an appropriate choice of song to open the service for a man who always had done things his own way, and as I walked into the church behind the mahogany coffin covered with flowers I was gratified to see just how many people had turned up to pay their last respects.

Phil's nephews and nieces took up several of the pews near to the front, some of them I barely recognized, it was so long since I'd seen them. Many of them were weeping for the uncle they could surely scarcely have known. I was pleased to see that Kayleigh was there to support Martin in spite of the recent differences reported by Louise.

The service followed its familiar pattern,

with prayers, and tributes from Phil's family and then the vicar began a reflection of Phil's life. I vaguely recalled him coming to the house and must have spoken to him about our years together. There would have been plenty of other family members around to fill in any gaps.

Listening to the story of our married life being related was a bit like hearing a fairy tale. How we'd worked so hard, supporting each other in our respective careers, achieved so much and then after twenty-five years of blissful marriage were about to be blessed with the child we had longed for — only for Phil to be tragically snatched away as the result of a freak accident while he was giving the father he adored one final motorcycle ride.

Some of it was true, some of it was pure fiction, but what did it really matter? At the end of the day, Phil was gone and it was surely better to leave everyone with pleasant memories.

The ear-splitting shriek when it came, took everyone by surprise and from the corner of my eye I saw someone coming from behind. A small figure dressed from head-to-toe in black ran forward to throw herself at the coffin, rocking it dangerously on the support-ing trestles and scattering flowers all around and wailing like a banshee.

Someone stepped forward, I think it was Rich, and tried to take her arm. She shrugged it off and turned to face the congregation. Her face was a mask of youthful tragedy, drained of colour and streaked liberally with mascara. I had a dreadful feeling of impending doom even before she spoke.

'It's *lies*,' Kayleigh said, 'all *lies*. It was *me* Phil loved, not *her*.' A finger was pointed directly at me, her eyes ablaze with pure hatred.

12

There was pandemonium as the Siddons brothers raced as one to the front of the church and Kayleigh was bundled unceremoniously out, shrieking and protesting all the way down the aisle past the shocked faces of the mourners.

I found myself standing with Jacquetta, surrounded by every one of my four sisters-in-law and their children. A solid, protective wall of family, making sure no more hurt could reach me. They would have ushered me from the church, but even in my shocked state I quickly realized the show had to go on or Kayleigh's outburst would be the only thing anyone would remember about the day — and I had a child's future to think of.

'I'm all right,' I insisted, 'and I would appreciate it if the vicar would please continue with the service. Kayleigh was obviously overwrought and delusional. She couldn't have known what she was saying.'

This was all said loudly enough for the congregation to hear and I was pleased to note my voice was amazingly steady. I don't think anyone there could have realized I'd just discovered the identity of my dead husband's mistress and that if he hadn't already been dead I would have done the job myself there and then.

As the day progressed I discovered I'd followed the wrong career path, because I was obviously a born actress. I played the grieving widow to the hilt, opened the house to the mourners after the service and burial with more enthusiasm than I had originally intended. It was a relief to find the caterers had overestimated so that there was plenty of food for all, and I made free with Phil's well-stocked wine cellar in a way that would have had him tearing his hair out; the latter gave me a vindictive kind of pleasure.

'I had to do it,' I told Louise when the final sympathetic — and very merry by then — mourner had left, 'it was about damage limitation. I can't have our child growing up knowing that his father was not only philandering, but even worse was playing around with a girl young enough to be his daughter and his nephew's girlfriend to boot.'

'I don't think anyone believed a word of it,' she assured me. 'I'm just so sorry that girl ever had anything to do with my family. She's broken your heart and Martin's, too, and neither of you deserve it.'

I shrugged, feeling there was nothing I

could say at that point to make her feel better. There was certainly nothing that was going to make *me* feel better about what Phil had been up to and with whom. It was almost a relief when Jacquetta came into the room.

'Mon dieu,' she said, 'what a day.'

I returned a heartfelt, 'You can say that again.'

'And again,' agreed Louise.

'I am so proud of you,' Jacquetta said then, taking me by surprise. 'Such a difficult day for you and made so much worse by that foolish girl. Thanks to you, it was dismissed as mere attention seeking — which of course it was. I never heard anything more ridiculous,' she added staunchly.

I thought about telling her the truth, but she was old and frail. Despite the effort she bravely continued to make with the heavy make-up, chestnut wig and carefully chosen outfits there was no doubt that the advancing years were catching up with her. She was also extremely vulnerable having just lost her husband of many years and favourite son. Nothing good would be gained from destroying her pathetic certainty that Phil and I would have been reconciled before her grandchild was born.

Louise went to speak, possibly to tell it how it was, so I poked her sharply in the ribs and said clearly, 'Oh, absolutely ridiculous, but no harm done and I think we did Phil proud today. Amazing turnout, though I don't think I'd ever met half of them.'

'You are a real lady, Alexandra,' Jacquetta accompanied the words with a look that made me feel certain she understood more than she was letting on, but that she knew — as I did — that from here on in it was all about putting on a united front and keeping up the fiction of happy families.

Rich appeared then from somewhere — the house seemed to be overrun with Siddons, but I had been more than glad of their help with the wake — he took one look at me and said, 'You should be taking it easy, Alex. It's been a long and very difficult day, especially for someone in your condition.'

With that he took the dishcloth I'd been using to wipe down surfaces out of my hand and led me through to the lounge, calling over his shoulder, 'Can someone make Alex a milky coffee and put in two sugars.'

'I'm all right,' I insisted, 'really.'

'You're as white as a sheet under that blusher and the strain shows in your eyes. If you won't think of yourself, then think of your child.'

'That's exactly what I intend to do from now on,' I collapsed on to the couch, suddenly realizing just how tired I actually was. Keeping up an act of such monumental proportions was obviously emotionally draining and it was still all far from over. 'Only a very few people knew that Phil and I were separated — most of them family — and even fewer knew he was having an affair or who with. That *is* the case isn't it?'

'None of it was common knowledge. I think even Phil must have been aware he would not only look like a complete idiot but a total bastard, too, if it became common knowledge that he was knocking off his own nephew's girlfriend. It would have fizzled out, you know. The novelty value of a very young girlfriend would soon have lost its appeal.'

'The affair was just the final nail in the coffin of our marriage, Rich. We had already decided we both wanted different things. When I moved into your flat the marriage was already over. Which reminds me, I should come over and collect my stuff.'

'Are you sure? I seem to remember you were adamant about not wanting to live in this house, even if Phil left. Don't feel you have to stay here, you can stay at mine for as long as you want.'

'Thanks, Rich, I would love to take you up on your offer, but the show has to go on. People will be calling to pay their respects, so if I'm to keep up the pretence that everything was all right before Phil died, I need to be right here and playing my part.'

'We could take it in turns to stay on for a while with you,' Rose came into the lounge with my cup of coffee, she was followed by Louise and Jacquetta. 'No one would think that was strange under the circumstances.'

'And you do need someone to take care of you,' Louise put in. 'You've had one shock after another recently and we mustn't forget you've already lost one baby. I don't think you should be taking any more chances.'

My independent streak made me want to refuse, but I really didn't relish the thought of staying on in what was a pretty big house alone, if I was being honest.

'What about Del and Tony, though?' I felt obliged to ask. 'Won't they mind fending for themselves? You've been here for most of the week as it is.'

'Everyone wants to help,' Louise said gently, 'it's just a pity it's taken all of this to bring us together. Del and Tony can manage for a few days and it's no hardship for Rose and I to continue living in luxury for a while longer.'

'I would like to help, too,' Jacquetta said unexpectedly. 'What have I to be at home for?'

Rose, Louise and I looked at each other and I could tell having her staying in the house, too, was the last thing they wanted. I hesitated, tried to harden my heart, but in the end I couldn't bring myself to send her away.

She needed no further bidding and with a speed that belied her years by the next day she had moved — bag and baggage — into the master bedroom and looked to be settled for a lengthy stay. I doubted I would ever want to sleep in the room I'd shared with Phil ever again, but I did take time to wonder what my life and home were turning into, and whether I was being too soft for my own good. After all the years as an outsider in her family I owed Jacquetta Siddons precious little, when all was said and done.

I might have managed to escape back into my work, but a visit from the doctor confirmed a slight rise in my blood pressure and — all things considered — he felt some time off was indicated. Even the idea of working at home was frowned on. He also discussed with me again the benefits of an amniocentesis test but I was grateful that he didn't try to persuade me otherwise when I explained I'd decided against it.

The changes in my life over a relatively short period of time were staggering when I thought about it. I'd gone from a happily married and childless career woman, to pregnant and single overnight, and then before I could even begin to come to terms with that unexpected status, I'd found myself a widow with any chance of a reconciliation gone forever.

In the end, one other change became increasingly apparent, and this was that the house actually benefited from the additional occupants. It had obviously been intended as a family home but, with only Phil and me to rattle around in it, had always seemed rather cold, friendless and empty: a show home with no soul. Bursting at the seams was an understatement. A hive of activity during the day, and with most of the bedrooms occupied at night, the whole place seemed to have come alive twenty-four-seven. The change was unbelievable.

Opening my eyes to another new day, I could already hear sounds of activity — someone singing in the shower, the rattle of crockery from the kitchen downstairs, which was followed shortly afterwards by a tap on the bedroom door.

'Come on in.'

'Hi,' Rose's smiling face appeared and then the rest of her bath-robed figure bearing a loaded tray. 'Only me.'

'Oh, Rose,' I struggled to sit up, 'you

shouldn't keep doing this. I'm quite capable of coming down to the kitchen for my breakfast.'

'Doctor's orders,' she insisted bossily, 'and if we're going shopping later, you need to conserve your energy.'

I'd forgotten all about the shopping trip. Yesterday I'd been coaxed into making a decision about turning the smallest bedroom into a nursery and today we were going to look at furniture and equipment. It would be fun, my sister-in-law had assured me and Jacquetta stubbornly refused to be left out.

At first I had found it strange that she never mentioned Randy's name, until I realized I was guilty of the same thing regarding Phil. It was almost as if the pair of them had never existed. How strange was that, given the length of our marriages? As Jacquetta didn't even have the excuse of an affair to blame for her lapse I did wonder what was going on in her head.

Even though she was French by birth and prone to emotional outbursts in the past, she had taken the British stiff upper lip to the nth degree and, from the day of Phil's funeral, I never saw her shed another tear. She rose each day and dressed and made-up in her own meticulous fashion. It would have amused me to see her dressing up to the nines to polish and vacuum, if I wasn't a little concerned about her mental state.

I might be pregnant but I was also years younger and obviously better able to cope. In fact, I felt remarkably calm and relatively cheerful, which even I thought was strange under the circumstances but considered that, as long as I was coping, it didn't really matter how. Maybe it was the very fact so many things had changed that was getting me through. I almost felt I was living someone else's life — and I was actually quite enjoying it if I was being totally honest.

Perhaps, I sometimes thought, I should be grateful to Phil for his misdemeanours, because if he had died under any other circumstances and while we were together, it would probably have taken me months, or possibly years to even begin to come to terms with his death.

I could see with hindsight that I had become totally dependant upon him during the course of our marriage, all of my happiness was tied up with his and I'd often bowed to what we both saw as his superior judgement.

It had taken years to build up Phil's confidence, due to his father's rejection and it was only now, looking back, that I wondered if I had gone too far and created a monster who truly believed his way was the only way.

I supposed it had never mattered greatly to me where we lived, what cars we drove or where we went on holiday, but I had become so used to going along with his wishes that I had almost accepted his ever-changing views about the unexpected pregnancy without question, too.

In some ways I had and — to some extent — still did understand his confusion. Discovering I was carrying a child, after accepting some years before that we would be childless, was a huge shock. If I was being truthful, I still had no real feelings, one way or the other, about the baby I was carrying — except perhaps a tinge of admiration for its evident determination to survive. How I would feel when it was born I really had no idea, but I had decided some time before to cross that bridge when I came to it — just as I had dealt with the many other unexpected hurdles in recent weeks.

All the thinking had given me a dull headache but I was amazed to see I had managed to consume the entire contents of the breakfast tray during my musings. Cereal, orange juice, marmalade on toast and a small pot of coffee had all passed my lips almost unnoticed. My appetite, previously miniscule, had appeared to grow apace with my now expanding belly and clothes were becoming a real problem. Elasticated waistbands had never figured in my extensive wardrobe so, perhaps along with the nursery furniture, it would be in order to purchase some maternity wear. It was well after the danger period now and high time I accepted I was obviously well and truly pregnant.

'Perhaps I may not come today,' Jacquetta said suddenly when we were discussing the day's plan of action.

Rose and Louise didn't even try to hide their relief and assured her she might well find the walking a bit much.

The old Jacquetta would have furiously denied that a bit of shopping was too much for her, but she merely acquiesced and said she might have a little lie down. I looked at her closely. She appeared much the same as usual, but it was difficult to gauge her mood beneath the defiant mask of make-up she showed to the world.

I suddenly felt quite protective of the old lady I had once viewed as the enemy, and found myself assuring her she would enjoy shopping for her new grandchild.

'We won't be walking too far at a time,' I insisted, 'not with my blood pressure.' It had actually been normal for several days, but I ignored that, *and* the looks my sisters-in-law were sending my way, to add, 'We can take our time and stop for coffee any time you like. We might even invite Vi along.'

The latter clinched it because, against all the odds, the two elderly women were becoming firm friends as they discovered they had much in common — though I had not yet managed to discover exactly what. I couldn't begin to imagine Jacquetta shopping for bargains at Sainsbury's or anywhere else for that matter, and Vi wouldn't have known a designer label if it had jumped up and bitten her.

'Shall I be the one to issue the invitation?'

She scuttled off eagerly when I nodded and as soon as she was out the door, Louise said, 'Oh, Alex, I know you mean well, but we'll get next to nothing done with those two tagging along.'

'I'm worried about her,' I said flatly. 'She's putting on a brave front, but she's been through an awful lot for a woman of her age and I would rather keep an eye on her.'

Rose nodded reluctantly and Louise said with a sigh, 'I suppose you're right, but you've obviously got a bigger heart and more patience than either of us where she's concerned. Didn't you even mind her taking over your bedroom — en suite and all?'

'It didn't feel like mine any more from the

time I knew Phil had been with someone else in there. I'm sure she won't stay forever and at the moment she's welcome to it. Perhaps one day that will change or perhaps I'll just go and live somewhere else. I've never been fond of the house, it was always more Phil's choice than mine.'

Rose spoke hesitantly, 'I must admit — lovely as it is — it's all a bit *spartan* for me, with all those emulsioned walls and not a knick-knack in sight.'

'Minimalist is the word,' I said ruefully, 'and that was Phil's choice, too. He couldn't abide clutter at any price and made sure there was plenty of storage so everything could be put away after use.'

'You can say that again,' Louise frowned, 'even the bloody toaster has to be hauled out of the cupboard every morning.'

'Well, from now on,' I decided with a little thrill at even so small a change in my own house, 'it can be left out on the worktop, along with anything else that gets regular use. You're right, it's a complete waste of energy to be dragging the thing out every time you fancy a bit of toasted bread. In fact,' I went to the cupboard and, lifting the appliance out, placed it prominently on the side, 'there you are, ready for use.'

It looked strange and out of place sitting

there all alone, but I was sure I would soon get used to it — especially once it was joined by other items of a similar nature.

Jacquetta bustled back into the kitchen, looking much more like her old self I was pleased to note. She was followed closely by Vi all dressed for the summer's day it was in a straw boater-type hat, floral dress and lightweight blazer and the sort of open sandals that my own mother used to favour. She carried her usual collection of shopping bags.

'Shall we take the Jag out of the garage,' I suggested, 'give it an airing and travel in style?' There was a moment of stunned silence as everyone realized I was referring to Phil's car, and then I saved them all from answering by saying, 'That's all decided then and it has a massive boot to take all the shopping we'll be bringing home with us. Are we ready, then?'

'Ooh, this is a treat,' Vi squeaked excitedly, cutting down the tension for those of us who realized that Phil would be hopping mad to see us making free with his very expensive top-of-the-range car.

'Actually,' Louise gave a little giggle of glee, 'would you mind if I drove. I'll never own a car like that in a million years, but I'd love to be able to say I've driven one. I have comprehensive insurance and Rich lied about me only ever driving around the block.'

'Go on then,' I agreed readily, and then asked Rose, 'Do you mind if I sit in the back? I think I'll be more comfortable.'

I was lying through my teeth, but as it was my idea for the two older ladies to come along on the shopping trip, I felt the least I could do was to make sure I was the one taking responsibility for them.

In fact the atmosphere in the car was quite jovial, with most of the conversation centring around the coming baby and the items we would be looking for. There was some debate about the changes over the years and how mothers used to manage in times gone by when there wasn't the labour-saving devices available. The idea of boiling soiled nappies in particular made me feel extremely grateful for the progress made.

Everything was fine up until the moment when a motorbike zoomed up so close to the car it was a miracle there wasn't a collision. As if that wasn't bad enough to frighten us half to death, it then raced forward and cut in front so sharply that, if Louise hadn't applied the brakes so hard we were all thrown forward against our seat belts, there would have been a serious accident.

The guy roared off, but not before he had

issued a defiant two-fingered gesture and leered at us over his shoulder, his eyes glittering through the helmet's visor. Obviously shaken, Louise quickly pulled over to the side of the road and stopped to ask if we were all okay.

Everyone began talking at once, condemning the guy for being an idiot, and assuring each other that at least no damage was done. It was only when I turned to Jacquetta that I realized she was very far from all right and was, in fact, unravelling in front of my eyes.

13

Finally tipped over the edge by a thoughtless act of road rage, all the grief Jacquetta had been burying with such grim determination came pouring out. I wasn't surprised it was the behaviour of a thoughtless motorcyclist that had brought it about, given all that had happened and the connection to that particular type of vehicle.

Between us we got her out of the car and sat her down on a low wall bordering someone's front garden. Luckily the road was a relatively quiet one and the few people around politely looked the other way and went about their business.

'Darling.' I got down on to my knees in front of her with some difficulty and looked up into the disaster area that was her face. Bright eye shadow mingled with mascara and made tracks through the thick foundation, forming muddy pools in the wrinkles and dripping sadly from the end of her wobbling chin. 'He frightened us all,' I told her, though I knew there was more to it than that.

She hiccoughed and gulped, barely able to breathe let alone speak. We surrounded her, protecting her as best we could from public gaze, offering tissues and patting her back, but feeling pretty helpless to deal with this sudden outpouring of emotion.

'Shall we take you home?' I offered, 'It was silly of me to drag you out like that, when you're clearly not ready.'

'No,' she sobbed harder, 'you must not think this. You have been so kind, so kind, much more than I deserve. I see your bravery, Alex, and I do my best to emulate it, but it is so hard — too hard sometimes.'

'Please, don't try to be like me, Jacquetta,' I pleaded, putting my arms around her and looking into her ravaged face. 'I'm not brave at all and I'm not even beginning to deal with what's happened. It's all too much to take and so I do my best to ignore it by shutting it all into a box of my own making and sealing the lid down tightly.

'If I try to take everything in, I fear I will drown in a sea of my tears and so I live my new life from day to day and refuse to look at yesterday for now. It's how I coped when my dad died and it got me through. So you see I don't know any other way.'

'Everyone has to find their own way of coping, whoever they are, and whatever life throws at them, there is no right or wrong way,' Louise put in, 'but I think you are both very brave indeed.'

'And so do I,' Rose chipped in, and Vi stood silently by nodding her own agreement.

'We can go home,' I said, 'another day will do for the shopping.'

'No, no,' Jacquetta seemed to pull herself together by making a supreme effort, 'you must go as you intended. I cannot, because I look,' she shook her head sadly, 'like the old woman I am. I shall take a taxi home, though I will be sad to miss the outing.' She managed to smile at us all and added, 'All girls together.'

'Look,' I said, touched by her attitude and her fortitude, 'Rich's place is only round the corner and I still have a key. Some of my stuff is still there, including make-up. What if we stop off, and give you time to make yourself presentable again?'

That's just what we did, and Winston was out of the front door before the car had even stopped. Whether he knew it was us, or greeted all visitors with the same enthusiasm I had no idea, but once he understood the situation he coaxed Louise, Rose and Vi into his flat with the promise of tea and homemade biscuits, while I took Jacquetta on up in the lift, intending to share the tea when we came back down.

'So kind,' my mother-in-law murmured

and she set to with a will to repair the damage to her make-up, rummaging in her handbag and making up the shortfall from items I had left behind. Leaving her to it I spent the time collecting personal possessions I discovered still scattered around the flat from my brief stay there.

When the phone rang we were both startled, and looked at each other wide-eyed.

'We should leave it,' I said, 'it's bound to be for Rich and will go to answerphone. Most people will know he's back on the oil rig.'

'It might be important.'

Jacquetta could well have been right, but I still had strong reservations about what I saw as interfering even as I reached out and lifted the receiver.

'Dad? Is that you?'

Well, there was no question that it had to be Amber, Rich's daughter and his only child. I was surprised, well aware there was little contact between them, and that this was more Amber's choice than Rich's.

'Amber, it's your Auntie Alex, but I don't expect you remember me. I'm here with Grandma Siddons, we just stopped by on the way to town as Grandma was feeling a bit under the weather.'

It wasn't exactly a lie, so I didn't feel too bad about saying it.

'Is my Dad there?'

'No, darling, he went back to work, but I don't know how we would have managed without his help after everything that's happened here. He's really been there for Grandma and for me.'

'That's nice. I'm truly glad for you, really I am, but it's just a shame he's never been there for me.' The girl didn't even try to keep the bitterness from her tone. 'I don't know why I thought he might be now. I'm an idiot. Tell him his daughter phoned will you — that's if he even remembers who I am.'

'Amber, Amber, wait,' I pleaded, 'let me give you your dad's mobile number. If you need him I know he won't let you down.'

'He,' she said viciously, 'has done nothing *but* let me down since the day I was born and I know he won't want me around now. He never has before. He just got right on with his life after mum and I left. It was just as if we never existed.'

'It was probably his way of coping, but he talks about you all the time and I know he keeps in touch. I'm sure he would visit a lot more but you live so far away and have a new life now. I'm sure he would be on the next plane if he knew that you needed him. Is that what you want — for him to come over?'

I knew I had to keep talking to the girl, it

224

was the least I could do for Rich after all he had done for me. Amber was obviously distressed or she would never have phoned the father she had always treated with disdain, and I had to find some way of helping her in Rich's absence. This might be his one and only chance of building some kind of relationship with the daughter he doted on.

There was a kind of hiccough. It could have been a sob and I tried again.

'Amber, do *you* want to ring him or shall *I*? Just tell me where you are and I promise you your dad will be there just as soon as he can be. He would do anything for you.'

'I'm at the airport.' Amber's voice was so low that I could barely hear her and I had to ask her to repeat herself. 'I'm at the airport,' she said again.

Seventeen years old she might have been, but I did wonder what her mother was thinking of letting her go there all by herself. Even with all the safety checks, airports were still not the safest of places to be, in my view at least. The security staff didn't carry guns for no reason at all.

'At the airport,' I repeated parrot fashion, 'what are you doing there?'

'I just flew in to Heathrow,' she told me, 'and I was ringing my dad to come and collect me.'

Stunned into silence, several things flew through my mind: the first was a realization that she was here in this country and had flown all that way, obviously on her own; the second was just how gutted Rich was going to be when he realized he'd missed this one chance to be exactly where his daughter wanted him to be, exactly when she wanted him to be there, and finally I accepted that it was going to be up to me to sort this out because there was no one else and no time to waste.

'Stay there,' I ordered, in a tone I sincerely hoped she would not argue with, 'there must be a collection point, so go there and I will come and collect you. I will be driving a green Jaguar. I'm on my way. Do you hear me, Amber, I'm on my way?'

'All right,' she agreed in a tiny voice. 'I'll wait for you.'

'Amber,' I told my mother-in-law unnecessarily and, as she would have picked up on only half the conversation, added, 'at Heathrow airport. I'll leave you with Winston and the others and go to collect her by myself. We don't want to scare her with a deputation. I can ring Rich on the way to the airport on Phil's in-car communication system. At least I have a great car for the journey, I must have known there was a

226

reason for bringing the Jag.'

We hurried to the lift and by the time I left Jacquetta at Winston's door we had decided the best course of action for them was to all take a taxi home. Quite obviously there was going to be no shopping trip that day.

The majority of the journey was under-taken in no time, but after that there was no point in putting my foot down since the roads approaching the airport were always notori-ously busy and I had no intention of hopping from lane to lane. My conversation with Rich had been brief and to the point. I knew he would get a ride on the next helicopter off the rig and I told him that, for now at least, Amber would be coming home with me.

'Alex . . . ?'

'If you were thinking of thanking me, Rich,' I told him, 'don't even think about it. It's the very least I can do after all you've done for me.'

I pulled up at what I hoped was the appropriate collection point and recognized Amber immediately from the photos scat-tered around Rich's flat. Tall, dark and very slim and pretty, dressed from head to toe in denim, she stood forlornly beside a large holdall.

Pressing the button that sent the window down silently, I leaned over and called her name. She looked startled for a moment and then came across dragging the holdall and, in spite of herself and her obvious distress, she whistled and said, 'Nice car, Auntie Alex.'

Pressing another button released the boot catch and I wondered aloud, 'Can you manage to get that bag into the boot, Amber? Only I shouldn't lift anything heavy?'

'Bad back, huh?' she guessed, and I didn't bother to correct her. 'Sure, I can manage,' she went on and demonstrated with ease, slamming the boot down with more force than was strictly necessary.

I thought Phil must have been spinning in his grave and thinking about him made me realize that if things had been back to normal there was no way *he* would have been making this airport run to pick up his errant niece — never mind *me*. It made me aware of what an isolated life we had led, uninvolved as we were in anybody else's troubles and with very few of our own. I seriously wondered which life I really preferred and had difficulty coming up with an answer that didn't make a mockery of the past twenty-five years.

I made a concerted effort not to fire a barrage of questions at Amber, but kept the conversation light and general, asking if she'd had a good flight, if she was hungry and how long she thought she'd be staying. All the time I was wondering what had sent her on this mad dash across the world and if her mother knew where she was.

'The flight was fine,' she assured me and then went on to regret the lack of reading material and bemoan the standard of in-flight entertainment, though the food, apparently, was acceptable. Eventually she asked, 'Where are we going?'

'I thought I would take you to my house for the time being.'

'No room for me at my dad's, I guess,' Amber still sounded bitter, but a little bit sad, too, I thought, as she added, 'with him living the bachelor life.'

I hadn't meant to tell her, but I suddenly felt she needed to know about the room all prepared and waiting for her — and sooner rather than later.

'That's not true, Amber,' I said, 'there is a room waiting just for you at your dad's flat and I would say that's always been the case.' I described it to her, even down to the big cream teddy bear.

She seemed stunned, and whispered, 'Really?'

'He loves you dearly, Amber, and the flat is full of framed photos of you. I know he bitterly regrets the breakdown of the marriage and its effect on you. He acknowledges his own failings, and the fact he didn't try harder to be a good husband and dad will always haunt him.'

Amber was silent for a moment and then she asked, 'How do you know all of this? My dad isn't the greatest talker.'

I didn't want to talk about my own problems, much preferring to leave them shut away for a later date, but this was no time for holding back and I was willing to use any of my own experiences to help this young girl to understand the problems adults sometimes face in relationships.

'Your dad spoke to me because, at the time, Phil and I were experiencing problems in our own marriage. I know he also spoke to Phil because he was terrified he was going to make the same mistakes and wanted him to realize the likely consequences of his actions. When I needed somewhere to stay your dad gave me the key to his flat and that's how I know about the room. I can tell you that I have never seen anywhere more lovingly prepared.'

Amber was silent, staring down at her hands — the nails bitten almost to the quick — in her lap.

'Your parents' problems were theirs, Amber.' I didn't know what to do but keep talking as the big car ate up the miles of motorway. 'If you had lived in England after the break up you might have had a more successful relationship with your dad with regular access visits and the chance to stay over with him.'

'That's just an excuse,' she said, her tone brittle and the hurt very apparent. 'America isn't on the moon. There are flights several times a day. He could have made more effort.'

'Yes, he could and he probably should — and I'm sure he would have if he had thought it was the right thing to do — but I'm guessing he thought in your new life there was little time or space for him. You had a whole new family, didn't you? A stepfather, a new school, new friends and maybe he didn't want to hold you back. I'm not saying he was right,' I went on as she went to interrupt, 'only that he probably didn't know what to do for the best.'

'Anything would have been better than the little he did,' Amber burst out hotly. 'I didn't want his presents and his phonecalls, I wanted him to be waiting when I came out of school once in a while, to come and see me in school plays and meet my friends.'

'I really wish you had felt able to tell him that.'

'How could I?' she demanded furiously, 'when I barely bloody knew him. I just feel so angry towards him. I'm a Siddons and yet I don't know anything about them.'

I felt like telling her that I was a Siddons too and until quite recently I hadn't known anything about them either.

'It was hearing that Uncle Phil had died,' Amber continued, 'that made me realize he was part of my family, but I barely even remembered him. One day that could happen to my dad and then it will all be too late.'

I wasn't even surprised when she burst into floods of hot tears. I felt very much like doing the same, but I kept my hands steady on the steering wheel and my eyes remained dry and focussed on the road ahead.

'I'm sorry,' Amber said, wiping her eyes on a wodge of tissues from the box I indicated in the glove compartment, 'here's me going on and on about me, after all that you've been through.'

'Don't worry about me,' I said, 'I can cope. I can completely understand your thought process and I really admire your determination to do something about your relationship with your dad before it's too late. None of us know how long we've got and someone always has to make the first move in these circumstances. Some things can't be fixed — like your parents' marriage,' and mine and Phil's, I thought, 'but others are worth making the effort for. I'm very impressed that you've come all this way and very happy to meet you, at last.'

'I won't be in the way, will I?' she asked anxiously. 'You must have a lot to deal with right now.'

I smiled, as we pulled up in front of the house and immediately, the front door flew open. Louise, Rose and Jacquetta rushed down the path to greet us. 'I'm getting lots of help,' I said, 'as you can see.'

'Are you *all* staying here?' Amber seemed a bit overwhelmed, sitting in the kitchen surrounded by three of her aunties and her grandmother.

'We're the regulars,' I pointed to Jacquetta and myself, 'and Louise or Rose have been taking it in turns to help out, but there are five bedrooms, Amber, so there's plenty of room and you're very welcome to stay as long as you like. Perhaps until you feel ready to move in with your dad or go home. I wasn't sure what your plans were.'

'Neither was I,' Amber admitted ruefully. 'I didn't think much beyond getting on a flight.'

A thought suddenly struck me and I said anxiously, 'Amber, you did tell your mother where you were going? She does know you're here?'

On reflection I should have realized Jessica

would never have allowed the girl to leave America, without checking first that she was welcome and that someone would meet her.

I hardly remembered Rich's ex-wife, but I didn't doubt her parenting skills, so I was barely surprised when Amber admitted, 'She thinks I'm staying over with a friend from school for a few days.'

Without a word I walked over to the cordless phone in the kitchen and bringing it back to the table, I placed it firmly in Amber's hand.

'Ring her right *now*,' I instructed, trying not to show my disapproval, 'if she rings your friend for any reason and finds you aren't there she will be out of her mind with worry and may even call the police.'

Between us we worked out the code and then I insisted we left her to make the call without us listening to every word of what was bound to be a difficult conversation.

We had barely settled in the lounge before Amber came in carrying the phone. Holding the instrument out to me she said, 'Mum would like to speak to you.'

'I'm shocked,' were Jessica's first words, and I agreed immediately, 'Me, too.'

By this time I was back in the kitchen, closing the door firmly behind me.

'However,' Jessica continued, obviously

recovering slightly, 'I can't say that I'm surprised. There are problems in my relationship with Amber's stepfather presently which haven't helped Amber's state of mind, but this has been a long time coming.'

'Yes.'

'I'm so sorry though that you've been landed with a teenage girl at what must be a very difficult time for you. I was stunned to hear about Phil's tragic death, though I barely knew him, he was still family for a while. Strange to think that he was on a motorcycle with old Randolph as I seem to remember they never really got along.'

I didn't really want to get into discussing Phil or his relationship or lack of it with his father. Instead, I said, 'I'm happy for Amber to stay with me until she decides what she wants to do. Rich will be on his way home as soon as he can get a lift off the rig.'

'Thank you,' Jessica said, 'it will be good for them to spend some time together. We all have our faults but Rich is a good man and I always felt bad about taking his daughter away from him. This is her chance and Rich's to make something out of their relationship.'

'I'll gladly do all that I can to help,' I told her, meaning it.

There was little more to say so I called Amber and she chatted some more to her mother, then I showed her around the house and upstairs to the spare room she would be using. We were just about to make our way back downstairs, and I was congratulating myself on how well things were going when, completely out of the blue, I suddenly became light-headed, dizzy and disorientated.

'Aunt Alex,' I heard Amber's shrill cry of alarm as I stumbled forward and then everything went black.

14

I couldn't think where I was, my eyelids were heavy and I had such trouble lifting them that I gave up and kept them closed. There seemed to be crowds of people and the babble of their voices ebbed and flowed around me.

Someone called my name, 'Alex, Alex,' and a cool cloth was placed on my forehead.

'We must call the ambulance.' This time there was no mistaking my mother-in-law's accented tones or the urgency and concern in her voice.

I made a concerted effort. I managed to open my eyes and to assure the concerned faces around me that I was all right and there was no need to call out the emergency services on my behalf.

'Where am I?' I asked. 'What are you all doing here and where's Phil?'

The stunned silence that greeted what appeared to me to be perfectly reasonable questions gave a strong indication that all was not as it should be. Reality, when it came back to me, didn't come in a trickle of awareness, but in a torrent that took my breath away and I had to fight against the darkness that threatened to claim me again.

I closed my eyes against a feeling of total despair, fighting to keep my composure and when I opened them again I was back in control, and everything had been returned to its box with the lid firmly shut down.

'Oh, silly me,' I said, keeping my tone deliberately light, 'Phil's dead, isn't he? I'm in my own house, though I don't think much of this room at all. Why am I in here?'

'Um,' Louise hesitated, and then said, 'Jacquetta is in your bedroom, Alex.'

'I must move out immediately,' Jacquetta made a move towards the door, as if she intended to do just that. 'I should not — how do you say it? — commander your personal room for my own use.'

'Stay there,' I said quickly, 'that's not what I meant. I just don't like the décor in here. It's very plain. Whose idea was that?' The looks were exchanged around the group again, and I nodded, 'Oh, yes. It was Phil's,' and I sank back against the pillows, too exhausted to care.

'I think we should call the doctor out,' Rose insisted, and Vi's voice came from the doorway, 'I've already phoned him. We share the same doctor,' she added, by way of an explanation of how she would have any idea

238

of who my GP was.

I hadn't even realized that Vi was still in the house. I couldn't begin to imagine what she thought of all these latest developments. However, I didn't doubt her discretion. Gossip she might be, but her loyalty to me since Phil's death could not be questioned.

'It's all been too much for you,' Louise sounded concerned, 'even the shopping trip was probably a bad idea, but you've been involved in a near collision that could have been very nasty, on top of taking off to drive all the way to the airport and back, and now look at you. It'll be a miracle if you make it through this pregnancy safely. We need to take more care of you.'

'You're pregnant, Aunt Alex,' Amber appeared at the end of the bed looking troubled, 'I hadn't realized. This is my fault. If I hadn't arrived out of the blue you wouldn't have been running up and down the motorway in your condition.'

I smiled faintly, 'Not quite literally, and I'm very happy that you're here, Amber. I'll be fine. The baby will be fine. In fact, I think I felt a faint movement just before I blacked out.'

'The quickening,' Jacquetta said, smiling knowledgably along with both of my nodding sisters-in-law.

'It was a good job that Amber managed to grab you,' Louise was quick to point out, 'because you could quite easily have pitched head first down the stairs.'

Eventually the doctor arrived and the gist of his visit was a confirmation that it wasn't unusual to feel faint the first time movement of the foetus was felt, a reminder that I *was* an older mother with a tendency to high blood pressure — and as such I should generally take more care — an order to rest for at least a couple of days and finally, a recommendation that I give up my lecturing job sooner rather than later. After he left, I lay back against the pillows and wondered if there was going to be anything left of my old life at all.

Everyone had appeared very excited about the foetal movement. I wondered why I couldn't feel even a little of their enthusiasm and what was wrong with me that I couldn't feel something — anything — towards the child I continued to carry towards full-term, in spite of the odds stacked against it.

I had been hoping against hope that my indifference would miraculously change and I would become overwhelmed with love for this child that Phil and I had created in the happier times that I could barely remember now. It hadn't happened yet and though there was all this talk of 'bonding', I didn't even know what it meant and was very afraid I was destined never to find out.

I didn't think I was a bad person and yet, if I could find no love for my own baby, didn't that make me as dysfunctional a parent as Randy and my own mother? The child wasn't anywhere near to being born, and I was already wondering if I could somehow bring myself to play the part of a loving mother for the next however many years in an effort to avoid damaging the child as Phil had been damaged by his father's neglect?

It was a common fact that we learned our parenting skills from our own parents, but could the excellent skills of one parent make up for a lack in the other? I could only hope that was so in my case.

I slept only fitfully and was up early in the morning against the doctor's advice, intent on making myself a cup of tea. The rest of the household slumbered on, which was how I came to be the one to open the front door to the first tentative tap and found Rich on the step.

'Alex,' he swept me into a great bear-hug, my face rubbing against the stubble on his chin. 'How can I thank you?' He held me at arm's length, looking deep into my eyes. 'How come I never realized before just what a

241

great woman my brother had the good fortune to marry?'

'How come your brother didn't seem to realize it himself at the end?' I countered and laughed to show it was a joke, even if it was in pretty poor taste.

He didn't respond, just hugged me again and stepped inside. With his arm draped around my shoulders, we made our way through to the kitchen.

'Everyone is still sleeping,' I said, probably stating the obvious, since the house was normally busy with people at all hours these days. 'Can I get you some breakfast?'

'I think I'm too excited to eat,' he smiled ruefully, 'does that sound a ridiculous thing for a grown man to say?'

'Not at all,' I said, 'but I think we'll both try a piece of toast.'

As I toasted and buttered and made the tea he preferred to coffee, we talked over what had happened, and how I came to be in his flat when the call came through.

'Thank God you *were* there,' Rich's relief was obvious, 'or I dread to think what might have happened to her. Don't worry, though, I'm here now and will take her off your hands.'

'Um,' I hesitated, unwilling to poke my nose into a relationship that obviously wasn't my business, yet feeling something had to be said.

'What?'

'It may not be that simple. Remember Amber hardly knows you, she might not be happy to simply move in with you before you've got to know one another a little better.'

He didn't argue, to my immense relief. The girl *was* his daughter, after all, and he was quite within his rights to tell me to keep my nose out of the decisions he made regarding his own child.

'What do you suggest, then?' he asked.

'Let her stay with me for a few days. You can come here whenever you like — stay, too, if you want to.' I heard myself say the words and even as I said them I was wondering what on earth I was playing at. I had a houseful as it was.

It was already too late to retract the invitation, because Rich's face lit up, his eyes a dazzling bright blue of hope, and I knew then that it was within my capability to help him build a relationship with *his* child, even if I had no idea how to build a relationship with mine.

'Really?' he said, 'you would do that for Amber and for me? You won't regret this, Alex.'

I had a feeling I already was.

I was chased back to bed, of course, when the household woke from its slumbers, but not before Rich had been filled in completely with the events of the day before and expressed his concern that the state of my blood pressure might be down to his absence when he was needed.

'I'm so sorry, Amber, that I wasn't there when you needed me, and though I can't thank you enough, Alex, for all you've done for her, I'm truly sorry that you had to pay a price for your kindness. If you'd rather I left after all you only have to say.'

'Nonsense,' I tried to dismiss it as nothing, but felt tiredness wash over me like a blanket and allowed myself to be ushered back to bed.

'Leave it to us,' Louise ordered, 'we can organize the sleeping arrangements, but are you sure all of this isn't going to be too much for you? You must feel you've been completely invaded by the Siddons clan these past few weeks.'

I managed a weary smile, 'I don't know how I would have managed,' I said, 'without you all,' and I found I actually meant it.

★   ★   ★

In the end, it was decided to leave Jacquetta where she was for the time being. I had no great desire to return to the master bedroom and the room I was currently using had its own en suite so it was no hardship to me even though it was smaller.

Amber was in the room next door to mine, with the one earmarked for the nursery next to that. Rich was across the landing next to his mother. With Amber and Rich comfortably ensconced there was no room or indeed any need for either Louise or Rose to sleep over, though they both assured me they intended to be around almost as much as before to make sure I wasn't overdoing things.

They were, they informed Rich severely, trusting him to make sure the household ran smoothly in their absence with minimal input from me. My protests that I wasn't an invalid went unheard.

Although Amber appeared slightly wary and on edge around Rich — so much so that she came across as abrupt to the point of rudeness in her manner toward him, which I'm sure he found upsetting — she seemed to enjoy her grandmother's company and mine.

I was almost certain that living in the same house as the father she barely knew and spending some real time together was all that was needed to bring a thaw in her attitude towards Rich.

Familiarity didn't always breed contempt, I assured myself, and I was sure I could come up with some way of getting them to work together.

With summer fast approaching, there was no great difficulty about my not seeing out the term. The university was being more than understanding in the circumstances, and my colleagues assured me they were more than happy to step into the breach wherever necessary, as I had done for them many times in the past, evidently.

There had, of course, been flowers at the time of Phil's death but when I went in to collect my things and to say goodbye, I found the department had very kindly made a collection and they presented me with something called a 'travel system', which must have been very expensive. I was assured that what looked like a very complicated pushchair was the very latest thing, with a seat that lifted out for use in the car, apparently.

Several people had knitted or bought tiny garments in white or yellow and I was more touched than I could say. After all, as I told Julie I barely knew most of them.

'I don't think you've ever realized how well

thought of you've always been,' she told me. 'Nothing has ever been too much trouble, and you've been generous with your time and your information. You don't have to be out socializing all the time with people for them to appreciate you, you know.'

A representation of my students made an appearance with their own contribution and that did almost bring me to tears. Besides a fabulous bouquet of flowers, they presented me with various items of baby paraphernalia which included a steam sterilizer, insulated bottle bag — they obviously didn't expect me to be breast-feeding, I thought with a carefully concealed smile — and a baby carrier harness.

They all seemed so pleased I would have the baby to help me over the loss of Phil that I wouldn't have had the heart to tell them he had already left me, or that neither of us had really wanted the child anyway. I could just imagine the shock on their faces if I had done anything of the sort and I didn't want to spoil their pleasure or mine.

At home, things had settled down again. After the disastrous shopping trip, it was decided it would be easier by far to order furniture for the nursery — and anything else that was needed — online. Catalogues were readily available and easy to flick through and soon a constant supply began to drop on to the mat. Indeed, I found with email and the telephone almost everything could be dealt with from home.

It was Rich's suggestion to decorate the nursery instead of leaving it plain. The idea was met with such enthusiasm by Amber that I saw it as the ideal scenario to get them working together and gave every encouragement to the project. In no time the dark head and fair were bent over wallpaper samples and paint charts, bringing favoured examples to me for my final approval.

'Is this what you and mum did when you were expecting me?' she asked Rich and he confirmed readily that indeed they had. His mistake he went on to say, within my hearing, was in thinking he had to provide much more in the way of material possessions than was ever expected of him.

'That's when I began to work longer and longer stretches away,' he told her regretfully, 'thinking the money I could earn would more than make up for my time. I was so wrong, Amber and I wish that I had listened when your mum tried to tell me that. It's a mistake I will never make again. I'm here now, for as long as you need me.'

Jacquetta was knitting — yes, knitting, I couldn't believe it but apparently Vi had been giving her lessons — and she looked up, caught my eye and smiled. I found it very easy to smile back and wondered again why we couldn't all have got along like this before. She couldn't have failed to enjoy watching, as what was left of her family finally all pulled together as any real family should.

'What about work?' Amber asked, looking into her dad's face for the reassurance she so obviously needed.

She couldn't have been disappointed when Rich replied, 'No job is more important to me than you are. I'm on indefinite leave.'

I watched the pair of them reach a joint decision on a Winnie the Pooh theme for the room, simply giving them the approval they looked for from me. Rich set to almost immediately with the enthusiastic involvement of his daughter. I felt sure she would be more of a hindrance than help, but her excitement and his pleasure were a joy to see.

I allowed Jacquetta and Vi full reign when it came to the choice of nursery furniture and enjoyed watching them cluck over this cot and that chest of drawers. I tried and failed to imagine my own mum's head bent over the catalogue beside theirs sharing their enthusiasm, and wondered with a pang if the birth of a grandchild might have finally brought us together.

I wished belatedly that I had made more effort with our relationship in her later years, but there are only so many times you can be rebuffed before you finally stop trying. It would have taken a stronger person than I was to persevere in the face of her evident dislike of her only daughter: a person like Phil, who had finally and against all the odds, seemed to win his father's approval and friendship, though the cost didn't really bear thinking about.

I tried not to think how disappointed in me as a daughter my mother so obviously had been and about the fact that she could never tell me why. I decided there and then that my son or daughter would never be made to feel responsible for my happiness.

The nursery, when it was completed, was a real picture with its yellow-washed walls and cartoon character border, matching lightshade and Scandinavian pine furniture. Even I was impressed, but it made me feel dissatisfied with the rest of the house, which seemed almost stark and clinical in comparison.

'Well, I know what you mean,' Louise agreed. 'I *like* my patterned wallpaper and little knick-knacks, though I know that sort of thing can feel cluttery to some people. The kitchen looks better though more homely now you have a few things left out on the worktops. It looked a bit like an operating theatre before and so immaculate that I was scared to cook in it. Oops, sorry to sound so critical.'

'No, have your say,' I encouraged, 'what do you think Rose, and you Jacquetta?'

'Well, this is a très beautiful house . . . ' Jacquetta hesitated, obviously not wishing to offend me, before continuing, 'but perhaps — how do you say it? — a little bit sparse.'

'Perhaps a few cushions and magazines in the lounge, a coat rack in the hall, pictures on the walls,' Rose suggested helpfully. 'I think we've definitely managed to make it look a bit more lived-in since we've all been here, but it's still sort of . . . '

'Bland,' I said, 'that's the word I'm looking for. It's always been too pristine, but that was the way Phil wanted it, and I just went along with that to keep him happy — though I've never really liked it.'

'Never liked what?' Rich came into the room with Amber close behind. She was carrying the Winnie the Pooh stuffed toy they had gone out to buy for the nursery. There was scarcely a day went by that they didn't bring back some little thing for the baby. I really didn't mind if they filled the little room from floor to ceiling as long as it brought them closer and it seemed to be working.

'The house,' I said, 'it wasn't really my choice, far too big for the two of us and looking like something out of one of those glossy celebrity magazines.'

'Ooh, yes, I know exactly what you mean,' Amber agreed, saying what everyone else was probably thinking, 'it's not very homey, is it? I still take my shoes off at the front door, and I wouldn't dare put my feet up on the couch or leave a magazine lying around. It feels like some posh hotel.'

'Amber,' Rich warned, 'that's not very nice, especially when your Aunt Alex has welcomed you here so warmly.'

'I'm only agreeing,' Amber defended herself, 'and the house doesn't suit her at all. If she was that house proud Aunt Alex wouldn't have let us lot in the front door never mind giving us the run of the house.'

'I've suggested cushions in the lounge and pictures for the walls,' Rose said, 'and maybe you could replace the vertical blinds with curtains.'

Amber shook her head emphatically. 'It'll take more than a few soft furnishings,' she decided, then her dark eyes lit right up and she positively beamed. I wondered what on earth was coming.

'I know,' she said, very aware that everyone's attention was on her, 'we'll decorate the whole house for you — from top to bottom.'

15

It was like trying to stop a runaway horse. Once Amber had the bit between her teeth about revamping the house there was no stopping her, but I loved her excitement and enthusiasm and it was certainly infectious.

The thought of the mess and upheaval such a project would incur was scary to say the least, but part of me was thrilled at the idea of finally having some say in my own surroundings. I'd never really liked the house or felt at home there but perhaps, with help, I could turn it into something I could live with.

'Dad and I will do it all,' she assured me, 'you won't have to do a thing but pick the wallpaper and paint of your choice from samples we'll bring to you.'

She made it sound ridiculously simple and Rich merely lifted his shoulders and said it was up to me, but they were entirely at my disposal. He looked happier than I'd seen him in a very long time, so what could I do but agree?

The dubious, 'yes', was barely out of my mouth before Amber threw her arms around my neck, almost throttling me in her enthusiasm. 'You won't regret it,' she told me, and I tried very hard to believe her.

It appeared that everyone was keen to be involved. Winston turned up on the doorstep dressed in pristine white overalls, before the materials had even been chosen, bringing back the pasting table and brushes Rich had apparently borrowed from him in the first place to do the nursery.

'This,' he said rolling up his sleeves to reveal sinewy arms, 'is a much bigger job and you're going to need all the help you can get.'

I could sense Amber brewing up to protest, and reminded her out of Winston's hearing, 'It's not just about the work — though you know what they say about many hands — I know you and your dad can manage just fine, but letting Winston get involved will be great for him. He gave up his job to nurse his mother and he's been at a loose end and so lost since she died. Don't spoil it for him.'

The crusty homemade bread and moist fruitcake Winston had brought along probably weakened her resolve more than my words did, but Amber made it very clear she intended to be the project manager.

I did feel bad when I realized the plan was to start in the master bedroom but, as Rich pointed out, I would need the extra space moving back into the larger room would afford me for the baby. When I said I thought that's what the nursery was for all the women — even Amber — laughed and assured me I'd be happier having the child in with me for the first few weeks, if not months. I kept my thoughts to myself and decided I would deal with that hurdle when I came to it. I had absolutely no intention of sharing my bedroom with anyone ever again, least of all a baby.

Jacquetta didn't seem a bit upset to be ousted, having already made arrangements to move in next door with Vi for as long as was necessary. Nobody bothered to point out she was paying rent on a perfectly good home of her own which was standing empty, and the unlikely pair seemed to be looking forward to sharing a roof.

I could only assume that, like me, they were finally beginning to appreciate the benefits to be found in the company of good friends. I just hoped Vi had plenty of wardrobe space.

Talking of wardrobe space, my clothes had eventually followed me to the spare room when I moved back from Rich's flat, Jacquetta had been using my evacuated space in the master bedroom for her own and all trace of Kayleigh's brief sojourn had long since been erased. Phil's garments, however, had remained untouched since his death and now I faced the prospect of getting rid of them. There wasn't going to be a better time and I metaphorically rolled up my sleeves and steeled myself for the task ahead.

I could have asked Louise or Rose to do it or even Rich, but I knew in my heart it was something I needed to do. Phil was in the past. He had already become part of my past even *before* his untimely death, and that had been his own decision.

I had to accept that had been the case and move forward into my future. I was already in discussions with a local businessman regarding the future of Phil's company. Even so, I didn't relish the immediate task that faced me, which somehow seemed far more personal.

Helping Jacquetta pack and move her things next door gave me an excuse to put off the inevitable, but I knew I was only putting it off.

'Now, you know you can come straight back when the room I'm currently in has been redecorated, don't you? If you want to, that is. The team have promised that will be the next priority.'

I wasn't quite sure if I was trying to reassure her or myself, and couldn't believe it was the mother-in-law I had detested for so many years that I was issuing such an invitation to. You'd have thought I would be glad to see the back of her, but I had to admit I'd kind of got used to having her around. She was a different person now that the dour Randy was no longer around — just as I had undoubtedly changed without Phil around to influence my choices.

Spending time with Jacquetta had increased my respect for her no end. She hadn't had an easy life and at her age — whatever that might be — she would be quite entitled to put her feet up and take things easy, but it was obvious no such thought ever occurred to her. She had the vigour of a woman half her age and she put a lot of that energy into making sure she appeared years younger, too.

She paused in the act of folding the sort of lace underwear Phil had always liked me to wear and looking at it I hid a smile. I should have known Jacquetta wouldn't have been seen dead in the kind of foundation garments my mother and possibly Vi, too, would have favoured.

'I cannot like the smell of paint, Alexandra,' she explained a little sadly, 'but that is the only thing that will keep me over the fence.' She came to stand in front of me and, very appropriately, a pair of silken French knickers dangled from the be-ringed fingers of one hand. 'This has been one of the saddest times — and yet one of the happiest times of my life. I have lost two loved ones — and I did love Randolph, despite his failings and whatever anyone might think . . . '

'No one could ever doubt that you did,' I assured her, telling myself it was not up to me to reason why.

'He brought me to my English life, which I have loved, and he gave me my family, my boys, who are everything. I have had to remind myself he was not responsible for my happiness, for we are each responsible for our own.'

I stared at her, wondering at her wisdom and realizing I should have known there was more to my mother-in-law than the apparently silly, self-centred, attention-seeking woman that was all I had ever been aware of at family gatherings.

'Jacquetta . . . ' I began, intending to put some of my thoughts into words.

She stopped me, placing a finger on the carefully painted mouth and shaking her head, 'I think you understand me a little bit better lately and maybe like me a little bit more, too. That is how I feel about you. Alexandra, you are far more of a person that the one I thought I knew all these years. I have become very, very fond of you. My son was a lucky man when he found you all those years ago. You lived for him — as I lived for Randolph — in the way he wished, but now we must live for ourselves.'

I hugged her. I couldn't help it, and she didn't seem to mind.

'And you'll be okay with Vi?' I queried, taking the knickers from her and putting them into the case with the other scanties.

'I never had a woman friend before,' she told me, and I was quite shocked, 'not since I come to England. First there were Randolph's biking friends and then the children's friends, but never anyone my own age and sex, just for me. We are quite different, Vi and me,' she added — and the words, 'you can say that again', almost escaped, but I bit my lip and kept them back — 'but we have many of the same thoughts and feelings. I think we shall do well together.'

'Don't tell me you'll be scouring for bargains in Tesco's with her, because I can't quite see it somehow.' I couldn't help smiling at the thought.

'You might be surprised,' Jacquetta nodded knowingly, 'at how much we learn from each other. Despite what they say, you *can* teach the old dog new tricks.'

With that she invited me to sit on the suitcase with her and we managed to ease the zipper around the bulging sides until everything was enclosed. We shared a high-five and smirked at each other. A sound from the doorway made us look up to find Derek standing there, watching us with a bemused look in his eyes.

'Look at you two,' he said, and then added by way of explanation, 'I let myself in and then came on up when I couldn't find anybody downstairs.'

'No one downstairs?' It was my turn to be bemused. 'Now, where can they be?'

Jacquetta nodded her head knowledgably, 'Gone off to Q and B again is what I'm thinking. It takes five of them to buy six screws these days.'

'Ah, yes,' I agreed, 'but they have to be the *right* screws.'

We all burst out laughing, even Del, but I was quick to warn him, 'I think your house will be next in line for a makeover. Louise is getting lots of ideas and collecting catalogues.'

'That's fine. She's having fun, and has more than earned the home she wants after all the years of scrimping. I might get your decorators — and I use the word loosely — over.' Derek's smile was rueful, 'I can't believe you're letting a bunch of amateurs makeover your house, but then I couldn't believe you'd let half of them move in, either.

You could have turned your back on us all, given what's happened, but you've given this family a new lease of life, Alex. Hasn't she mum?'

Jacquetta nodded, going to stand in the circle of her eldest son's arm. He looked down at her fondly and dropped a kiss on the chestnut wig.

'But I haven't done anything,' I protested, wondering where I might have been if they hadn't all rallied round.

'Oh, yes, indeed you have,' Jacquetta insisted firmly, 'more than you will ever know. Perhaps now, in spite of everything, we can become a real family and I can share my time equally between *all* of my sons, now that I don't feel I have to spend my time making up to just one for the lack of his father's love.

'I can even visit Barry — the Isle of Man is not so very far away — and Simon in Scotland, which I would never have dreamed of doing before. You can get flights there for next to nothing, you know, and I've never been on a plane.' She looked excited and regretful all at the one time, and added, 'It is sad that it sometimes takes a tragedy to heal a family.'

Through the open window came the sound of wheels on gravel and then the sound of car doors slamming.

'Sounds as if the decorators are . . . ' I began, when there was the sound of raised voices and one of them was definitely Amber's.

'This was *my* idea and now you've all just taken over,' she yelled, but I could hear the edge of tears in her shrill tone. 'Well, you can just get on with it. It's time I went back to America, anyway. I wouldn't want to outstay my welcome.'

I heard a deeper, placatory voice, it might have been Winston or Rich, but Amber was having none of it.

'Oh, get lost.'

The front door opened, then slammed behind the girl and there was the drumming of her feet as she pounded up the stairs. Her figure was little more than a blur as she passed the open doorway without acknowledging our presence, before the house shook as she banged the door of her bedroom — hard.

'Shall I . . . ? Del looked awkward, but he took a step towards the door.

I shook my head. In my heart I knew I'd been expecting something like this since the day Amber had arrived in England. It had all been too calm and reasonable, but all that hurt, the pain of her parents' broken marriage, the loss of her dad's presence in her life, had to come out sometime.

'Take Jacquetta's case downstairs and stop anybody coming up, would you? Let me see what I can do.'

'We will make tea,' Jacquetta said firmly, giving Derek a little push in the direction of the door. 'Alex can handle this if anyone can.'

I just wished that I had her confidence in my ability to pour oil on troubled waters. I actually felt quite nervous as I walked along the landing and tapped on Amber's door. There was no reply but I could hear the sounds of cupboards and drawers opening, so she obviously wasn't going to waste a minute getting her stuff together.

'Amber,' I tapped the door again. 'It's me. It's Aunt Alex. Can I come in?'

'Yes,' the tone was sullen, and as I pushed the door open, Amber said without looking at me, 'It's your house, after all. I suppose you've come to sort me out or have a word.'

I almost smiled at those very English phrases, probably picked up from a British soap opera, but quickly suppressed it. 'Actually,' I said, 'I was wondering if you would help me to do a job that has to be done, but which I've been dreading. You can say no, if you like, but I really could do with a hand.'

She'd have loved to say no, I could see it written all over her face, but good manners finally won and she asked grudgingly, 'What is it?'

'I need to clear the clothes and stuff from the big bedroom ready for it to be decorated.'

She frowned, 'Do you mean Grandma's? There aren't any of yours in there, are there?'

'None of Grandma's either. We just packed them up and Uncle Del is taking the case across to Vi's.'

'Whose, then?'

'Phil's.'

I think Amber realized what I was going to say just before I said his name. I saw her eyes widen and was immediately sorry I'd asked.

'Don't worry,' I said, 'I can manage.'

I had actually been counting on her better nature and for a moment I thought I'd made a mistake. Thankfully, I had been right to trust my instincts.

'No,' she said, 'I want to help. You've done enough for me. In fact, you've been great, and it's the least I can do.'

Together we walked along the landing and into the master bedroom that Jacquetta had so recently vacated. It looked — I searched for a word and could only come up with the

265

word — abandoned, with the king-sized bed already stripped and the surfaces cleared of any toiletries.

My hand trembled as I reached to slide a wardrobe door back but I wasn't going to let a slight reluctance on my part prevent me getting on with the job in hand. A new start meant getting rid of the old. I couldn't help reflecting that Phil had appeared to be only too happy to remove all trace of me from *his* life, and at a speed that was not only hurtful but bloody insulting.

That thought was enough to stiffen my spine and the door slid back noiselessly to reveal row upon row of expensive shirts, colour coded and neatly pressed, just as I had last seen them.

'Wow,' Amber breathed, 'why would a man possess so many clothes? Did he ever wear them all?'

I smiled, 'Pretty much. It was nothing for Phil to change up to three times a day, if he had meetings. The only shirts he probably never got around to were the more brightly coloured ones I bought him in an effort to cheer up his appearance. It never worked. When we get to his suits you will see they are mainly shades of grey with the odd navy or beige one thrown in. Shame really, but I think he had this image of how a successful business man should look and never wavered from that.'

'Shall we make a start then?' Amber suggested.

'Mmm,' I lifted an empty suitcase on to the bed, saying, 'I thought this would be better than black bags. Phil wouldn't have appreciated black bags.' I refrained from adding he'd obviously had no compunction about disposing of my things in them.

'Charity shop?' Amber queried as we started lifting hangers down and neatly folding each shirt as if Phil were setting off on holiday.

I nodded, 'Unless there's anything his brothers would like to have. It's all expensive stuff and very good quality — but that would be up to them. I suppose I should think about his vehicles, too. I quite like the Jag, so I might just let my car go and keep that one, but the four-by-four I would have absolutely no use for. His business almost runs itself because Phil built up a good team over the years, but I've already put out feelers with a view to selling to one of his competitors. It only took a phonecall and he seemed keen to strike a deal.'

Amber looked at me curiously. 'Don't you find this upsetting at all?' she asked.

I shook my head. 'I know I should feel something, but at the moment I feel nothing.

I know that's strange after so many years together, but I had already lost Phil, you see. I was getting used to a life without him in it. There was a lot of anger between us when he died. I doubt if he would have shed a tear for me either, if the boot had been on the other foot and it had been me who died.'

'A fresh start, then?'

I nodded, 'And it's all been so different, with all of you around, and now with the house changing so much that I'm actually beginning to enjoy living here. I can see that I've lived quite a lonely life, even during the years I spent with Phil. My dad was the only one who acted as if I was family but he died while I was still quite young. We were very close, but once he was gone it was just my mum and me and we didn't really get on.

'I never found it that easy to make or keep friends either, that's why it was so easy to accept Phil's way of living as the right way. I didn't see anything wrong with living only for each other all those years. I can see why he would have needed my undivided attention — he was used to having his mother's — and my approval was crucial because of his father's condemnation of everything he did.'

'I don't remember much about grandad,

but he wasn't a very kind man, was he?'

'Not as far as Phil was concerned,' I agreed, 'but we have to respect that he must have had his reasons, even if we don't understand or agree with them, though you'd have thought that, as grown men, they could at least have talked their problems through. Perhaps they did at the end. I would like to think so.'

'I suppose I should be talking to my dad about our problems,' Amber said thoughtfully, 'because we haven't, you know. We're both being so careful not to criticize. On the surface we seem to be the best of friends, but underneath I really resent the fact he just let me and mum go without a struggle.'

'Talk to him about it,' I advised, careful to keep my tone neutral, accepting it was really nothing to do with me, even if they *were* living in my house, 'about how you really feel. Allow your dad the chance to explain how it was for him, too.'

She nodded, 'I will,' she said, and I hoped she wouldn't wait too long.

We'd been working steadily, filling one suitcase after another and when we closed the final one all trace of Phil had gone from the room we had shared for just a small part of our marriage. I had a feeling it wouldn't be long before I had erased every sign of him from the house.

I wondered how much longer it would take to expunge the bitterness I felt towards him from my heart, and how on earth I was going to live with a child who was going to remind me of Phil and his rejection every day for the rest of my life.

16

The house quickly began to resemble a bombsite, but my bedroom — the master bedroom becoming 'my' room the moment that particular bit of decorating was done — became an oasis of calm.

I'd refused to have the baby's cot or any other infant paraphernalia in there, saying it was tempting fate. There was nothing of Phil in the room at all and the décor certainly wouldn't have been to his taste, but everything — every little thing — was to mine.

I had stayed with the cream walls but my choice was less of the insipid magnolia emulsion favoured by Phil and more the rich colour of Cornish clotted cream on wallpaper that was randomly patterned with splashes of terracotta. Together with a terracotta carpet it warmed and brightened the room, the bedlinen followed this theme with the addition of plump cream cushions piled high on the bed and the lace, draped curtains also in cream. It looked very feminine and very gorgeous and I was as thrilled as I could be with it.

Pictures of my choosing had been hung on the walls, where before they had been bare, and a few ornaments had been scattered around on sills and cupboard tops. My late husband would have hated it with a vengeance, but I loved it so much that resting as the pregnancy progressed became a pleasure rather than a pain.

At every antenatal check I was assured the child was growing and developing exactly as it should. Thanks to the efforts of my lodgers and visitors the house grew and developed around me into the home I had never even realized I'd *always* wanted. Looking at it that way, perhaps when the baby was born I would be able to appreciate it as the child I had never realized I had always wanted, too. I hoped so, but the doubts persisted.

As it was, I had nothing to do in preparation for the birth except to follow the midwife's advice to take it easy. Everything else was being taken care of with great enthusiasm by my 'family'.

Nursery items appeared as if by magic. Sometimes it was Vi who turned up with a 'bargain' find, sometimes Winston 'caught sight' of something in a shop window. The rest of them unashamedly went out on expeditions, trawling Mothercare and Adams and trying to outdo one another with gorgeous clothes and luxury items for the baby they were all so excited about.

I ooh-ed and ah-ed with the rest and then left it to them to find room in a nursery that already appeared to be stuffed from floor to ceiling. I felt I did my bit by taking seriously the responsibility of carrying the child, eating well, keeping active, but resting too, and whatever else was expected of me. All the time I looked forward to the day I could pass the responsibility over to the nanny I had recently decided would be vital to my well-being after the birth. There was no doubt in my mind by this time that I would be returning to work.

However, I kept such thoughts to myself, instinctively knowing such decisions would not be well received, far less understood. It was surprising that I found myself unwilling to relinquish the approval I had so unexpectedly acquired from the Siddons family members now so involved in my life.

Deep in thought I jumped at the sound of a voice from the doorway. I had thought the house was empty for once.

'Sorry, did I startle you? I was just making tea and wondered if you'd like a cup,' Rich said.

'That would be nice, but it would be nicer if you'd sit and talk to me for a while. I'm bored with my own company now and there are only so many daytime soaps and reality shows I can stand at a sitting. I have to stay put for a while to give my ankles and blood pressure time to go down.' I patted the bed and Rich obediently sat on the end. 'So,' I went on, 'how's it going?'

'We're nearly finished up here,' he said, 'so Ma can move back if she has a mind to, and if you don't mind.'

'I don't mind at all,' I assured him, meaning it, amazed that I actually missed Jacquetta quite a lot especially since she'd carried out her threat to visit Simon and his family and taken herself off to Scotland. I had Vi wandering in and out of the house like a lost soul, too. 'That wasn't what I meant, though, Rich. I wondered how it was going with Amber after the little spat you had a while ago.'

'There have actually been a few, so I'm relieved if you haven't heard them all. It's pretty bad manners to be fighting in your house.'

'The house *you* are all making into a home at last,' I reminded him, 'not just with the decorating, but by being here. If we were a real family there would be arguments, so I guess we're pretty normal.'

'Is that what we are?' he looked at me

strangely, 'a real family? I like the sound of that. It seems a long time since I was part of a real family and I miss it. I'll always regret that I didn't try harder to make my marriage work but I really think Amber and I are beginning to understand each other at last. We lose our rags a bit with each other sometimes, but that's when the truth comes out, and a lot of it needs to be said so that we can deal with it and move on. You've taught me that much at least.'

'Have I? I'm glad,' I said, and then asked, 'Have you ever showed Amber the room you've always had ready for her? You should you know.'

A look of concern crossed his good-looking face. At times Rich looked very like Phil, and yet there were subtle differences that I couldn't quite put my finger on. He was certainly less uptight in his manner, that much at least was very apparent and he was always more than willing to look at things from another person's perspective.

'Oh, dear, is that a hint?' he queried, looking a bit stunned, 'time for us to move on, and all that? Not that I would blame you, you must be sick of tripping over us Siddons every time you turn around, not to mention Vi in and out and even Winston is becoming something of a fixture. You must be used to a much quieter life. Of course, we can go any time — the flat is plenty big enough for the two of us and all ready for us to take up residence.'

Before I got the chance to interrupt, he went on, 'I know you only asked us to stay in the first place to give us time to get used to each other and it was extremely kind of you. It would have been hard for Amber moving straight in with me, having other people around has really helped us to bond without any pressure — despite the arguments.' He went to get up, saying, 'You've certainly done more than enough and we really shouldn't be taking your hospitality for granted the way we have. I should have realized there was a possibility we were outstaying our welcome.'

'Stop. Stay.' I caught at his fingers and there was an extraordinary moment when we both looked at our joined hands, then at each other and then quickly away. I released my hold on him immediately. 'I don't want you to go. I like having you here — all of you,' I added belatedly. 'Please don't feel you have to leave.' Suddenly realizing it sounded as if I was pleading, I turned it into a joke, 'At least stay until Jacquetta comes back, or I shall find myself rattling around on my own, with no one to make tea for me.'

'Talking of tea . . . ' This time Rich did get

to his feet, 'I'll go and put that kettle on. Got to look after the mother-to-be. I know it's a bit late for regrets but it's a pity you and Phil didn't have kids years ago. If it had happened when you were younger it might well have made all the difference,' he smiled then, 'but you're going to be a great mum. You're brilliant with Amber.'

I think it was a good job he left the room then, so he didn't see the look on my face. How come no one — not one person — doubted my parenting skills, except me? I was already well along in my pregnancy and no nearer identifying that strong rush of mother-love I had read and heard about. The bump I carried was little more than an inconvenience, just as I was sure the child would be when it arrived.

I was totally confused about what I wanted. There were certainly elements of my old life I did want back, though they were limited and I was shocked to discover they didn't include Phil or the lack of social contact and absence of visitors that had been far more his choice than mine.

I didn't think I was the only one who appeared to have skipped whole chunks of the grieving process, either, as I believed Jacquetta was finding life without Randy actually had quite a lot to offer. I had a feeling we had both mistaken control for love, though I doubted either of us would ever come right out and admit it.

'Poor baby,' I patted my swollen belly, 'you'll never know the chaos your conception caused if I can help it. I just wish I could look forward to your birth the way I should be doing, I'm just hoping all that will change when I hold you in my arms, because I want to love you, I really do.'

'I've been thinking,' Rich came in with the tea, then, cutting the one-sided conversation short, 'about framing a few photos to put around the house. It's something the place lacks, I feel.'

'Phil didn't like pictures on the walls,' I said by way of explanation, 'and he detested having his photo taken — unless it was for publicity purposes, of course.'

'Phil isn't here now,' Rich pointed out gently, 'and it might be nice for the baby to grow up with photos of his family around. He or she will need to know Phil even if it is only from pictures. I've heard that it's important.'

I nodded, 'You're probably right.'

'We could set Winston to work when the baby is born, might be just the thing to get him back into the swing of things. He's a great photographer and it's a shame to let all that talent go to waste. Anyway, I thought I'd pop out and buy some frames, do you have any preferences for wood or metal?'

'Anything, as long as it goes with the new décor.'

Rich set the cup down on the bedside cabinet and straightening up, he said, 'No time like the present. Will you be okay until the others get back? They shouldn't be long now.'

I indicated the bump and my still swollen ankles and said, 'I won't be off running a marathon, if that's what you're worried about.'

'Just stay put, then,' he ordered with mock sincerity, 'and don't do anything to send the blood pressure up. It will be worth the hours spent resting if you get a healthy baby at the end of it all.'

'Mmm,' I reached for my tea and leaned back against the pillows as I listened to the sounds of Rich making his way downstairs and leaving the house.

He'd only been gone a matter of minutes when the doorbell rang. Either he'd forgotten his key or the others didn't have one between them. Any excuse to cut short my resting period was welcome as far as I was concerned. Boredom always set in quickly and with a vengeance when I was on my own, so I heaved myself to my feet and made my way downstairs.

I was smiling when I opened the door and was quite unprepared to be thrust to one side as a very unexpected — not to mention unwanted — visitor barged her way in.

Despite the fact it was my house, I felt distinctly at a disadvantage, and I had to take a minute to catch my breath before following Kayleigh through to the kitchen.

She looked very much at home as she filled the kettle and reached into the cupboard for cups and saucers, saying, 'I take it you'd like a cup of tea?' She looked me up and down insultingly before she added, 'You look as if you could use one.'

I couldn't compete with her and she knew it. She was about twenty-five years old, long blonde hair ironed to perfection, her size ten body, toned and tanned. What chance did I stand twenty years older and heavily pregnant into the bargain?

'What do you want?' I asked evenly, taking a seat at the table to hide the fact my legs were shaking and could barely support me. 'You must know you're not welcome and the others are due back at any moment.'

'Others?' she stared at me insolently. 'Oh, you mean Phil's 'family', the famous Siddons?' she made quote marks with her fingers. 'Yes, I heard you were as thick as thieves with them. Shacking up with Rich already, by all accounts. Didn't waste much time, did you?'

'Shacking . . . ?' I couldn't believe what I was hearing, but decided — with difficulty — not to rise to her bait. 'For your information, Richard is staying here with his daughter — and Jacquetta, too,' I added for good measure.

'Very cosy,' the girl sneered, her pretty face marred by the venom in her expression. 'Yet you've had no time for them all these years, nor they for you. Phil told me all about it.'

'I expect he did,' I kept my tone even with great difficulty.

'Yes,' she went on, 'he did. How you came between him and his father. It was only when the two of *us* got together that they began to sort things out.'

'Good for you.'

'He never loved you, you know.'

'Really?'

'That's right. He called you a controlling bitch. Imagine thinking you could keep him by getting pregnant — at your age — when you knew full well he never wanted kids.'

I actually couldn't trust myself to reply to any of that. I remained silent, but could feel my blood pressure rising through the roof.

'A few more weeks,' Kayleigh placed her hands flat on the table and leaned forward until her face was practically touching mine and I could see the hate for me blazing in her eyes, 'and all this would have been mine. You were well and truly out of the picture.'

'That's true,' I agreed, wondering why she had come and if she was angry enough to physically attack me.

She straightened up and spun away from me. 'Stupid, stupid,' she fumed, and I thought for a moment she was still talking about me. Then she continued and it became apparent she was actually talking about herself. 'Getting the motorbike out of the garage and back on the road was my idea and Phil loved it. For the first time he and Randy had something in common.

'How was *I* to know he was going to try and impress the silly old bastard by going faster than the speed of sound? I can't believe it,' she spun around and thrust her face into mine again and it was all I could do not to lean back away from her. 'I was *this* close,' she held up her hand, the forefinger and thumb almost, but not quite touching, 'this close, to getting the life I'd always dreamed of — only to see it snatched away.'

I could almost begin to feel sorry for her, though I didn't know why. With a determination like hers she was bound to succeed eventually. There would always be another

Phil with a wife who no longer understood him. In fact I actually said as much and Kayleigh seemed to take it as a compliment and was mollified by the suggestion.

I thought it so sad that she didn't seem to think it was worth working for the life she wanted with someone of her own age, but I carefully kept that opinion to myself and watched with relief as she left without even one final parting shot. She had obviously said all she came to say.

The last few weeks of our marriage were one thing, but I couldn't believe that Phil had *never* loved me. If that were true it made a complete mockery of all the years we had spent together and I didn't think I could live with that notion.

Phil hadn't been a great one for photos — as the bare walls of the house testified — but I had been meticulous about filing those we did have into albums over the years. Even before Kayleigh's visit I'd decided to follow Rich's suggestion and was going to dig them out with a view to filling some of the frames he'd gone to buy, but now I had a pressing desire to look at them in the hope of discovering the truth about my marriage.

I knew where they were — still in the loft where Phil had placed everything that he'd identified as 'clutter' when we'd moved in.

The minimalist approach didn't allow for mementos of the past and storage was limited, despite the size of the house. That was Phil's verdict and, as usual, I just went along with his wishes in the matter.

I knew I should wait. I had lived for many months without seeing the photos, but Kayleigh's visit and the claims she'd made had shaken me more than I could have imagined.

Before I would even allow myself to question the sense of what I was doing, I was back upstairs and retrieving the hooked stick I had seen Phil use to open the loft hatch and pull down the ladder. I belatedly remembered him complaining bitterly because a house of this calibre didn't boast a better way of gaining access to the roof space.

A tap with the rubber-tipped end of the stick brought the hatch swinging down, but I had to climb on to a chair to comfortably reach the ladder and pull it down. I was a bit stuck when it only came down halfway, but then I recalled Phil fiddling with something at the side and found a button that released the second length to floor level and it clicked into place.

If I was honest, I had been expecting someone to return and take over the task of retrieving the photos. That hadn't happened and since I had managed this far I thought I might just as well continue. As I put my foot on the first rung, I wasn't totally convinced I was doing the right thing, but I had come too far now to leave the task until later.

It wasn't as difficult as I'd expected, and even heaving myself up through the hatch didn't present too much of a problem. There was a light switch right in front of me and I blinked in the sudden brilliance and looked around the boarded space with interest at the piles of boxes, the contents all neatly identified on the outside in my own hand.

I had totally forgotten doing any such thing, but now I had good reason to bless my organizational skills as I very quickly located the container holding the albums. In no time I had retrieved a couple of albums and prepared to make my descent, but I soon found that with only one hand to grasp the side of the ladder the journey down was going to be precarious, to say the least.

I did contemplate dropping them to the floor below, but the probable resulting damage made me reconsider that option and I decided to take it slowly, leaving the books at the edge of the hatch until I was partway down. This method worked well and I had the albums in my grasp when everything began to go wrong.

One moment I was feeling with my foot for the next rung down and then the books began to slip. Trying to grasp them *and* the ladder proved impossible but, somehow, I just couldn't let them go, and I felt myself falling.

For a long moment I lay there on the landing carpet, stunned and wondering what damage I had done, though everything seemed to be intact when I tentatively moved my limbs. With a sigh of relief I rolled on to my side and found myself staring at a wedding picture of Phil and me from all those years ago.

Heaving myself into a sitting position, I picked it up and studied it. I was taken aback by how young we looked, little more than children really, with me all dressed up in satin and lace and Phil standing proudly beside me in a suit from C&A.

Looking into each other's eyes, there was no denying the love between us on that day and probably for many of the years since. I was filled with so much relief that I began to cry.

That was when the pain ripped through my body like a knife. This was no gentle contraction warning of the onset of labour, but a vicious stabbing that had me twisting my body in an effort to escape both the pain and the knowledge that my foolish actions had brought me to this.

With no phone near enough to be of any use, I faced giving birth prematurely and all alone. This early in the pregnancy the child would have only a slim chance of survival — without the benefit of immediate medical care I was very afraid there was no chance at all.

17

Surely there was supposed to be a break between contractions, but the rolling pain just went on and on and on. Any hope of making it to the nearest bedroom was dashed and I could already feel the baby's head making its presence known. Everything was progressing with a speed that was frightening.

Struggling out of my underwear, I then ripped my skirt from hem to waist and spreading it beneath me prepared for my child to be born. I should have been scared to death, but there was no time to be afraid.

Hearing the front door open and close, I yelled with all the breath I had left and it was Winston who shot round the corner of the landing just in time to ease the tiny scrap of humanity into the world. I had never been so glad to see anyone in the whole of my life.

Carefully hiding his real feelings — which had to have been of complete panic like mine — he wrapped the baby in the remnants of my skirt with one hand and, reaching into his pocket for his mobile phone, dialled for an ambulance with the other. Ominously, there was no sound from the child.

With a glance back at me he stepped into Amber's bedroom to make the call. I could only hear one side of the conversation and precious little of that, but they seemed to be issuing Winston with instructions regarding the baby and asking him questions.

I lay exhausted and bloodied where I had given birth, in no fit state to try to move. All I felt at that moment was an unbearable sadness, not just for another child who had fought a losing battle for survival, but for all that had gone before and the realization that in the end it had been for nothing. At the end of a pregnancy that had torn lives and relationships apart there was nothing to show — and then from the bedroom came the thin mewling of my firstborn child.

★   ★   ★

Within days I was ready to go home and, if it weren't for a little soreness where I had been stitched, I wouldn't even have known I had given birth. My figure seemed to be already shrinking back to its slender pre-pregnancy shape with no effort at all on my part.

The baby would remain in the neonatal unit in an incubator, which I thought was by far the best for both of us. I had no idea of how I would have coped with a bouncing

289

healthy bundle, so the very thought of dealing with this frail scrap of humanity scared the life out of me.

I was spared the indignity of expressing milk several times a day, because the full breasts I was assured would be mine had never materialized. All anyone seemed to expect from me were regular visits to gaze fondly upon this tiny mite and I found I could manage that without too much difficulty.

Dressed in just a nappy with a feeding tube and the incubator the only signs of medical intervention, she was quite sweet, with her mop of dark hair, but the sight of her did not arouse any strong feeling in me beyond a very genuine respect for her obvious determination to be a part of my life whether I wanted it or not.

This baby had made up her mind long ago to battle adversity and in doing so had made my mind up for me. I had no doubt at all that she was here to stay, but whether I would ever grow to love her — well, that was another story. I had my doubts.

I knew my behaviour was unnatural, but amazingly no one else seemed to be aware there was even a problem. They were all too busy bonding with the baby themselves to notice any lack of real interest on my part. It was a relief to be able to go home and plead exhaustion to account for the limited visits I made to the hospital. I had no difficulty consoling myself that there was always someone there, and a baby that age wouldn't even be able to tell the difference.

That it was going to be a different story when she came home, I was only too well aware, but I just decided I would deal with that when I came to it. It was how I'd managed everything else and seemed to work well enough. Meanwhile the makeover team were going flat out to finish the decorating before the baby came home.

'It's looking fabulous,' I said, walking into the lounge, which was the last room to get a makeover.

The papering was well underway and the lightly patterned walls were a welcome change from the bland magnolia that had previously dominated every room. I'd never realized before quite how much I'd detested it. I suppose I'd become used to never voicing an opinion on the choice of décor for any of the houses Phil and I had lived in over recent years.

Winston was the one up the step ladder easing the paper into line and matching the pattern, Rich stood beneath him taking the weight of paper and making sure it didn't stick to the wall until Winston was good and ready. Amber was waiting brush poised, ready to begin pasting the next sheet. I was impressed with the teamwork and organizational skills and didn't hesitate to say so.

All three of them turned to look at me, standing just inside the door, 'That's all well and good,' Rich said, 'but do you *like* it. I did feel we were just a bit too keen to influence you and it is still your house when all is said and done — despite the fact you seem to have been invaded by Siddons.'

'Rich,' I went over to him, and leaving the paper hanging to the very capable Winston, he turned to face me, 'you see before you one very happy lady and that's despite everything that's happened. You've given me something I've never known before,' I paused and suddenly realized what I was sounding like and that Amber especially was looking at me with a very bemused expression on her face. I hurried on. 'You've given me a house that finally feels like a home — *my* home — and the biggest bonus is that between you you've all filled it with the laughter and love of a family. Phil and I thought we were so independent and self-sufficient, but I can finally begin to see what we were missing all those years.'

'You're not the only one,' Rich said

emphatically. 'I really think that Phil and I made the same mistake and that was to put money before family. Jess and I might have broken up anyway, but me being so bull-headed about being the big provider certainly hastened the demise of our marriage.'

'Well, as long as you realize it,' Amber said a trifle tartly, 'you won't make the same mistake again, will you?'

Rich gave her a long, thoughtful look. 'I doubt anyone else would even have me with my track record,' he said finally, 'or have you already got someone in mind. She knows everyone up and down your road, you know,' he turned to me again. 'She has a word to everyone during the course of the day. It makes me quite nervous to think she might already have a prospective stepmother lined up.'

I laughed, but then said, 'Talking to the neighbours — apart from Vi — is more than I've done.' A bit shamefaced, I was shocked to find my niece had managed in a few short weeks what I hadn't bothered to achieve in all the months I'd lived in the area. 'Yet I think they all sent flowers and cards when Phil died. I seem to recall someone even brought round a casserole.'

Amber shrugged. 'We live in a small

community in America and everyone knows everyone else. Sometimes it feels a bit like Big Brother, with everyone knowing your business, but we all look out for each other and it's kind of cosy. You only have to smile at people, you know — anywhere in the world — and they can't help smiling back. That's all it takes to start a friendship — just the one smile.'

Rich shook his head. 'Hey, how did you get to be so wise?' he asked, adding, 'It must come from your mother,' and he was smiling so proudly that the look on his face brought a lump to my throat.

It made me wonder if there was the slightest chance I would ever look at my daughter that way. Somehow I didn't really think so. I always felt slightly stunned when I was reminded that I even had a child, the birth already felt as if it had happened to someone else, the baby as if it belonged to someone else. I didn't know how that was ever going to change.

'Let's get everyone round,' I said suddenly, desperate for some sort of distraction. 'All the family, to say thank you and, of course,' I told Winston, 'that includes you and Vi, too.'

He nodded, concentrating on getting the next piece of paper straight, but I didn't miss the pleased smile and the little cough he always gave when he was trying to hide his feelings. He had no family. Being a grown up orphan just like me, there was no doubt Winston had been a lonely man until first Rich and then the rest of us became his substitute family.

The realization had begun to dawn, too, that I had actually been quite a lonely woman — yes, even when Phil was alive — and it had taken far too many years of my life to understand how important family was and to learn that family doesn't necessarily mean just those who are related.

I was getting into the idea of a family gathering, the more I thought about it. 'The dining room looks fabulous,' I enthused, thinking of all the best crystal and china and how candles and flowers would set it all off.

How silly, I thought, that we'd had such a wonderful room for entertaining and yet Phil and I had probably used it only once or twice and that was for wining and dining Phil's more important clients. His family would have been the last, the very last people that either of us would have given a thought to inviting round.

It wasn't as if I didn't like cooking, though I'd done precious little of it of late, and my mind was already racing ahead choosing and discarding menu choices.

'Can I help?'

My immediate instinct was to refuse Amber's request. When I was cooking — and I mean really cooking something special — I liked the kitchen to myself, but this was another me and somehow I couldn't throw the girl's hesitant offer back into her face.

'Of course,' I said with a warmth that was only partly put on, 'we'll do it together. You can help me plan the menu,' I added rashly and was glad I had when I saw the way her face lit up. Interference in my kitchen was a small price to pay for making someone that happy and anyway, the food was less important than the company. I blinked at another lesson learned relatively easily.

'Perhaps,' said Rich, thoughtfully, 'you should do it sooner, rather than later, before the baby comes home. She's doing so well it can't be too long until she's discharged and there won't be much time to spare after that.'

'Why don't we make it a celebration of her birth?' Amber suggested brightly, flicking back her dark hair as she pasted another piece of paper. She was concentrating on what she was doing and not looking at me as she added, 'You can let everyone know what her name is going to be at the same time.'

Amber might not have been looking at me, but Rich was, so I had to school my features into a smile and try to match the brightness of Amber's tone, when I said, 'Oh, that's a good idea,' hoping I was giving no indication that I had absolutely no idea what the child was going to be called — and very little real interest, either, if I was totally honest.

I shuddered and suddenly felt dreadful for even admitting such a thing. What kind of person was I, anyway, that I could have time for all and sundry and none for my own daughter?

'I'm going to the hospital,' I said suddenly, 'we'll sort out a date for the dinner and discuss menus when I get back. I won't be too long.'

Pausing only to grab a jacket and my bag, I left the house before I could change my mind.

Walking into the maternity unit of Brankstone Hospital was harder alone. Every other time I'd been there I'd had one of my in-laws with me and whoever it had been, they'd chatted excitedly about the progress the baby was making, who they thought she looked like and how great it would be to finally bring her home. All I had to do was to make the correct response at the appropriate time.

I rang the bell at the locked door of the special care baby unit. The midwife who opened it instantly recognized me and welcomed me with a smile and the news that the baby was now out of the incubator and feeding without the benefit of a tube.

Instead of being filled with delight by my baby's evident progress, all I could think was that the midwife must have an excellent memory. Either that or that by sheer good fortune she had been working her shift on each of the few times I'd visited.

I made my way through the maze of incubators, each occupied by a tiny scrap of humanity that clung to life — precariously, to say the least it had to be said in a few cases. Some babies had anxious parents hovering, but not all. I guessed the strain of watching your child struggle to survive could become too much to bear sometimes.

Promoted to the neonatal nursery, my baby, when I reached her looked almost robust in comparison. A healthy pink colour, she might have been small at just over four pounds, but she was also perfectly formed and free of the mass of tubes attached to the far more premature and therefore weaker babies. It was like looking at a stranger's child and standing there I couldn't believe the tiny individual would ever feel like mine.

'Would you like to feed her?'

'What?'

I turned to stare at the midwife. It was the

same one who had let me in and she stood there smiling and holding out a bottle of milk. Before I had time to protest or refuse I was sitting with the baby in my arms and watching her suck furiously on a teat that looked too big for her tiny mouth as if her life depended on it — which, of course, it did.

I stared and stared at her, as if I'd never seen a real, live baby before. Actually, I probably hadn't, not this close. I'd always avoided other people's children like the plague, equating their proximity with sticky fingers and drooling mouths — and that was just the teenagers. My own joke brought a little smile to my lips, though I didn't feel much like smiling.

'I wish I'd thought to bring the camera.'

I looked up to find Winston had come in and was watching me. I realized guiltily that he thought I was smiling at the baby as any normal mother would.

'I thought you might like some company,' he went on, when I didn't reply. He indicated the other parents through the doorway and I took his point. In almost every case there was two of them.

'They'll think you're the daddy,' I managed to joke.

He shrugged and smiled, 'Probably thought I was parking the car and then followed you in. I just said the name was Siddons, but I meant the baby, not me. Well, I don't mind if you don't, and I do have a vested interest in the baby I helped to bring into the world.'

'You probably saved her life,' I said. 'In fact, there's no probably about it. She wouldn't be here now if it wasn't for you.'

Winston reached out and ran one long finger down the child's tiny face in a gesture so infinitely tender that it brought tears to my eyes and I had to blink quickly.

'I'll take care of you.' I knew he was talking to the baby, but then he added almost under his breath, 'I'll take care of you both,' and I wondered whether I'd heard him right. We were hardly his responsibility, after all. He was just a friend and a relatively new one at that. Before I could think about it further he became brisk, asking in a knowledgeable fashion, 'Have you brought up her wind yet?'

'Brought up her . . . ?'

Taking the child from me he showed me how and was rewarded with the smallest belch I'd ever heard. He looked so inordinately pleased with himself that I couldn't help smiling, but realized it was just one more thing in a whole list of things that I didn't know how to do for my own child.

I looked at the nametag on the incubator, at the labels on the baby's minute wrists and ankles, identifying her as 'Baby Siddons', and a sudden thought came to me.

'Winston,' I began, 'what's your favourite girl's name?'

He was about to ask me why. I could see the word forming on his lips, and then he looked from me to the baby in his arms and back to me again.

'*I* can't decide,' he protested.

'No one has more right than you do,' I pointed out, 'and I really don't have any preferences. Please help me out or she will end up being registered as Baby Siddons and will grow up as such and never forgive me.'

'If you're quite sure,' Winston didn't object again, which was just as well or I would have felt I was forcing him to make a choice. 'I think the name Mia would be perfect for her. It's a beautiful name and also the Italian word for 'my' and because of the circumstances of her birth I guess a part of me will always look upon her as partly mine.'

'Mia.' I liked the way it sounded. I liked that Winston had chosen it and told myself it was because I was desperate and fast reaching the point of getting the whole family to put names in a hat and pick one at random. 'It's perfect, Winston. Thank you.'

'No, thank you,' he replied quickly, 'I'm very honoured, though I have to say Mia doesn't seem that impressed.' He nodded down at the baby now sound asleep in his arms. 'Do you want to put her back?'

It was my turn to speak quickly. 'You do it, we don't want to disturb her.'

When he held her towards me, for a moment I couldn't think what he wanted, and then I realized he was waiting for me to kiss the child goodbye. I could hardly refuse, and so I touched my lips to the smooth softness of her tiny cheek, taking in the sweet baby smell and wishing I could feel something — anything — apart from relief when she was safely back into the perspex cot and I could walk away from the responsibility for another day.

18

When we got back home, it was to Amber and Rich looking mightily pleased with themselves having put the finishing touches to the lounge in our absence. They hadn't even waited for the paper to dry before arranging the furniture in a far less formal way, with the chairs grouped in a fashion that positively invited a relaxed atmosphere and cordial conversation. The scarlet scatter cushions I'd chosen from a catalogue and had been delivered were also a welcome and very homely addition.

'Dad wouldn't let me hang pictures yet in case the paper got ruined,' Amber explained, 'but do you like it, Aunt Alex? Do you really like it?'

I didn't have to pretend, my enthusiasm was absolutely for real. I finally had a lounge where relaxing seemed like a great idea, with the bright cushions adding colour to the cream leather of the expensive suite, and matching rugs breaking up the oceans of cream carpet.

This was a room where a guest could kick their shoes off without embarrassment, put their feet up — should they wish — and sink back against the plump pillows. In this room I could certainly enjoy reading a book for the pure pleasure of a story well told and not with a view to impressing anyone. I could catch an episode of Corrie or Emmerdale without fear of my choice of viewing being put up for ridicule, and watch a cheesy romantic film for pure enjoyment or sing along to a Westlife CD without apology simply because that was my kind of music.

It seemed so incredible now that I had allowed Phil to dictate my choice of reading matter and TV viewing, and to ridicule my taste in music to the point that I'd kept all my favourite CDs in the car.

'I love it,' I told Amber, catching her hands and spinning her around in a real expression of joy. 'Thank you, thank you all of you for giving me the home I probably always wanted yet never realized was possible. I know I can be happy here now.'

'Our job is pretty well done, so we must be thinking of packing up and leaving you to enjoy your home in peace. It's been great but it's time we were heading back to Mallory Court and getting out from under your feet.' Rich was smiling at our exuberance and for a moment I didn't take in his words or their meaning.

Amber's face was a picture and I was quite sure that within seconds mine was, too, as we stared at Rich as if he was quite mad. I wasn't quite sure what I would have found to say but, luckily, Amber got in first.

'Leave?' she said, 'leave? We can't leave now. There's the dinner party to arrange and then the baby will be coming home. Aunt Alex is going to need all the help we can give her. Aren't you?' She turned to me for verification, her eyes clouded with concern.

'Oh, absolutely,' I agreed quickly.

'Hey,' Rich said, but gently, 'don't you *want* to come home with your dad? You really mustn't put Alex on the spot like that.'

She ran to him, flinging her arms around his neck in a gesture that would have been unheard of only a very short while ago. 'I already feel like I'm at home with you. This,' she gestured around the newly decorated room, 'feels like my home. Living here with Aunt Alex — and you, too — has given me back the family life in England that I lost when you and mum split up. I even have the next best thing to a baby sister.'

Rich was obviously lost for words and so was I. It was left to Winston to say, 'I know what Amber means. Sometimes family doesn't have to be family to *be* family, if you see what I mean.' He wasn't actually making any sense at all, and yet we did know exactly what he meant.

The thought of them leaving filled me with the most awful apprehension, but I was very aware I couldn't let my feelings influence their future plans. Each person had already, and with great generosity, put their life on hold to help me through a very bad time in my own. The problem was, having them all in my life had shown me with great clarity everything that my life had previously lacked. I finally understood what real family life was all about, and now I couldn't imagine ever wanting to be on my own again.

'Being family doesn't mean we have to live in each other's pockets,' Rich pointed out. 'We can all still spend lots of time together.'

'But there's the dinner party and the baby coming home,' Amber wailed, and then she played her trump card, 'and what about when you go back to work? You can't expect me to stay on my own in the flat. I'm only seventeen.'

'Very nearly eighteen,' Rich pointed out, 'and what about your education? I thought you planned on going to university.'

'Yes,' Amber trumped her trump card, 'over *here*. That was my plan, to look into the possibility, but I *had* planned on taking a gap year to make sure we would get along first.

Now it's worked out here so much better than I thought, I might try for a last-minute place through clearing. There's still time.'

'But — what about your mother?'

'Oh, Dad, she'll be cool about it. I'll go home for the holidays and she always thought it would be great for me to spend some time with you. It was me who had the problem — until now.'

'Well,' I felt it was okay for me to say something at that point, 'it seems you have a lot to discuss and plan, and whether you do it there or here is up to you, but we did promise Amber she could help with the dinner party — and with the baby when she comes home . . .'

Rich held up his hands, laughing, 'Okay, I know when I'm outnumbered, but I can't help feeling you must be sick of Siddons camping on your doorstep and will be relieved to get your life back.'

Even Rich who was usually so sensitive, seemed to have missed the essential point, which was that I could never get my old life back. Too much had changed for it to ever be the same again. The one person who had been of any real importance to me was gone forever taking with him all the illusions I had held about us living the perfect life during our years together.

Other people — the very last people I would ever have expected — had come into my shattered life and helped to make it whole again, but I was becoming aware they could just as quickly go, leaving me with the one person responsible for every recent change my life had seen, the daughter I had to take full responsibility for. The daughter I didn't know how to love.

★ ★ ★

The size of the dinner party grew slightly bigger than I had originally planned when Simon and his wife Susan made known their intention to drive Jacquetta back from what had apparently been a most enjoyable visit to their Scottish border home. They saw it as the ideal opportunity to spend some time with family and revisit the south coast and it seemed only right to arrange the meal to coincide with their stay.

Jacquetta was full of enthusiasm about returning home, though undecided about whether to return to her room in my house or the one at Vi's.

'She could do with the company, you see,' she told me over the phone, 'but then you might need a hand with the baby when she comes home, though you must tell me if I would be in the way.'

I had to be very careful not to influence her decision, but I knew if Amber and Rich were leaving, I could seriously do with the company. I couldn't even begin to think about dealing with the baby and her needs on my own, the very idea filled me with terror.

'I cannot wait to see the petit chou,' she said excitement making her French accent all the more apparent. '*Voilà*, and there she is the very minute my back was turned and many weeks before she is due. How that could happen I do not understand. It was all I could do not to climb on to the very next plane, but the family are taking care of you, n'est-ce pas?'

'I couldn't have managed without them, Jacquetta,' I said honestly.

'And the little one? Tell me again how she looks, about her funny little ways and how much she has grown. She *is* definitely healthy, isn't she? For they are keeping her in hospital for so long.'

The actress in me came to the fore and the enthusiasm in my tone would have fooled a far more intuitive person than my mother-in-law. She was happy to coo over my description of dark curling hair, eyes of the deep Siddons blue, pink limbs of perfect proportions and tiny fingers and toes tipped with minute nails.

In the end there would be twelve of us sitting down to eat including Rich, Amber and me. I was looking forward to seeing Louise and Rose with their respective husbands, Del and Tony, and there would be Winston, Vi and Jacquetta together with Simon and Susan.

The only one of Jacquetta's sons who would be missing — apart from the dear departed Phil, of course — would be Barry. At fifty-six years old his place in the family was between Tony and Simon. Barry had sent his regrets but explained that as he and his wife had already taken time away from the hotel business they ran on the Isle of Man to attend both Phil's and Randy's funerals they didn't feel they could absent themselves again so soon leaving the staff to cope at one of their busiest times. I wouldn't have expected it and was just surprised at how disappointed he'd sounded.

'Are you sure you can manage such a large group?' Rich queried, 'and will they all fit around the table?'

'Dad, will you just stop fussing,' Amber advised, with more confidence than I felt. 'Just sort the wine out and leave the rest to us.'

Louise and Rose also offered their services, but again Amber vetoed any outside interference, insisting we could manage and they should just show up on time with an appetite.

'I'm not doubting *your* ability to cope,' I insisted when I queried the wisdom of turning all offers of help away, 'just my own. It's been a very long time since I cooked a meal of this magnitude and I'm feeling extremely nervous I don't mind telling you.'

'I want us to do this,' she said, 'throw a dinner party like a real family, with dad going off to do the wine and you and I doing the cooking just like a real mother and daughter.'

I was really touched, so I said no more and allowed Amber free rein with the choice of menu and even down to who would be sitting where.

Very sensibly, she kept everything simple, with a melon and parma ham starter, roast beef and all the trimmings for the main course, and the dessert was sherry trifle or apple crumble and custard.

She seemed to know exactly what she was doing and happily told me that her mother had entertained all the time, mostly business colleagues of her stepfather, but often for friends and neighbours, too.

'They've always seemed happy enough, though they don't always see eye to eye, and it is hard to tell with grown ups,' she told me, setting me to the task of peeling potatoes. 'I hoped for years that she and my dad would get back together, but if that can't happen then I would like to see dad happily settled, too. I'm sure he will meet someone one day soon.'

'Oh, so am I,' I agreed enthusiastically, 'he's far too nice to stay on his own for very much longer. In fact, I've been giving it a bit of thought. He's a bit young for Vi,' we both laughed, 'but there's Julie at work. She'd be just the right age and she's really nice. I'm sure they'd get along well.'

'What about you?'

'Me? Oh, I'm not bothered about meeting anyone.'

'That's not what I meant,' Amber didn't look at me as she continued relentlessly, 'I meant — what about you for my dad?'

I didn't even see it coming and the potato I was peeling dropped back into the water with a splash that soaked the front of my t-shirt.

'Can't you see how perfect it would be?' she pleaded, her gaze steady on my face.

'No,' I said, determined to nip this in the bud, 'I can't.'

'But he really likes you and I know you like him.'

'Not in the way you're thinking, Amber. We're friends, good friends, and that's all there is. Anyway, it's hardly appropriate, is it? He's my brother-in-law.'

'You're not related by blood,' she pointed out, obviously unwilling to let the matter drop, 'and anyway, I went to the library and checked. There's nothing to stop you from marrying my dad.'

I was almost speechless — almost, but not quite. 'The 'nothing' to stop me marrying your dad is that there is *nothing* between us. I'm horrified that you're talking this way and he would be mortified if he could hear you.'

'But . . . '

'But — nothing. Remember what I just said — there is nothing — and your dad deserves something more than a convenient family arrangement cobbled together to suit his daughter.'

Thankfully, Amber finally dropped the subject, but her words had an effect on me and made me see possibilities where there were none before. As a consequence my manner around Rich lacked some of its former ease and I became terrified of giving him the wrong impression.

Amber must have got her idea from somewhere, I reasoned, and I didn't want her dad coming up with the same one. Perhaps it was time they went home, after all.

When everything was under control we left Rich to fiddle with his wine choices and to keep an eye on the simmering pans and disappeared upstairs to get ready. It was a long time since I had dressed up for anything. I didn't even know if my clothes still fit since, after the baby's birth, I'd taken to comfort dressing in a big way and lived in the jeans and t-shirts so favoured by the likes of Louise, Rose and Amber.

Even plugging the ceramic straighteners into the electric socket was like a whole new experience, and that was from a woman who had never previously left the house — or indeed stayed in it — without the full treatment. All that seemed like a world away and I wondered why my appearance had seemed so important to me for all those years. The answer was Phil, of course and living up to his exacting expectations.

However, there was no harm in taking a pride in your appearance, and the effort I was making paid off, I thought, because I looked and felt good. My hair, newly cut, was flicked into a similar style to the one sported by Jane Fonda the last time I'd seen her on Parkinson a few months before. It had looked fabulous on her and I'd been hoping for a similar result. I wasn't displeased with the effect.

My post-pregnancy curves were shown off to full advantage in a strappy dress in the browny autumn shades that suited me best, the asymmetric hem and killer-heeled shoes really flattering my legs. For the first time in a very, very long time I knew that I was dressing up for me and no one else and that felt good. In fact, it felt great and so did I.

Amber and I met on the landing. She was much more casually dressed than I was, in khaki cargo pants slung low on the hips with a fitted halter necked top showing off the light tan she had managed to acquire through the unpredictable British summer.

'You look . . . ' we both spoke at once.

'Stunning,' I finished.

'Great,' Amber completed, and we both burst out laughing and shared an affectionate hug.

I had to admit to becoming incredibly fond of her in a relatively short space of time and knew that I was going to miss her cheerful company far more than I would ever admit. This happy family thing was definitely going to have to come to an end, though, as I was beginning to realize and accept. It should probably be sooner rather than later, before we all started believing that it was the real thing and not just a convenient arrangement that had helped us all out for a while.

Amber insisted she needed no help in the kitchen and practically drove me out of the door. Feeling a bit like a spare part I went to check on the table and found Winston polishing glasses and fiddling with cutlery. Red wine was already open and 'breathing' and I knew the white wine was chilling in the fridge.

'That's supposed to be Rich's job,' I joked, straightening a serviette, 'I thought you stopped being his labourer once the decorating was finished.'

He looked up and then couldn't seem to look away.

'Wow,' he said in a hushed tone.

'Wow, yourself,' I answered back trying not to look as awkward as I felt, and doing my best not to stare back. Used to seeing Winston dressed casually in jeans or chinos, I'd have had to be blind not to notice that he cut a fine figure in a dark suit and white shirt. He still had the look of a bandit about him — I think it was the moustache that did it — but a very dashing one at that.

It was a huge relief when the doorbell chimed demandingly and I was able to rush off, without it appearing that I was running away, to greet the influx of Siddons who appeared to have arrived en masse and were congregating on the front doorstep.

'Mon Dieu, look at you,' Jacquetta cried, lacquered nails gleaming a deep red as she waved them in my direction, begging everyone to, 'look my beautiful daughter-in-law. Would anyone believe she has so recently given birth?'

Would anyone believe those remarks came from the mother-in-law who had given every indication of detesting me over the years? In fairness, I had to admit that my own previous efforts to build a relationship with her had amounted to very little.

Everyone agreed politely that they would not as they were ushered towards the dining room — now gleaming by the light of the many candles that Winston had begun to put a match to the moment the doorbell heralded the arrival of our dinner guests. Rich had obviously gone round to collect Vi, as she arrived on his arm soon after, joining the others around the extended table. Almost immediately Amber served the first course.

It turned out to be unlike any other of the Siddons family celebrations, dominated as they always had been by Jacquetta's attention-seeking behaviour and Randy's dour disapproval.

Jacquetta looked to be the same delicately painted be-wigged French doll she had always been, but the change in her attitude was remarkable. Though she took part in the lively discussions around the table, she also appeared equally happy to see others take centre stage and the contentment on her face as she enjoyed the company of most of her family members was a joy to behold.

The conversation flowed as easily as the wine that Rich had chosen and he made a grand job of ensuring everyone's glass was kept topped up. Amber had made a supreme effort with the food and would allow only minimal assistance from me to serve courses and clear plates. Everyone was full of praise and she glowed under the warmth of all the approval.

'The house looks wonderful,' Louise said warmly, 'I might move the whole makeover team over to my house when Del gives the go ahead.'

'Damn good idea,' said Del, with a real gleam of delight in his eye. 'Shall I book them all up now and get them to put it in writing to make sure they can't back out when they've sobered up?'

'Was it a family effort, then?' came from Simon's wife Susan, who had seemed to fit right in and appeared to be enjoying herself hugely.

Somehow, I didn't feel the same could be said for her husband. I tried to feel charitable towards him, and make allowances for the fact he lived too far away to be closely involved with the family, but I didn't appreciate the speculative looks that were directed my way from time to time. It was as if he knew something I didn't and was smirking at me behind his fat hands.

I'd always thought, from the limited number of times I'd seen Simon over the years, that he was the one brother-in-law who was the most like his father in manner and behaviour. So far I'd seen nothing during the course of the evening to change my mind about that. He had a way of looking down his nose that really got up mine.

It was Rose who piped up, 'Oh, yes, and the whole idea came from Amber. She's been staying here with Rich, since she arrived in England, so it was their way of paying Alex back for her hospitality. Winston, here, also got very involved. He lives in the flat below Rich's and met Alex when she was staying there for a while.'

I was in the kitchen dealing with the coffee I had insisted on making after Amber's efforts in producing the marvellous meal we'd all enjoyed, when Simon's voice behind me made me jump. I hadn't even heard him come in.

'All very cosy,' he said, but not in a nice way at all. 'So, tell me was this thing with Rich and you going on when Phil was alive?'

Somehow, I wasn't even shocked, and I

turned to glare at him. 'There is no 'thing' going on with Rich, not now and not ever.'

Simon continued as if I hadn't spoken, 'I'm sure Phil would be thrilled to see his feckless brother step into his shoes so quickly and enjoy the fruits of all his years of labour. What's the matter? One Siddons not enough for you?'

My hand connected with the smug face before I was even aware of my instinctive reaction. The red mark that bloomed immediately on his plump cheek gave me no end of satisfaction.

'Why don't you just *fuck off*, Simon, and take your disgusting innuendoes with you? The company is in the process of being sold to a local businessman — a competitor of Phil's — and the money will be put into trust for our baby. There is and never has been anything going on with Rich and me but, let me tell you, if there was, it would be none of your damn business — or anybody else's, come to that.'

'Bravo.'

We both turned to find Rich standing in the doorway, clapping his hands softly.

'And just so you have the full story,' Rich said, throwing his brother a look of sheer disgust, 'Jess is on her way home. Her second marriage hasn't worked out and there's every chance we will be trying to make another go of things. Make an effort to put your brain into gear for once — or at least try to get your facts right — before you open your mouth in future, why don't you, Si?'

Simon glared at us both, then spun on his heel and left the room.

Soon after that I heard his strident tone boom across the hallway as he advised his wife, 'It's time we made a move. We have an early start in the morning.'

Rich shrugged his shoulders and advised, 'Ignore him. I'm afraid he always did have a dirty mind,' but I could tell from the look in his eyes that he was as uncomfortable about his brother's accusations as I was.

If it was true about Jess and him, I was very pleased for them. A second chance was something Phil and I had been denied, though if he had lived — well, who could tell what might have happened, anything was possible.

Something about my previously easy relationship with Rich had been irreversibly changed — first by Amber's outspoken comments and then by my brother-in-law's snide remarks. For the first time I felt really awkward in his company and I knew for sure then that the days of sharing a roof were coming to an end.

I'd become incredibly fond of him and of Amber in a relatively short time and the thought of facing the future without their support seemed not just bleak, but absolutely bloody terrifying.

19

I did my best to put Simon's spiteful and totally unfounded comments to the back of my mind, so that I could concentrate on enjoying having what — in the past few months — had become my own little family around me while I still could.

All thoughts of the future and especially of coping with the baby had been ruthlessly ignored, which was why it came as something of a shock when my carefully cultivated bubble of oblivion was suddenly burst by a handful of words on my next visit to the hospital.

'You'll be glad to be finally taking little Mia home.' It was the same nurse as before greeting me with a smile, and total confidence that my reaction was going to be the pure joy of every other normal parent on receiving such news. 'We expect her to be given the all clear some time today or tomorrow at the latest. I bet you can't wait.'

'Taking her home?' I repeated, quickly going on to protest, 'but she's far too tiny.'

'Nonsense,' the jolly girl laughed, 'she's as tough as old boots and more than ready to leave. It's only natural to be worried, which is why we arrange for mothers to 'room in' for forty-eight hours prior to discharge. It allows new mothers to get used to looking after their babies with the staff on hand to offer advice and assistance.'

Christ, I didn't know what was worse, to be thrown in at the deep end by suddenly finding myself at home with this child who had never yet managed to become more than a stranger to me, or finding myself under the microscopic supervision of the hospital staff who would surely see through any pretence at a maternal instinct in a minute.

My visit that day was even briefer than all the brief visits before it. The thought of the impending 'rooming in' with Mia filled me with terror and by the time I had made my excuses and left I was shaking from head to foot. I had to walk round and round the hospital grounds before I felt anywhere near safe enough to climb into the car and drive myself home.

Once there I couldn't even bring myself to mention the impending arrival of the newest member of the household, let alone the plans for the forty-eight hour period prior to that happening. Instead, I spent a lot of time thinking about returning to work — even though my maternity leave was nowhere near used up — and hiring a nanny as soon as possible.

I was scared and fully prepared to admit it. Nothing in my past could have prepared me for what lay ahead. There were so many decisions to be made about my life and future — and not just mine. I had never been responsible for anyone else before and I didn't feel old enough to be responsible for anyone else now. My forty-five years and wealth of experience counted for nothing in my current situation.

I just didn't know where to start or what I really wanted. I couldn't even say I wanted my old life back — which I could quite see would be a normal reaction after losing a partner — because circumstances had taken that away even before I was widowed anyway.

I wandered around the house aimlessly, appreciating all the work that had been done. Noticing just how much those people who had taken up residence had brought the place to life and changed the whole ambience of the house turning it into a home.

I found myself in the nursery, wandering around touching things and trying — and absolutely failing — to imagine caring for the tiny baby who would eventually be my sole responsibility for the foreseeable future.

* ⋆ ⋆

The next few hours passed in an anxious blur. How nobody picked up on my state of perpetual panic was a mystery and I got sick of hearing what a wonderful idea it was to allow parents of premature babies to get used to sleeping with them before they were discharged from hospital.

In no time I found myself arriving at the hospital with a small suitcase. The room I found myself in was basic, with little more than a chair and a bed — and the perspex cot with my sleeping daughter in it.

How I got through those two days, I will never know but, thankfully, the child slept a lot and I was sure I was managing to give a great impression of coping and even caring. I was sensible enough to avoid spending time with other mothers in the same situation, convinced they would see through me in a minute.

I wouldn't have harmed a hair on the tiny child's head, but in my heart I knew I was letting her down. Telling myself I was lucky to have a healthy child at the end of what had been a pretty traumatic few months — for her and for me — didn't help. All I could feel was a deep sadness for us both, and a fear that I was damaging her emotionally because I couldn't be the mother she needed or love her in the way she deserved to be loved.

*   *   *

Luckily, I had Louise with me, when Mia was finally bathed, dressed and ready to go home. Her calming influence helped me to keep a grip on the last remnants of my own precariously balanced commonsense.

Without her, I think I'd have dropped the infant's car seat, shrieked, 'I can't do this,' and simply taken off out of the situation as fast as my feet could carry me.

Instead, I thanked everyone most profusely, proffered the thank you card and chocolates of the grateful new parent, fastened the child into her car seat with trembling fingers and brought her with me out of the safe environment that had kept her cocooned from the reality of her life.

'All set then?' Louise peered at me through the rear-view mirror then, satisfied that we were all safely strapped in, put the green Jaguar smoothly into gear and started the drive home. All too soon we were turning into the tree-lined avenue where I would be facing my life as a single mother — a life from which there could be no turning back.

'Oh, my God,' Louise laughed delightedly,

'would you look at that? I knew they were going to do something, but — well — bloody hell.'

Bloody hell indeed, I stared through the window of the car in a daze. A small crowd was gathered outside of a house that was decked from brick paving to plastic guttering with banners, flags and balloons informing the world, 'It's a Girl', and 'Welcome Home'. Phil would have had an absolute fit, was the one thought in my mind as we pulled into the curved driveway.

I stepped out of the car to a sea of smiling faces, several of them neighbours I barely knew, every one of them apparently delighted to see my baby brought safely home — except me. I tried hard to keep a grip, I really did, but suddenly the past months and the enormity of everything that had happened caught up with me and all I could do was burst into tears.

It was as if the floodgates had opened and all the grief, all the doubts overwhelmed me totally. I couldn't remember losing control, not *really* losing control to such an extent, ever in my life before.

I saw the smiles turn to shock on the familiar faces and then turn very quickly to concern.

'It's all been too much for her,' I heard

Rose say, before I was ushered inside and found myself cocooned once again in the love of this family of Siddons.

For days, I did nothing much at all. I certainly did nothing for the child as aunts, uncles and cousins took over the day-to-day care Mia needed. They must have made a wonderful job of it, because I rarely heard her cry for more than a few seconds. Even my apathy didn't seem to phase them. The possibility of postnatal depression was discussed — it was pointed out it would hardly be unexpected after the trauma I had suffered throughout my pregnancy, all of which was followed by the terrifying circumstances of the premature birth.

'I don't need a doctor,' I insisted, 'just a bit of time to adjust.'

That I was making no effort to adjust at all must have been apparent to everyone. Even I could see that eventually they would all lose patience with me, so how could I blame them when finally that's what happened.

First Louise and then Rose pleaded other commitments. Jacquetta reluctantly but with determination took herself off to visit Barry and his family, though I could see she was crying when she left. Finally, I found Amber's and Rich's cases standing by the front door.

'Why are you all doing this?' I pleaded,

'Can't you at least stay until I've managed to employ a nanny?'

'That's not the answer and you know it. You can't just hand the responsibility of your child to others, and I know that may sound hypocritical coming from me, but I had thought you might have learned from my mistakes,' Rich said, he didn't add that he was disappointed in me, but I could see that he was and that hurt me more than anything. 'You've managed to deal with everything else,' he went on, 'and you can deal with this if you'll only try, Alex. Mia deserves better from you, just as Amber deserved better from me.'

'Mia is just a little me,' Amber was crying so much she could hardly speak, 'and look how you've cared for me all this time.'

'But *you* did all the caring, I've done *nothing*.'

'You underestimate yourself,' Rich said sternly, but still with a hint of underlying sympathy in his tone, as he turned to go. 'Now you know where we are, and if you *really* need us we will be here — just as we always have been — but I think you are tougher than you think and will manage perfectly well without us.'

I was frightened. Realizing even *they* really were going and leaving me to it was very hard to accept, because they obviously just didn't understand that my feelings — or lack of them — were out of my control. Then I got angry.

'Go then,' I spat, 'I don't need or want any of you. Where were you all those years anyway? I managed without a family throughout my marriage to Phil and I'll manage now. Go on, get out, and don't bother coming back.'

The sound of the front door slamming behind them sounded so final and, as I slumped against it, I felt all the fight and anger go out of me. It was all I could do not to wrench open the door, run after them and plead with them not to leave me.

Instead, I listened to the sound of the car as it drove away and upstairs, almost immediately, the baby began to cry.

For as long as I could I ignored the plaintive sound, hoping that someone would have second thoughts about the appropriateness of leaving someone so clearly unsuitable with a helpless baby.

I drank tea, I tidied, I even put the TV on, but the mournful wail increased almost perceptibly in volume until ignoring the sound was no longer an option. It was obvious something was going to have to be done and — quite simply — there was no one else to do it.

The nearer I got to the nursery the more my nerves jangled and all I wanted was for the crying to stop. By the time I reached her, the baby's face was scarlet, her hair stood up in angry tufts and her tiny fists beat the air in a temper so fierce it shocked me to see it in one so small.

Standing by the cot, I hesitated, and she stared up at me for a moment before taking another breath in as she prepared to take the screams up another notch. Realizing I really had no choice, I finally picked her up with a hand under each arm as carefully as if she were a bomb primed to explode.

The crying hiccoughed to a halt and I held her at arm's length as we surveyed one another. The serious expression on her face was quite certainly mirrored on my own.

There was nothing, no sudden rush of mother love, just a feeling of overwhelming responsibility and of helplessness, but also the knowledge that something had to be done and that I was the only one there was left to do it. I just wished with all my heart I could remember even one of the things about childcare I had been taught during my forty-eight hour 'room in' at the hospital.

'Well, Mia,' I said, feeling incredibly stupid to be talking to someone who was, quite obviously, not going to be talking back, 'it looks as if it's just you and me, and I think we're going to have to show them we can manage just fine.'

That seemed okay, in principle, and the solemn look on the baby's face told me she was taking the information in. When her eyes creased up the next minute and the tiny mouth opened to emit a huge roar, it was clear she had some very definite reservations of her own about my ability to cope.

'When babies cry they are either wet or hungry.'

I suddenly recalled my mother-in-law's decisive tone when she had made this statement and decided to see if she was right, in the absence of any better plan.

Everything was to hand. Even I recognized a changing unit when I saw one and placing the wriggling child on to the changing mat I reached to undo the poppers of her pink Babygro with a confidence I was very far from feeling. The screaming reached a crescendo as I fumbled to remove one wet nappy and replace it with a dry one, remembering to make use of wipes and cream in the process. All the time the little legs thrashed and struggled to escape my grip in an effort to thwart any progress and by the time I'd finished we were both crying.

The yelling from us both subsided as the

job was accomplished, with me apologizing through my tears for the length of time it had taken me. 'I know,' I told this little scrap of humanity that was all Phil and I had to show from twenty-five years worth of living together and loving, 'I'm useless, and even Amber could do a better job, but I'm all you've got at the moment, so you'll just have to put up with me, I'm afraid.'

' ... and me,' said a voice from the doorway and I spun round. Of all people, Winston was the very last one I expected to see leaning against the frame but boy, was I glad to see him. 'Not that I can be much help,' he went on, 'never having had anything much to do with babies.'

'It's enough that you're here,' I told him and absolutely meant it.

He came to stand beside me and together we looked down at the helpless mite and I could see a bemused expression on Winston's face that was probably mirrored on my own.

Mia wore a solemn look, as if she was sizing us up and making yet another decision about our capabilities. I could tell she wasn't ready to be impressed when the eyes narrowed again and a thin wail rent the air.

'Hungry now then, I guess,' I hazarded, and lifted her up as before with a hand under each armpit.

Carrying a baby, even one as light as Mia, in such a fashion, wasn't ideal and I soon transferred her weight into the crook of my elbow, leaving a hand free to grasp the banister as I made my way downstairs. It felt safer that way. Winston followed on behind obviously anxious to help but probably not quite knowing how he was going to manage it.

To my relief there were bottles already made up in the fridge, the bottle warmer on the worktop was easily recognizable and already set to what I presumed was the correct temperature. I did pause to wonder how I had managed to notice so little of what went into the process of caring for this baby.

Winston made tea and toast as I coaxed Mia to take the bottle she had screamed for and now had no real interest in. I drank the tea, left the toast, went back upstairs to settle the baby in her cot, and went straight to bed myself exhausted and tearful, only to be woken little more than two hours later by a cry I was already beginning to recognize as one of hunger.

I hadn't realized Winston had stayed, but when he came up the stairs wearing a dressing gown I recognized as Rich's and carrying a warmed bottle, I could have wept all over again.

I was tired and upset, the baby was fretful and difficult to feed, and by the time she was settled I was beside myself and convinced it was all beyond me.

'I can't do this,' I told Winston, sinking on to my bed and hating the weak tears that dripped down my face. 'I just can't.'

Sitting beside me, he held me close and insisted, 'Yes, you can. Just take it one day at a time.'

'But I never wanted her and I don't love her.'

There I had said it right out loud and to another person. The sky hadn't fallen in and Winston hadn't pushed me away in disgust.

'Was it Phil who convinced you you couldn't be a good mother?' he asked calmly, adding, 'Why don't you try listening to your heart? Love doesn't always come like a bolt from the blue, sometimes it just needs the chance to grow and thrive as it did in the family who finally came together under your roof. You'll be a great mother, Alex, just give it time.'

I wasn't sure I believed him, but I wanted to. Winston held me close, talking to me softly and convincingly through those dark, doubtful hours, I gained comfort from the strength of his arms and from his simple belief in me. When I finally fell asleep I had learned that the true meaning of friendship was simply being there.

Over the next few days the nappies eventually went on the right way round and no longer leaked once the sticky tabs were being applied correctly. I learned how to mix bottles, and to clean and sterilize them. I even managed to establish some sort of routine and to use the time that Mia spent sleeping for laundry and household chores.

Winston was quietly supportive, yet unobtrusive, simply given to appearing at any time of the day or night. Though he did little more than occasionally vacuum, heat bottles and pass cotton wool, at least he was *there*. I realized I never before knew the real meaning of hard work, though in my ignorance I would once have pooh-poohed the notion that motherhood was actually a pretty tough job.

I finally began to appreciate the amount of support I had received from my in-laws, bitterly regretting the way I had summarily dismissed the family when they finally lost patience and handed over to me the role that should have been mine all along.

'I think they must be very cross with me,' I told Mia, as I held her slippery little body in the bath water and watched her kick enthusiastically, 'even Vi scarcely shows her face over the fence to ask me how I'm doing. It's bad enough you'll have to grow up without a daddy and now, because of me, you'll have no other family. I'm so sorry. I'm so sorry — for everything.'

Her gaze so deep and blue was wide and steady on my face, and the tears that still came far too easily dripped on to the soft down of her hair as my grief and regrets were finally acknowledged. She really did deserve so much more and I wished with all my heart that I could be the one to give it to her.

And then she smiled. It was a wide toothless smile of pure joy and I could do absolutely nothing else but smile back at her through my tears. There was no way of knowing if the smile was a genuine one, or just the result of wind. I preferred to think it was the former, and I lifted her from the water and held her wet little body against my breast, caring little for the water that soaked my clothes, and feeling the wall I had so carefully erected to protect my damaged heart finally begin to crumble — just a tiny bit — and hope for the future crept stealthily through the gap.

20

I held my child, this little stranger, close to me and made her a promise I would have thought not only unlikely but impossible, even a few days ago.

'It will be okay,' I told her, 'somehow I will make everything right again and give you back the family you deserve.'

'Of course you will.'

I looked up and smiled at Winston, knowing he could convince me it was possible if anyone could.

'What the family did in their desperation is, I believe, called tough love,' he said, coming into the room, 'and it wasn't easy for them to walk away and leave you to it.'

'I know that,' I nodded, wrapping Mia into the warm folds of a white towel and hugging her to me, 'they did what they felt was the right thing, and it probably was, but I'll always be glad you also did what you felt was right and stayed. You were the only one who could have done it, because with your lack of experience matching my own I could hardly leave Mia's care to you. Your company and encouragement were all I needed and I do thank you for that.'

'You helped me to come to terms with my mother's death and move forward,' he said simply, adding, 'I was feeling sorry for myself and your arrival at Rich's was a sharp reminder I wasn't the only one finding life difficult. If I've done anything at all to help you to come to terms with your daughter's birth then I would say we're quits, wouldn't you?'

'Thank you,' I said, 'that's a lovely thing to say. I have a feeling we'll be all right now — *all* of us,' and right on cue I swear Mia smiled.

Winston stared at us thoughtfully for a moment, and then mused, 'Do you know, for the first time in a very long time, I feel like giving my camera an airing?'

I beamed up at him. Surprised and more pleased than I could say by what could only be seen as a positive sign, I encouraged, 'Why don't you, then? The only photo I've got of Mia is the one they took at the hospital on the day she was born, and there are all those frames Rich bought to fill.'

It was a case of striking while the iron was hot, because I understood from the things Rich had said that Winston hadn't been near any of his photographic equipment since his mother's final illness — and it was quite

340

possible he wouldn't go near it again if I allowed the moment to pass.

'Stay there, don't move,' he ordered, 'and I'll be right back,' and the next minute the front door slammed behind him.

Well, of course I didn't stay there I leapt into action. I still had my pride and I wasn't about to be captured on camera soaking wet and bedraggled, with Mia wearing only a towel, not even for Winston, who was my only friend in the world at that moment. By the time he'd raced across town and back, Mia and I were all dressed up for a photo session and looking pretty damn hot.

'Not quite as natural, but you'll have to do, I suppose,' he joked, checking the light and camera angles like the true professional he was, and then continued thoughtfully, 'I've been thinking that this is something I might enjoy doing. You know, family portraits and celebrations.'

I felt like punching the air and yelling, but just agreed, 'That's a great idea. I can see you with your own studio in town, advertising yourself as a 'photographer for every occasion — family portraits a speciality'. You can use some of these photos as examples of your work and I'm sure the rest of the family won't mind being guinea pigs. It's only me they're not talking to.'

'The family — and I'm including Vi — just need to know that you forgive them,' Winston assured me. 'A phonecall is all it will take.'

I hoped he was right, but I wanted to make a bit more of an effort, so instead I sent them each one of the photos. On the back I wrote, 'I'm still learning but you were right — I *can* do this and be the mother Mia deserves — forgive me for doubting you. PS She now needs to have around her again the family she deserves and would love to see you all at her christening — we both would.'

Love to me meant wanting to say how sorry I was for failing to accept that the family who had become my dearest friends had only ever wanted what was best for my baby and me.

Celebrating the life of the child who had initially brought us all together seemed the perfect way to heal a rift that was all of my own making — shutting people out wasn't the way to a happy life as my years with Phil had taught me. From confident lecturer, I had made the return to hesitant student with some difficult lessons to learn before I could adapt from what my life had once been to what it had become.

★ ★ ★

Coming around the corner of the churchyard, I saw them all before they saw me and I paused to take in the sight of 'my' family grouped together in the autumn sunshine.

The men were fidgeting in their dark suits, checking their watches surreptitiously when they thought no one was looking and tugging at the unaccustomed constriction of a formal collar and tie.

'Been brushing up on your hymn singing, I hope,' came from Del and there was a laughing response from Tony that I didn't quite catch though it brought a smile to Jacquetta's prettily painted features.

She was going to make a wonderful picture — just as she always did — dressed for the occasion in an eye-catching black and white ensemble. A stark black knee-length dress showing off the shapeliest pair of pins this side of a fashion show catwalk, encased in sheer black stockings with her tiny feet shod in eye-catching black and white high-heeled shoes.

The whole outfit had been teamed with a white jacket and was set off by the familiar shiny chestnut wig and a striking black hat edged with white piping. She looked simply fantastic. After all that she had been through, she hadn't changed a bit in that respect and I was more proud than I could say of her.

'Mon Dieu, all those years of Sunday school were wasted on my sons,' Jacquetta told Winston ruefully. She shook her head a little too enthusiastically and then had to reach up to prevent the hat from tilting to a rakish angle.

'Oh, I do hope they have *Amazing Grace*, don't you, dear? I'm extremely fond of anything Scottish,' Vi a vision in silk enthused, the choice of a tasteful floral two-piece showing definite signs of Jacquetta's influence. Even from a distance I would have sworn Vi was wearing a touch of lipstick, too, and there wasn't a shopping bag in sight.

They were as unlikely a pair as you could hope to see, yet the friendship between them had been the making of two elderly women who would appear to have little or nothing in common apart from an enviable zest for life.

'I wish I could have arranged for Simon to turn up in a kilt, then, Vi,' Louise responded, with a little laugh at the thought, 'but he was reluctant to make the journey for some reason, so you'll have to make do with our men all scrubbed up in their suits.'

My sisters-in-law were dressed respectively in bright turquoise and hot-pink trouser suits and both looked absolutely stunning. Gone was the faded prettiness of the middle-aged housewife, to be replaced by extremely attractive ladies who could easily slash ten years from their real age and were obviously all too well aware of the fact as they flirted with their besotted husbands.

'It's time to go inside. Alex will be here soon.'

It was Amber, stunning in a red dress, who called them all to order. She stood close to the father she had barely known only a relatively short time ago and turning to take his arm she followed the others into the church.

I was able to stand unnoticed for a while, watching through the doorway as they took their places, and then waited patiently for me to join them. Looking at them all — the majority of them a family who had once been little more than strangers to me — I thought back to the journey we had taken together through the incredible ups and downs that life had thrown our way, challenging us and changing us forever.

I was in no hurry and savoured the moment. Apart from the initial watch checking — they showed no sign of impatience, but were content to wait at my convenience.

Finally, I stepped forward with Mia in my arms and, as one they turned towards me smiling with the warm approval I had come to expect from them because I was part of their family, because they all wanted what was best for me and because they trusted me to know what that was.

At the front of the church I could see Amber, Rich and Winston waiting and as I moved steadily towards them my little girl spotted them, too. Dressed to match Amber in the red that was her favourite colour Mia began to struggle, pointing and laughing. I could do no other than set her on the floor and watch in disbelief as she took her first tentative steps forward and was lifted high into Winston's arms.

There wasn't a dry eye as Amber handed me my bridal bouquet, Rich produced the rings, and the family who had become friends watched with love and approval as the man who had become so much more than my best friend in the months since the christening became the family Mia and I deserved.

We do hope that you have enjoyed reading this large print book.

Did you know that all of our titles are available for purchase?

We publish a wide range of high quality large print books including:
Romances, Mysteries, Classics
General Fiction
Non Fiction and Westerns

Special interest titles available in large print are:
The Little Oxford Dictionary
Music Book
Song Book
Hymn Book
Service Book

Also available from us courtesy of Oxford University Press:
Young Readers' Dictionary
(large print edition)
Young Readers' Thesaurus
(large print edition)

For further information or a free brochure, please contact us at:
Ulverscroft Large Print Books Ltd.,
The Green, Bradgate Road, Anstey,
Leicester, LE7 7FU, England.
Tel: (00 44) 0116 236 4325
Fax: (00 44) 0116 234 0205

HIGH INFIDELITY

Pamela Fudge

When a brief affair in Tina Brown's past resulted in an unplanned pregnancy, the decision was made not to share the news with the father, Calum Stacey. Tina raised the child alone, having decided to provide her with the full facts when she is eighteen years old. With her birthday just months away, Leanne is rushed into hospital with suspected meningitis and Tina feels she has no choice but to contact Calum without delay. Calum's engagement to a famous celebrity makes him newsworthy and there is mounting speculation surrounding his past. Can Tina and Calum protect their daughter from sudden media intrusion?

WIDOW ON THE WORLD

Pamela Fudge

Widowed at 46, Denise has come to the end of that first year alone and survived. It's time to get back out in the world and live her life. However, life — and her own family — seem to have other ideas, as her mother and daughter move into a house now bursting at the seams. A battle of wills ensues which Denise is determined to win, because only when she has sorted everyone else's lives out can she get on with her own. Romance doesn't figure in her calculations — but Denise should know that life doesn't always go according to plan . . .

GLISTER

John Burnside

Leonard and his friends, living in the decaying and industrial ruin that is the coastal community of Innertown, exist in a state of suspended terror. Every year or so, a boy from their school disappears, vanishing into the wasteland of the old chemical plant. Nobody knows where these boys go, or whether they are alive or dead, and without evidence the authorities claim they are simply runaways. The town policeman, Morrison, knows otherwise. He was involved in the cover-up of one boy's murder, and he believes all the boys have been killed. And although seriously compromised, Morrison — along with the local children — wants to find the killer's identity.